THEIR LAST
BEST HOPE

THEIR LAST BEST HOPE

Robert P. Coutinho

TATE PUBLISHING
AND ENTERPRISES, LLC

Published by Tate Publishing & Enterprises, LLC
127 E. Trade Center Terrace | Mustang, Oklahoma 73064 USA
1.888.361.9473 | www.tatepublishing.com

Tate Publishing is committed to excellence in the publishing industry. The company reflects the philosophy established by the founders, based on Psalm 68:11,
"The Lord gave the word and great was the company of those who published it."

Book design copyright © 2012 by Tate Publishing, LLC. All rights reserved.
Cover design by Shawn Collins
Interior design by Cheryl Moore

Published in the United States of America
ISBN: 978-1-62024-066-3
Fiction / General
12.06.05

DEDICATION

For Frank and Nancy

ACKNOWLEDGMENTS

This book would not be possible if not for the following people and organizations: My wife and children who supported me throughout the writing, Mrs. Rowell (my own first-grade teacher), Mrs. Sullivan (my seventh-grade English teacher who encouraged me to become a writer), Frank and Mildred Raymond (my in-laws and adopted god-parents), Officer Candidate School in Fort Benning, GA (December class of 1985), Ketil Horn (an internet buddy and fellow, aspiring writer), and especially Malwina (Inka) Allen, PhD (Chemistry) and Steve Allen, PhD (Physical Metallurgy).

PROLOGUE

Robert Crandon heard a voice. At first, he thought he was still day-dreaming, but he felt a touch on his face, and when he opened his eyes, he saw a familiar face. "Oh, thank God Almighty!" the voice said in an Irish accent. "I don't believe my eyes."

"Robert, can you hear me?" Father Jeff asked.

"Yes, Father, I can hear you." Robert forced his voice through enormous pain in his chest. He then tasted blood in his mouth and blew it out to try to be able to continue talking.

"Don't force it, son," Father Jeff cautioned. "I need to tell a doctor. I'll be back, I promise! Okay?"

"Of course, Father," Robert gurgled and fell asleep once again.

When Robert opened his eyes again, he saw things around him looking as if they emanated light. He figured that he was seeing things in a "fuzzy" manner. He tried to make out a face and saw his academy priest sitting near his bed. "F-f-father?" he gurgled out.

The tiny priest was on his feet immediately. He put his face a few inches from his nine-year-old altar boy's face and asked, "Are you still awake, Robbie?"

"Yes, Father," Robert responded. "Where am I?" he asked.

"You're in Fort Waterline Hospital, Robbie. You have been attacked. Do you remember anything?"

"Yes, Father..." he said through pained breathing. "I remember. Cadre Captain Gerralds, sir."

"That's right, Robert. Do you remember *all* that happened?"

"Begging your pardon, Father—and I'll gig myself if you think it impertinent of me—but how would I know if I remembered everything, sir? I mean, if I didn't remember something, wouldn't I be unlikely to know that, sir?"

The priest let out a sigh of relief and laughed. For the first time in four days, he laughed loudly and strongly. "Don't even think about gigging yourself for that, cadet! Yes, you're right. You can't possibly know if you remember everything. Do you think you're up to telling me what you *do* remember?"

"Well, Father, I remember that I was serving All Saint's Day Mass with you, sir. I mean, as an altar server, sir."

"Yes, of course, Robbie. Please continue."

"Well, sir, Johnny and I—that is, Cadet Freeman—we were serving as your altar servers. A lady came to the side church door as we were just about to head up the corridor to the sacristy. She said you had an urgent call, so you told us—that's me and Cadet Freeman, sir—to go ahead and clear the altar, put away our vestments, and go to class.

"We did all the things you asked, hung up the vestments really carefully, and headed off to our classes. We met Cadre Captain Gerralds at the side door, and he told us that we were in big trouble, sir. He said that we were skipping class. I told him that we just got out of Mass, and he told us that Mass had ended at least five minutes ago. We tried to tell him that we were altar servers and had just finished clearing the holy items and putting our vestments away, but he wouldn't listen.

"He grabbed hold of our arms and pulled us into the sacristy, sir. Then he took his metal, umm … *swagger stick?* Would that be the right word, Father?"

"As good as any other, Robbie, go on."

"Well, sir, he took his metal swagger stick, turned me to the wall, and hit me with it eight times on the … the—um … well, sir, the bum." Here Robert paused and blushed. The priest gave a reassuring smile, and Robert continued. " … And all the while, Johnny—that is, Cadet Freeman—was begging and pleading for Captain Gerralds to *please* use some other form of punishment on *him*. Cadet Freeman, well, Father, as you know, he's a plebe more or less, and he had never been hit by *any* of the cad—RAY..."—Robert remembered to add the last part just in time—"... before. I could see that he was really, really scared. I just couldn't take it any more, Father. I know that I probably got a bunch of majors for interfering, but I just couldn't stand to watch Captain Gerralds attack another pleading, little boy.

◆"I jumped in front of Johnny and yelled, 'Leave him alone you, you, sadistic creep!' Cadre Captain Gerralds struck me again and again with his metal rod. I looked behind me and saw that Johnny was kind of awestruck, so I yelled at him, 'Run you nut! Don't stay here! I'll give you as much time as I can! Go!' Captain Gerralds really started in on me then, sir. Johnny started moving slowly away and finally did start running. Captain Gerralds then kicked me in the chest, and I just lost all my air and—well, Father—kind of crumpled to the floor. As I looked back, I could still see Johnny's back, so as Captain Gerralds began to run after Johnny, I threw my arm out and tripped him.

"I didn't *hurt* him!" Robert insisted in an apologetic voice. "I just kind of slowed him down. Well, after that, he was hopping mad. He kicked me in the back, and I felt a stab in there. Then he got up, smashed my arm, the one I tripped him with, sir, my right one, with his swagger stick, kicked me in the face, and said, 'I'll find him anyway, cadet!' I think he hit my legs, too, but it's kind of fuzzy."

"He left me there and ran after Cadet Freeman. I tried to get up because I figured that Cadre Captain Gerralds had hurt me really badly and I would need help soon. I didn't think that Cadre Captain Gerralds would be coming back to save me, and I wasn't sure how long you might be gone. Nobody else would even think to go into the sacristy, so I tried to find some way to move, sir.

"My legs just wouldn't do what I told them to do. My right arm was clearly broken. The only things that seemed, well, sir ... workable, were my left arm and my hip. I kind of crawled or shuffled—or whatever you would call it, sir—to the rectory and threw rocks at the doorbell until the door opened. I couldn't stay up any longer after that … I mean by 'stay up' that I was turned onto my left side to throw rocks, sir, so I rolled onto my chest and … well sir, I heard some shuffling feet, then I heard some more shuffling feet and heard you ask me what happened. I tried to say, 'Cadre Captain Gerralds gave me a punishment for skipping class. Now he's trying to find Johnny to do the same to him!' But I don't think that I got all that out, sir." Here, Robert looked quizzically at the priest.

"All we heard was 'Gerralds,'" the priest corrected. "That was enough."

Robert tried to nod his head, felt explosions going through his skull, tried to move his arms to hold his head in pain, felt a sharp pain in his broken, right arm, and gave up entirely. For a few minutes, he did his best to control his breathing, and finally continued his tale.

"Anyway, sir, that is all I remember really. I remember waking up here a few times … I think, but not much else, sir. Is that enough, sir?" Here, the young cadet seemed truly apologetic as if he worried about disappointing the priest.

Father Jeff had tears in his eyes as he thought about a nearly destroyed little boy creeping toward his rectory over the pavement and grass to get to his door, and the boy's first concern was that he might disappoint Father Jeff because he might not remember anything else. "It's everything, Cadet Lieutenant Crandon. It is far more than any of us have any right to expect from you."

"Father Jeff?" Robert prompted.

"Yes, son?"

"Father, I hurt really badly. I could go to God now, right? Would that make the hurts stop?"

"Don't give up now! Please! You have come so far! You'll be alright, I'm sure! I know it hurts, but you can make it!"

"Father, I have never gotten a pass. I have not been able to speak to my family, my parents, for three years. Would you please write a letter for me and send it to them? I also have not been allowed mail privileges."

"Of course I will, Robert. Let me get a pen and paper."

Dear Mother and Father and my sisters and brothers,
I asked Father Jeff to write this for me, and he is taking down what I say. He's really nice, by the way, and has always been really kind to me. I am one of his altar boys now.

Mother and Father, this part is for you alone. Please, please, please forgive me for whatever I did! I don't know what I did to make you think that I should come to this awful place, but it must have been really bad! Even if you found out that I didn't do the things in Mrs. Rowell's letter, you still must have had some reason to think that I did do them. Whatever it was, I promise that I won't do it again. I am so sorry that I made you ashamed of me. I wish and pray every day that I can somehow make you like me again. I love you and miss you so much. I wish I could be with you now.

For everybody: I love you all and pray for you, although probably not as often as I should. I have thought about all of you each day. I hope and pray that you are all doing well and are happy. I wish that I could see you, but that does not seem to be likely any time soon.

I've done okay here since I came to Waterline Academy, except for getting passes. I have not written to you before because I have never gotten a pass. It seems pretty odd that I have not gotten one because I don't get many gigs or punishments. There are four times each year that cadets may be allowed to go to their families: Thanksgiving, Christmas, Easter, and the Fourth of July. I have been banned every time. If we are banned from leaving the academy, then we are also banned from writing letters, since we will not be allowed to get or use postage stamps. If you have written to me, I would not know because those who are banned are also prohibited from *receiving* mail as well. These are the reasons that Father Jeff has to write the letter for me. I would appreciate it if you never told my

Cadre, because that would be a *major, big time* punishment, and I really don't like those.

Please say hello for me to Grandmother and Grandfather McPhee, Grandmother Crandon, Great-Grandfather Lowry, Aunt Jenna and Uncle Jim, Uncle Dennis, and Uncle Jack and Aunt Lisa.

I am currently in the hospital here at Ft. Waterline. I don't know how badly I am hurt, but Father Jeff agrees that it is bad. Earlier, I felt like I was dying, and if that is the case, I didn't want to leave you without saying that I'm very, very sorry and that I love all of you. I have tried to make up for all my sins and bad behavior. I wish that I could see you all. I miss you all so much.

Your son,
Robert Joseph Crandon
Cadet Lt., USAS
Waterline Academy

Dear Mr. and Mrs. Crandon,

Your son has been attacked by one of the most sadistic cadre officers in the history of the academy system. His injuries are, in fact, life threatening. When he arrived at the hospital four days ago, he was given less than twenty-four hours to live. The next day he was given two days to live. The doctors do not understand how he has lasted this long. They assure me that he is one of the fastest healers they have ever seen; however, Robert has challenged me. He wants to know why he has never been allowed to go to Massachusetts to visit you in all his three years.

He explained it as follows: he was the first (and only) plebe cadet (first year at the academy) to achieve no more than three major penalties in his first year. The rules of the academy are that if a cadet has three majors (penalties) before Thanksgiving (from the September starting period) then he is banned for that Common Week (weeks where the cadets may be allowed to go home). If a cadet has four majors before Christmas, he is banned. This continues five for Easter, and six majors will get a cadet banned for the entire school year. Your son accepted his bans as simply another part of the way that Waterline Academy operates. However, he has never received another major penalty before the Fourth of July in any year. That should have permitted him to visit you.

He has challenged me, saying that he wants me to discover why he was banned. If I am unable to tell him, he may lose the will to live. Without that will, he won't survive. It may be very difficult to determine why he was banned, particularly considering his meteoric rise in the cadet ranks. The reason for the difficulty is that there need not be any reason attached to why a cadet has been banned. Nevertheless, I suspect that the culture of

Waterline Academy has let your son down in this matter. I will take my request directly to the Waterline Academy Commandant, explaining in *vivid* detail why he should cooperate with this request.

I wish that I could offer you more hope. You son is the most resilient child I have ever seen. He is also one of the most loving children I have met on my journey through life. You should be very proud of his achievements here at the academy. He was made a fire team leader after only half a year (while most cadets would take a minimum of two years to obtain such responsibility). He was promoted to Squad Leader at the beginning of his second year (obviously also unprecedented) and, finally, has been promoted to Platoon Leader at the beginning of his fourth year. No other platoon leader has ever been at the academy for less than five years. Due to the young age at which your son entered Waterline Academy, he is also correspondingly the youngest (by far!) to achieve all of these positions. In addition, he has earned numerous citations for outstanding achievement in both academics and "Academy" (meaning the cadre system) requirements.

If I can be of any help to you at all, please contact me. My address and telephone number are on the envelope.

—Father Jeffrey Lions

PART ONE:
THE EARLY YEARS

★★★★

FIRST GRADE

"My badges of honor," Robert Crandon told himself. The small, bandaged, nine-year-old boy reflected back as he did his best to withstand the obvious pain he was feeling. His reddish-brown, very short hair was showing in only a few places through the bandages wrapping much of his head. Both of his legs were in plaster casts—along with his right arm—preventing any movement of those extremities. Every time he tried to take a deep breath, he felt stabbing pain in his chest and shoulders. The effects of the damage, the pain, and the bandages made thinking just about all he could spend his time doing. So, he thought back to how it all began, how he came to be in that particular bed at that time.

Roberta Crandon, a fiery redhead, was pleading with Sister Ann Jacobs, "If you'll just talk to him, you'll see that he's clearly ready for kindergarten!" Sister Ann was the head of the nuns at St. Paul's Church. She ran the Catholic Christian Doctrine (CCD) programs and the parochial kindergarten. Mrs. Crandon was desperate to get her youngest child, Robert, into the 1968-1969 kindergarten class. Robert had been learning Nancy's schoolwork ever since the girl entered second grade; Nancy was four years older than her youngest brother! Robert's second-oldest sibling had wanted to "share" with her baby brother. The three-year-old Robert had taken to the learning immediately.

"We're not supposed to take any child who was born after June first," Sister Ann repeated. "I'm not sure that the public schools will take him into first grade next year—even if he *has* completed kindergarten." Sister Ann had been cautioned about taking children early into the parochial kindergarten. The public school system had regulations about the ages of children entering first grade. St. Paul's did not have an elementary school—all of the children in Coventry went to public schools from first grade on.

"We can worry about that next year," Mrs. Crandon suggested. "Won't you please at least talk to him and see?" She knew that her youngest child was more than capable of handling any academics that the kindergarten teachers would ever consider trying to teach him. He appeared ready for second grade, never mind kindergarten.

Sister Ann went over to where the four-year-old child was sitting on the play floor. He was looking at a book that had been in one of the cubbyholes of the schoolroom. "Hello Robert," she offered. "What are you doing?"

"Reading," the young, blond-haired boy answered. He was wearing a green, striped shirt with green shorts. His sturdy, little feet were contained in black sneakers with white socks.

"Would you read to me?" Sister Ann asked.

The boy began. "He did not want the people of his town to get hurt, so Samson went with the soldiers. After a while, he came upon the jawbone of a donkey. Samson took the bone and attacked the evil men who had taken him. He killed all one thousand one of the soldiers."

Sister Ann was impressed. She stopped his reading when she asked, "How high can you count to?"

Robert looked thoughtful for a while and then answered, "I don't know. I'm not sure how long I'll live." Mrs. Crandon did her best to suppress the smile that came to her face. She had not expected the answer, but she understood what her youngest son meant.

"Why would it matter how long you lived, Robert?" Sister Ann asked.

"I'm not sure how far I would get before I died," the boy answered.

A stunned look of understanding came upon the nun. "If you were to live as long as you needed, how far could you count to?" Sister Ann clarified.

"Umm … I guess to nine hundred ninety-nine trillion, nine hundred ninety-nine billion, nine hundred ninety-nine million, nine hundred ninety-nine thousand, nine hundred and ninety-nine," Robert answered. "I don't know what comes after that. Nancy never told me."

Sister Ann immediately admitted Robert into St. Paul's Kindergarten for the upcoming school year.

Nancy Crandon was short for her age, had brown hair, was thin of frame, and had piercing blue eyes. Her voice resonated certainty and surety of action. Nancy was the only sibling of Robert's who had actually completed kindergarten. When her youngest brother was just three years old, Nancy began teaching him all the things she had learned in first grade (she began second grade at that time). Mrs. Crandon had suggested to her daughter that Robert would be too young to learn, but that did not prove to be the case. Although Nancy's efforts with Kevin and John had not gone well, her youngest brother proved to be both eager and capable of learning.

Nancy started off by telling Robbie that he should always find fun in learning. She also told him to make up songs when he memorized stuff, "like the Alphabet song." Nancy was the leader of the Crandon children, in spite of being two years junior to her sister, Marie. Robert and Nancy had a very special relationship with each other. Robert trusted her completely.

"How was your first day of kindergarten?" Nancy asked her little brother.

"It was great! It was super great!" Robert answered. "We learned some songs and read the words that Sister Mary-Brenda held up. The cards had pictures of the thing too, but that's okay. I met this guy named Jerry. He's from Coventry too! I guess everybody's from

Coventry. *Anyways,* we colored next to each other. Oh! And I got a sticker too!" Robert proudly showed his sister the cartoon bear sticker on his arm. Robert always said, "Anyways," in a singsong manner when he was excited.

"You got one already? Wow, what did you get it for?" Nancy asked.

"I got it for learning my name, address, phone number, and parents' names," Robbie stated proudly. "Robert Joseph Crandon, son of Paul and Roberta Crandon, 275 Main Street, Coventry, Massachusetts, 617-555-3445."

"I'm gonna learn all the other kids' names and parents so I can help them too!" Robert suggested.

Robert completed the task of learning his classmates' names and information by his third day of kindergarten. He helped his friend Jerry to learn his identification information. Soon, the intrepid little four-year-old had helped every classmate learn his or her information. Sister Mary-Brenda eventually noticed that Robert was often alone rather than with the other children. He would sit aside reading a book from one of the cubbyholes. "Why are you reading instead of playing with the others?" she asked one day.

"Oh, they said that I couldn't play. I guess they think that it's not fair; I would mess up the teams. They're playing the word game, and I already know all the words. It's okay, Sister. I don't mind. They said I can play the next game." Robert smiled and blinked a cute, impish blink. Whenever he sported that signature blink it usually meant that some embarrassing consequences would happen to someone else.

Sister Mary-Brenda could hardly believe that this young boy had already learned every word on every card in the deck. She took him to her desk and obtained her own copy of the word deck, while her counterpart, Sister Nora, continued with the team competition. Robert recited each word—without needing to look at any of the pictures.

First grade was to start and Robert was sick. "This is yucky!" he grumbled to himself. "I'm stuck with my aunt, drinking yucky, weak tea. All the other kids get to meet their teacher and start school. I'll be behind even before I start, and who knows what will happen?"

He got over his stomach bug in four days and was so excited to finally go to "Big Kids' School." The school was near his home in the southern portion of town. He, his two brothers, and his two sisters all walked to school together. Marie, his oldest sister, allowed him to carry her books for her. He was beaming from ear to ear.

In his hospital room, Robert pictured that blond-haired little kid walking down the shaded road to South Side Elementary School. His hair had turned reddish-brown since that time. He smiled as he thought about it, and this caused him to wince a little. *One more badge of honor for me,* he thought.

Robert was in the first- and second-grade playground. It was all cement and had no swings, slides, or other playground equipment, but it was filled with children who were laughing, screaming, running, and having all sorts of fun. Robert did not know what he was to do, so he did what he usually did in such circumstances: he watched the chaos around him and tried to figure things out. He saw a "grown-up" and wandered over to her. "My name is Robert, and I'm kinda new here," he told the grown-up. The woman had to run to a small group to break up some roughhousing, and Robert was far too shy to pursue her. After what seemed like an eternity but was probably about ten minutes, a loud clanging sounded out.

"Line up in your class lines," a teacher called out. "Mrs. Rowell's class here, Mrs. Jander's class here…" The list went on, but of course, Robert did not know into which line he belonged. He stood where he was, bewildered at what to do. With a tear in his eye, he approached the speaker.

"Please, I don't know which class I'm in. I've been sick, and this is my first day."

"Don't worry," she suggested, "your teacher will figure it out, I'm sure."

Robert stayed there and waited. Teachers were coming to the front of their class lines and starting to take attendance. When Robert heard his name called, he raised his hand and shouted, "Over here." He scrambled around the bigger children and tried to find out who had called his name. He saw a young woman standing in front of the line that the previous woman had named, "Mrs. Rowell's class." The woman had dark, brown hair, brown eyes, and rosy cheeks. "I'm Robert Crandon," he declared.

"Okay, Robert. Is this your first day?" Robert nodded. "Don't worry, dear. Just go ahead and stand in line and everything will be just fine." Mrs. Rowell smiled at Robert, and he knew that he was in perfect bliss. He got to the end of the line behind a taller boy.

"You're new here?" the taller boy asked.

"Yeah. My first day," Robert responded. "I was sick for four days," he added in explanation.

"I need to talk with you after school," the boy intoned.

"Why after school? Why not now?"

"Because it has to be after school." Robert was naïve, so he agreed to meet the new boy without further question.

School was all Robert had hoped for and more! Mrs. Rowell was beautiful, fun, loving, caring, all the things Robert had hoped she would be. He followed her instructions as carefully and intently as he possibly could. He was going to get along perfectly there!

After lunch, which Robert had gone home to eat—even though most of the students ate in the cafeteria—Mrs. Rowell handed out short, white-lined pieces of paper. "Okay, class. It's time for your spelling test," she announced. Robert took up his pencil and got ready. "Dog," Mrs. Rowell began, "The dog ran up the hill. Dog." Robert wrote as quickly as he could. "Cat. The cat says, 'Purr.' Cat." The list went on. About halfway through the test, Robert was totally frustrated. Mrs. Rowell noticed this and went over to him. "Robert?" she asked. "What's wrong?"

"Well ... you're going so fast that I can't keep up!" Robert explained. Mrs. Rowell looked at Robert's test paper:

Dog. The dog ran up the hill. Dog.

Cat. The cat says purr. Cat.

Hat. The man is wareing a hat. Ha

Tree. The tree is losing its leav

Ten. I can count to ten. T

Send. Pleez send me you

"Oh!" she exclaimed. "You don't have to write the entire sentence. You only have to spell the first word." Robert looked at her bewildered. "I just gave the sentences so you could know how the word is used," she gave as further explanation. Robert finally understood that he needed only to spell "dog," "cat," "hat," "tree," "ten," and "send." He could not, however, understand why she gave so much time for anyone to write just one, little, easy word.

The school day closed and the tall boy reminded Robert to meet him "around the back." Robert assured the boy, Roger, that he would be there.

Roger sat next to Robert in class. He never seemed all that interested in the things Robert loved on that first day. He would interrupt the teacher, throw papers at other children, and generally make a nuisance of himself. Nevertheless, Robert went right instead of left out of the school building. Roger was waiting, and Robert asked him what was so important. "This!" Roger yelled in a hostile tone. He pushed the younger, smaller boy; Robert instantly fell over another boy who had positioned himself behind Robert on hands and knees. Robert began to cry as his head hit the ground with a loud and painful thud. The other two boys jumped onto Robert and began punching him. He could only struggle to put his hands over his face.

After the two assailants had left, Robert continued to cry. He struggled his way back onto his feet and ran to where his brothers were waiting. "Where have you been?" his oldest brother, Kevin, demanded.

"Two guys just beat me up!" Robert wailed. He showed his brothers where he had been attacked, and they took him home to their mother.

Mrs. Crandon was always busy. She and her neighbor, who lived across the little street leading to the back of South Side Elementary School, each had five children. This kept them both very busy, so just before school let out for the day, they always shared a cup of tea and talked with each other. When Mrs. Crandon saw her youngest coming home crying, she leapt up from Mrs. Jass's table and rushed to her boys. "Robbie got ambushed," Johnny declared as an explanation. The entire story came out, and Robbie, as his family always called him, was instructed to never meet with "that boy" again, and his brothers were instructed to watch over their little brother.

The next day, Robert ran home to his mother after meeting his brothers. He was excited because he had received his first graded paper.

"Mommy, Mommy, guess what I got? I got my spelling test back and I got an A!"

Mrs. Crandon praised her little boy and gave him a hug. "Everything's going well then?" she asked.

"Yep! Mrs. Rowell is great! I love big kid's school so much!"

Robert's sixth birthday had gone by in mid-September. He was small for his class and young as well. Nearly all the other students started first grade already having achieved the age of six by June 1. Robert was an exception because he had attended parochial kindergarten.

He refused to talk to Roger, even though the boy sat right next to him in class. He was not going to get fooled twice!

Robert attempted to learn everything that he could as quickly as he could. Whenever he finished work that Mrs. Rowell had assigned him, he would approach her and ask for more. The teacher had twenty-five other students to teach as well, so she often took a book off of one of the shelves and gave it to her brilliant pupil to read. Robert read the entire beginning science series by the end of the second week. He finished his extra reading book by the end of the third week. He also showed excellent skill at handling a pencil—writing both numbers and letters with ease. Mrs. Rowell was wondering what she could do to keep her star pupil occupied.

After five weeks had passed since the beginning of school, Mrs. Rowell passed out "teacher's notes" to Robert and Roger. Both children were instructed to make *sure* that their parents read the notes. Robert asked permission to go to the boy's room and left his letter on his desk.

Roger was not a very bright student, but he knew, since he was repeating first grade for the second time, that his note was not likely to contain good information. His parents had threatened to put him into the Academy System if he failed to perform correctly. Roger had heard the horror stories about those places! Since no one was looking, Roger opened his note. He did not see his name or his parents' names in the letter. He could not read most of it, but an idea had come into his head. He grabbed the letter lying on Robert's desk and took it out of the envelope. He placed his letter into Robert's envelope and Robert's letter into his own.

Now, of course, this evasion was not going to help Roger in the least. His parents would soon know that this was a deception, but poor Roger did not have any clue that the plan was doomed to failure from the start. Robert had no clue that any such plan was even in the works. This began a chain of events that led Robert down a very different path than his parents or his teacher had ever intended.

BOUND FOR
WATERLINE ACADEMY

Robert lay back in the hospital bed and began to weep. The last memory was just too painful. "Use it as a badge of honor," he could hear his first platoon leader cautioning. Struggling to contain his emotions, Robert continued to look back on his early life.

"What kind of rotten, little beast did we raise?" Paul Crandon yelled. "How *dare* you do such things while telling us all along that everything was fine?" Robert's father rushed into the adjoining room and got down "the belt"! Robert's world exploded in pain! His father continued the punishment whenever the man saw his youngest son. No matter how hard Robert protested his innocence, his father was no longer going to believe his "lies." To Robert, it felt like his father repeatedly whipped him throughout the weekend. Robert spent the bulk of his time trying to hide from both his parents.

His mother had been shocked when Robert had gotten home and handed her his teacher's letter. She called the school principal to check up about her son's letter. Principal Edwards confirmed that Robert had been given a Teacher's Note. He looked up the listing for Mrs. Rowell's class and saw that the teacher had recommended two of her students for the Academy System. Mrs. Rowell had already left, so he did not see the need to pursue the matter further. Roberta headed to the school district headquarters and immediately got the paperwork to send her youngest son into the Federal academy system (as suggested in the teacher's letter).

Sunday night, Robert meekly came downstairs at his parents' insistence. "You have just one more chance to admit what you did!" Paul Crandon intoned menacingly.

"I didn't do anything."

"That's *it!*" his father roared. "Since you still won't tell the truth, I'll tell you what: you bring home a note from your teacher tomorrow telling us this is all a huge mistake, or I'm putting you in the toughest, strictest academy that exists! No exceptions, no excuses!"

Monday, Mrs. Rowell was sick. Robert asked the substitute to write a letter, but of course, she could not contradict anything the regular teacher had written. Robert walked home alone. He had endured two and a half days of physical torture, and now he was heading home without the needed letter.

" … beating up the other children, throwing papers around the class, tearing up his school books, ambushing children on their way home, bullying the children … " How could his teacher *say* those things? How could she even think them? He was doomed and he knew it.

That night, he told his father, in vain, that his teacher was sick. He knew that was not going to help, since, if he was the liar his father now believed him to be, he would make up just such an excuse. "No exceptions. No excuses," his father had said. Robert knew that his father was a man of his word. The beating that night was not nearly as bad as Robert had expected. Mr. Crandon seemed more resigned than angry. "You will bring the paperwork directly to the office yourself! Your mother is going to check, so don't try to get out of it this time!"

Tuesday morning, Robert took the yellow envelope with his paperwork into the school up in the "big kid" region, to the office where the secretary and principal worked. "Excuse me, Miss Sattie … " he prompted. "My parents said to hand this directly to you and insist that you"—Robert struggled for the exact words—"'process it immediately,' they said."

"Thank you, dear," she said and continued her typing.

Mrs. Rowell was sick again on Tuesday, and Robert went home with dread, knowing that his fate was sealed. He carried a white envelope with the officious-looking words "Academy System" written on it in big, bold letters. Robert handed the envelope to his mother and waited for the words he knew were coming, and the instructions he suspected were accompanying those words.

"So," his mother chided, "you finally did something you were told, huh?" Robert's face flushed with anger. He wished that his mother would get hurt or something. That would show her! She opened the envelope and read the letter. "It says here that you will meet a van at a quarter to ten tomorrow morning. Do you still remember how to tell time?" Robert nodded his head. "You have to bring this envelope with you. If you try to hide it, they will just spank you, so *don't try anything! Got it?*" Robert nodded again, meekly. He went upstairs, plopped onto his bed, and cried.

At supper that evening, Robert's father just glared at him whenever Robert looked his way. After supper, his father said, "Get out of my face, you little beast. I don't want to see you anymore!" Robert went up to his bed and cried some more. The next day, his father had left for work without speaking to him. His mother was busy with all the other children. She just pointed to the envelope and waited for him to pick it up. He didn't want to walk to school with his brothers and sisters. They had joined in the verbal abuse, calling him a bully, an idiot, a thug … whatever *that* meant. He walked to school alone, slowly and sadly.

Before school, in the schoolyard, Robert just stood dejectedly near the wall next to the doors for the first and second graders. When the bell rang, he got into line near the end and simply raised his hand when Mrs. Rowell called his name. The teacher led her class to their classroom. Robert immediately approached her desk. "Mrs. Rowell, I won't be in class. I have to wait upstairs for my ride," Robert said, choking back tears.

"Robbie, what's the matter?" Mrs. Rowell asked, concerned for her star pupil.

"I have to wait for my ride, Mrs. Rowell," the boy simply repeated.

"Ride to … where?" the woman demanded in a soft and caring tone.

"To Waterline Academy, where you suggested!" Robert cried out. He could take no more. He rushed out of the room with his orders and ran up to the office area. The secretary told him to wait on the wooden bench that sat opposite the principal's office. Although it was the only seating in the entire small area, other than the secretary's chair, all the children had named it the "naughty bench."

Robert waited a while and then saw Mrs. Rowell running up the stairs to the office. "Stay right there!" she demanded, and Robert saw no reason to argue with such a request. He heard some shouting, screaming, and a lot of heated conversation going on in the principal's office. He really did not care. Mrs. Rowell came out of the principal's office and headed down the stairs, presumably back to her classroom.

More time passed, and Robert saw his mother come into the school, right at the office area. Roberta Crandon was dressed in a deep-blue skirt and light-blue blouse. Her hair was up in a bun. She looked a little disheveled; she had rushed to the school on foot—the Crandons had only one car. The school was built on a hill, so although there were stairs leading from the early grade classrooms up to the office, the office was still the main floor. "What did you do this time, you little beast?" his mother quipped rhetorically. Robert's face flamed in anger. He looked away.

In a very short while, he saw Miss Sattie get up and head toward the first and second grade classrooms. Mrs. Rowell arrived a short time later and ran into the principal's office. There was a lot of yelling and some frantic shuffling going on in the small office. Eventually, Robert looked at the clock and saw the big hand pointing at the eight. He decided there was no point in waiting. He decided that if he was stuck going to a disciplinary academy, at least he could do it without resisting. He took the envelope with his orders and went out of the front door.

When the van arrived, Robert jumped in and handed his envelope to the police officer who was to attend him. Robert stared at his feet and cried some more.

HOW WATERLINE WORKS?

When Crandon, Robert Joseph arrived at Waterline Academy, a man in a light-blue uniform told him to strip off his clothing. Waterline had a policy of integrating its ne'er-do-wells harshly and devastatingly. Robert removed his shirt, trousers, socks, and shoes. "Everything, cadet!" the man demanded menacingly. Robert removed his tee shirt and undershorts as well. While standing there stark naked, he was given a can of liquid and told to soak the clothes in it. He was then handed a small torch with fire at the end of it. "Light'em!" he was told. Robert pressed the flames to his clothing and watched them turn to smoke.

"Get him his uniforms, cadet!" the man demanded of a much older and bigger boy. This boy was also dressed in a light-blue uniform. The older boy crisply saluted the man.

"Yes, sir!" he said to the cadre officer. "Follow me, cadet," the older boy ordered. The two marched over to the Quartermaster Building. The older boy told Robert, "I'm Cadet-Lieutenant Darryl Marks. I am your student platoon leader. You will remember your platoon and company at all times. We are First Platoon, Alpha Company. Have you got that?"

"First p'ltoon, Alfer Campanie?" Robert asked meekly.

"First … PLAtoon, Alpha COMpany," the cadet intoned.

"First Platoon, Alpha Company?" Robert tried again.

"First thing you've got to know is that the cadre officers are in charge. They are in charge of everything. Second thing is how to salute." The older boy showed Robert how to hold his hand and keep his elbow and arm locked. They finally reached the Quartermaster building. Lieutenant Marks gave three sharp knocks on the door.

A man, dressed similarly to the cadre officer who had met Robert (and had had him burn the clothes), said to the older boy, "Got another one, huh, cadet?" Robert noticed the man's nametag: "Thomas."

"Yes, sir!" Marks answered. He kept his head straight and his shoulders level, and he stood in a perfect, upright posture.

"Okay, bring him in, cadet," the quartermaster officer said. He measured Robert. It was apparent that the quartermaster officer had not had a child that small ever before. He had him try on various pieces of clothing. He altered some clothes, shortening the sleeves and pant legs. He checked and double-checked and then, when satisfied, said, "That should do it, Darryl. If anything seems to be fitting wrong, bring it back, and we can try again."

"Yes, sir!" the platoon leader intoned sharply. "Thank you, sir!" he added. He helped Robert lift the large duffel bag that now contained Robert's uniforms and bed linens.

Robert's platoon leader led him to a large building, of which there were two other very similar structures, one on either side. The buildings were painted in off-white, drab color. "We're up here, on the top floor, cadet," Darryl informed his young recruit. "Your bunk is in room"—he hesitated and took out a small book from his left, breast pocket—"three fourteen." The two boys walked down the corridor and stopped at Room 314. Robert saw "Crandon" next to another word he could not pronounce just above the doorway. "You use your combo lock—that is the combination lock—on your wardrobe. That's the big, closet-looking thing over there. You put your jackets and trousers in that, along with some other stuff that you will be getting—books, blotter paper, that sort of thing. I've put you with your squad leader, Sergeant-Cadet Wohljokowski. That's pronounced "wole-joe-cow-ski," okay?" Robert repeated the name. "He can show you the ropes and help you out in the early going.

He'll help you make your bunk when he gets out of class. This"—Lt. Darryl handed Robert a green-covered book—"this is your gig book. Any time you misbehave, do something wrong, you get a mark in that book. You must carry it at all times—for the rest of your time in the academy. If you are ever caught without it, except during PT, you can expect an automatic MAJOR. Got it?" Robert certainly did *not* get it, but expected that he would very shortly.

Lt. Darryl showed Robert around the entire academy campus. The three similar-looking buildings were barracks for each of three companies. Each company had three platoons, and each platoon could have up to forty-two cadets. One of the buildings billeted the student battalion officers, of which there were three—the commander, the adjutant, and the "XO," as Lieutenant Darryl named him, the executive officer. Each student company commander had his own room, as did the student platoon leaders and platoon sergeants.

Platoons were broken into four squads each. The squads all had a squad leader and an assistant, known as a "fire team leader," although Robert had no idea, at the time, what that meant. He only knew that the boys who were better at keeping all their things in proper order and memorizing all the "required knowledge" seemed to be those who were promoted to the "student officer corps."

On his first night, Robert was summoned to his platoon leader's room. He moved down the corridor, knocked, and, when told to enter, opened the door, saluted, and cried out, "Sir, Cadet Crandon reports as ordered!" in the same tone he had seen his platoon leader using all day when speaking to the cadre.

"Sit down, cadet," the older boy said in a much calmer tone than he had used earlier in the day. "I don't know what you did to get put here in maximum security and most of the guys don't like to dwell on it, so I don't need you to tell me, okay?" Robert nodded. "Usually, if a cadre officer asks you a question like that, you *must* respond with 'Yes, sir,' like that. It's their way of commanding respect. Got it?"

"Yes, sir," Robert responded.

"Now you're getting it, Rob ... uh ... Robert ... Bob ... say, just what *do* they call you?"

"Robbie?" Robert responded in a meek voice.

"Okay, Robbie it is, for now. Anyways, in front of any Cad, that is cadre officer, you will probably be called Cadet Crandon. You may as well get used to that. Oh ... and don't use the term *cad* in front of one of the cadre.

"As I was saying, I don't know what you did to get put into maximum security, but either you did something really, *really*, bad"—Robbie shook his head no—"or there had to be a major, goofball mistake. I have never, ever heard of *anybody* being put into any disciplinary academy, never mind Waterline, at six years old. Either way, it really doesn't matter. You're here, and you're going to stay here. There is no way that anybody can get you out before your time.

"All cadets are signed into Waterline for a minimum of six years, and it would take an act of Congress to reverse it ... and Congress ain't gonna act," he said with an accent on the last phrase. "I waited to talk to the other plebes, that is, the newbies, until I found out just how nasty they were. I'm going to give you the tricks of the trade early. There are all sorts of ways to get gigged. You have to write down each gig and what each assigned punishment is for. By the way, can you write?" Marks asked, remembering just how young this newbie was.

Robbie nodded his head in assent, froze, stood at the position of attention, and shouted, "Yes, sir!"

Marks smiled. "Okay, that's good, because you're going to be writing an awful lot in the next few months. Anyways, you have to write down every gig and punishment, not counting when they hit you. Ten gigs equal a minor punishment. Ten minors in one week get you a major punishment. Got that?" The platoon leader continued on without looking for feedback. "Punishments—minors, that is—are usually things like polishing the handles on the cadre's doors, sweeping the cadre office for an hour, cleaning the school windows, that sort of thing. Majors are *very unpleasant.* The cadre officers take turns trying to come up with nastier things to make you do or to do to you.

"This part is very important. Most guys don't get it, and you may be too young to really understand, but … here it is. There is a way to, well, to survive in this place. You are going to be in pain. That's just the way Waterline is. You can either accept that pain or fight it. If you try to fight it, you will lose. You will fail to fight it, I mean. The way that most of the guys make it here is that they play *the game.*"

THE GAME IS HARD

Robert began coughing, which gave him sidesplitting spasms in his ribs. He thought that his eyeballs might pop out from his holding back the pain. The nurse in charge of the intensive care patients came over to his bedside and asked him if he was in pain. "No, ma'am," he responded. "I'm fine," he continued through clenched teeth. The nurse shook her head, adjusted the intravenous drip attached to the boy's arm, and left his bedside sadly.

The game, Robert thought once again and drifted off into sleep. When he awoke, he continued his review of those things that had happened to him in Waterline. The game was the cadets versus the cadre, "the cads" as all the cadets thought about it when thinking about the game. "When you're in Waterline," his platoon leader had said, "you are going to be in pain. While getting hit or whipped or beaten, it's okay to cry, since that's at the time. During any punishment or task, though, you never, ever complain. You try to out-cad the cads. *Your pain is your badge of honor.* If you can keep from complaining, whining, bellyaching about anything the cads make you do or do to you, then you win and they lose. They try to break you. If you whine, they win. If you blubber afterward, they win. If you complain, they win. Don't be a loser, be a winner."

Robert changed his focus to the rules of survival in Waterline Academy. Waterline had the strictest rules in the country. All cadets were there for their own good. Waterline was their last, best chance to remain out of prison for the rest of their lives. Waterline had the reputation of receiving some of the worst ne'er-do-wells and turning them into productive citizens. "Never argue with a cadre officer, never correct a cadre officer, never, ever fight a cadre officer," his first platoon leader had told him. "They are here for our benefit. They are our world, our salvation, our last chance. Without the cadre we wouldn't eat, we wouldn't have clothes, we wouldn't have a roof over us in the rain, and we certainly wouldn't straighten out our lives. You can play pranks all you want, that is, so long as you're willing to accept the punishment if you get caught, but you never harm a cadre officer."

The cadets had other unwritten, inviolable rules. *You never steal.* Since the boys were not allowed to own anything, it was irrelevant to steal in Waterline Academy, but most of the plebes who had larcenist tendencies had to get straightened out by the Cadet Officer Corps. You could change the location of anything in the academy world, but you never even considered stealing personal items from Cadre, teachers, or any outsiders. The Cadet Officer Corps had devious ways of enforcing their will—Robert knew that as fully as any cadet could.

You do not get into fights. This particular rule was typically enforced by the cadet platoon sergeants. If two cadets wanted to fight, a platoon sergeant would give them extra lumps to remind them why they should *not* fight. This caused a lot of cadets to have "slipped on a bar of soap" many, many times. The cadre did not question the claim of the cadets; the men in charge knew, of course, what happened, but allowed the unwritten policies to be enforced.

You never lie. If you want to give partial truth or simply be silent, that is permissible, but you never lie. "What if a cadre officer asks you to turn in another cadet?" Robert had asked his platoon leader.

"Then you just say, 'Sir, I did not do such and such' or 'Sir, you would have to ask the cadet in question.'"

That reminded Robert of the cadet motto of the school, the unwritten motto: Cadets help cadets, cadets don't turn in cadets.

That one could get sticky sometimes because a cadet might be doing something illegal and patently dangerous. The other cadets usually got around such incidents by *suggesting* to the cadre officers that they just might want to look out the window, or that they just might want to go to Charlie-3 (3rd Platoon, C Company). The only allowed exceptions to the motto were if cadets needed to turn in a cadet for the continuing safety of other cadets or if a cadet tried to escape. There were, after all, some things that even the Student Officer Corps might not be able to handle. Robert, however, had not seen any such thing in his three years at the academy.

The Cadre is always right. No matter what they do, the cadre officers are there for your benefit. Whatever they tell you to do or do to you is so that you can make it in *Their World.* This was drilled into the cadets weekly, sometimes even daily. No cadre officer was to be questioned. All orders were to be followed immediately.

Robert remembered his first week in Waterline Academy. He had been a latecomer for the year, but that did not mean that he was given any time to adjust. He received ninety gigs in his first week. Some of those had been for "required knowledge." The Academy had seventeen pages of required knowledge—and the contents changed each September 1. Most of the cadets had failings in required knowledge, but the cadre seemed to be especially intent on gigging the plebes.

Gigs meant loss. All of your credits for "buying" boot polish and brass cleaner—and treats at the Post Exchange (PX)—were dependent upon you passing through with few gigs. If you could get a "merit," you got a huge infusion of credits. If you managed to get an achievement medal, you could buy smoothies for your entire platoon—or so Robert had been told. Due to his being banned, he had never visited the PX. When he became a platoon leader, Robert did not even have to use credits for boot polish or brass cleaner; Captain Thomas was authorized to give it to the senior officer corps for "free".

Robert studied his required knowledge intently and had it all memorized by Friday of his first week. He took the first shower of his life on Thursday morning, right after physical training. Robert followed Sergeant First Class Cadet (SFC) Thompson's and Sergeant Wohljokowski's recommendations about how to polish his brass and boots, how to make his bed, how to set up his uniforms, and other requirements that were a major source of gigs.

By the time preliminary inspection came—at the end of October—Robert had learned enough and worked hard enough that he actually passed. Darryl Marks, Robert's platoon leader, was amazed at how quickly his youngest plebe was taking to the Waterline requirements. Darryl's cadre adviser had told the newly promoted cadet to keep a close eye on Robert. Darryl told his battalion commander, Cadet Lieutenant-Colonel Ted Washington about the situation. He also kept Ted appraised of Robert's progress.

In addition to the cadre requirements, Robert had to deal with the cadet requirements. Those were not technically binding, but they were requirements that the cadet took just as seriously. He exercised his fingers and toes in order to be able to move on them—and nothing else. He practiced moving silently in the vents an hour each day by going back and forth behind Lieutenant Marks's ventilation screen. Lieutenant Marks would tell Robert each time he could hear him, so the boy would know to change his movements.

Robert needed to learn many things for his cadet duties. Darryl Marks and Harry Tromp, having been the vent rats prior to Robert's arrival, taught him how to sneak around, pick locks, take things from people's pockets, and read the codes. Ted Washington taught him how to forge letters, distract cadre officers and strategically plan out his forays. He was told that no one had been in the files for years, so the order of the files—a critical part of the code—might have been changed. Robert would have to put them back into order.

Robert recalled one of the few times that he specifically did not follow an order. The cadets were marching on the parade field. Robert jumped out of formation and ran about fifty meters. Cadre Captain Summers grabbed him by his jacket and roughly dragged him back to his platoon. Later, Darryl asked Robert what had happened.

"There was a bee!"

"It doesn't matter. I told you before that you would be in pain sometimes. It doesn't matter if a bee, a yellow-jacket, a wasp or anything else tries to sting you. You still have to keep following directions."

"But sir..."

"No buts."

There were three times that the cadet officers court-martialed cadets. The Senior Officer Corps told the cadre that they needed to conduct disciplinary training. The cadre knew exactly what this meant. Robert had learned all of the procedures from the Cadet Archives. He had not witnessed any of the trials; he was marching with most of the rest of the cadets. He only knew that all three cadets were unable to walk out of the school building afterward. He later made entries into the Archives listing the offenses: one of the cadets attacked a younger and smaller cadet, another had tattled to the cadre, the third one had repeatedly taken other cadets pencils without permission. As always, the cadre was told that the cadets had, "...slipped on a bar of soap."

ACCELERATED EDUCATION

Dr. Darlene Lawson was the principal of the Waterline Academy School. She had taught history and psychology before being promoted in 1968. She had been chosen as one of the best and brightest educators back in 1957. She had been invited to join the academy system, and being young and ambitious, she jumped at the chance. She married in 1963; she and her husband, Dick, lived in Riverton, South Carolina. He worked in a private law office, and she did her best to educate recalcitrant boys.

She loved her work for the first ten years. But by 1969 she was disgusted with the behavioral problems. She had expected behavior problems from the cadets; she did *not* expect such problems from the cadre. She seriously considered resigning after just her first year as Waterline's principal. Then she met Robert Crandon.

The boy entered the academy at much too early of an age—he was only six! Darlene had been notified by Joan Dickinson that a first grader had come into the school. She almost did not believe the news. Waterline had not had a first grader in over seven years. When she found out how young the boy was, she immediately requested a reevaluation of Cadet Crandon's status. No six-year-old should ever have been admitted into the academy system.

Robert was the first—and only—cadet from the state of Massachusetts to enter Waterline Academy. The Waterline Academy cadre was not about to short-change a state that was so under-represented. The reevaluation was denied. She researched the child's background and could see absolutely no reason why he had been sent to maximum security. Nevertheless, he was there, so she was going to determine where in the school he belonged.

Within five minutes of talking to Cadet Crandon, Darlene knew that she had a gifted student on her hands. That ended her quest to change the cadet's status; she wanted to use her academic skills and Robert was the perfect target. During his first two weeks, Darlene had multiple teachers subject the boy to a battery of tests designed by and for Bethesda and Berkeley Gifted Academies. The tests had been designed to determine potential as well as knowledge. Robert tested at the top one percent—for gifted students!

Darlene had a PhD from Johns Hopkins and knew several of the professors who had influence at Bethesda Academy. She called in some favors and obtained classified information on how Bethesda Academy taught its gifted students. She implemented the suggestions and modified them as time went along. The entire staff at Waterline Academy wanted a shot at educating their "resident genius."

Christina Ruchala was the first teacher to "get her crack" at Cadet Robert Joseph Crandon. She covered addition and subtraction in one session. Mrs. Rowell and Sister Janice had already covered both with Robert. The next session, Professor Ruchala introduced Robert to multiplication. She left the boy learning the "times tables" for the rest of the day. The next day, she tested Robert on multiplication through the "twelves." He was perfect. She next began trying him out on three-digit addition and subtraction, and he seemingly had already taken that instruction as well. She was at a loss as to where to start with such a quick learner. She introduced fractions and found that he had no idea what they were.

She next covered two-digit multiplication and division. That was a "starting" place. It did not take long for the cadet to master those. When she introduced remainders, Robert took two days before he was proficient. She next began on simple fractions—explaining that the line was the same as division. Robert took to the arithmetic like a fish to water. By the time her two weeks were finished, she had already taught Robert decimals. She wanted to keep him, but she knew that his reading, English, and other academic subjects needed to keep pace.

Rachel O'Connor got the "resident genius" next. She saw that he could already read at the middle of fifth grade in reading level. She introduced him to spelling and vocabulary. It was still a time when Robert was trying to master all the cadre requirements, so Rachel had to give the boy some leeway. She told Dr. Lawson about the difficulty and was given another entire week to keep Robbie.

During her first three weeks with the cadet, she saw him soak up knowledge like a sponge soaking up water. He showed not just willingness, but an eagerness to learn everything that he could. She used nearly all of her time with him to show him how to look up words, spell, sound out difficult ones, and place definitions into context. When she had to let him go on to his next course of study, she gave him a reading list of over one hundred books. She had expected him to read perhaps fifteen or twenty of them by the time he came back, a monumental achievement even by Bethesda standards.

Robert's vocabulary began to expand enormously due to Professor O'Connor's teaching. The boy would constantly ask others to help him to find the precise word whenever he felt that he could not find the "right" word he was looking for.

Mary Planter was the next instructor to receive Cadet Crandon. She was assigned to teach him elementary science. She had her master's degree in elementary education but had her bachelor's degree in general sciences. She spent the first day with Robert, showing him many of the different types of "scientific" wonders that his world held. She then gave him a test the next day about those items he had seen—telling him that she was not going to "gig" him for wrong answers. She had learned that the boy was very sensitive to negative criticism—little wonder after he had been forced to lose an entire day of school to dredge out a field latrine!

Robert could not give all the answers on the test; that was far more than anyone would have expected. Nevertheless, he did answer the majority of the questions. Given the short time that Mary had covered some of the topics, she was amazed. She immediately went to Dr. Lawson and told her that Cadet Crandon should be allowed to come to her one hour daily. He would be far better able to benefit from her instruction that way. Mary got her wish and was Robert's science teacher for his first year at Waterline Academy. By the time he finished his first academic year, he was ready to begin secondary education in science. Mary Planter had covered everything up through the sixth grade.

Luiz Rodriguez was permitted to start Robert on his "bilingual" path. Spanish was the chosen second language due to the large Hispanic population within the United States. Rodriguez also needed to have the boy show up for an hour each day; this was also granted. Rodriguez had recommended that Robert also begin other language classes, but those had to wait. After half a year, Robert was started on other languages—albeit not as accelerated as his Spanish.

Andrea Marda was the next professor to see Robert Crandon. She was assigned to teach him his beginning history and geography. It took her only four weeks to cover everything she needed to cover. The boy had completed all the social studies work from first through sixth grade in that time. She was sad to have to let him go and envied Lizzy Gemme—who taught secondary level social studies and history.

When Robert got back to Professor O'Connor, he had only completed seven of the books. "I can't get through them very fast, Professor," he explained. "I'm not allowed to take them with me when we do our drills and chores."

Professor O'Conner decided that *that* was not going to slow up her star pupil! She got Dr. Lawson to ramrod a permission slip for the boy to take his reading books *anywhere*. She also began to teach Robert how to speed-read.

Professor O'Connor and Professor Ruchala traded Robert off to each other each day from December 1969 onward. Robert had classes in Spanish and science each day, but the bulk of his learning for the rest of the school year occurred in arithmetic and reading, spelling, writing, and vocabulary.

After Robert's first academic year, Principal Lawson wanted to grant Robert Crandon an achievement medal for each grade's worth of work in which he obtained mastery. Cadre Captain Gerralds put his foot down. The school could issue no more than four achievement/commendation medals in any given school year to any individual student. Robert Crandon had already received all four of those for which he was eligible. Robert had also received medals for achievement from the cadre.

Robert's classes were usually conducted in the chemistry classroom. Dr. Lawson taught Robert psychology and sociology (although she usually called it Social Studies) in her office during the time when the chemistry class met. Since there was typically only enough students for one chemistry class, that classroom seemed the most logical choice. That left the young boy in a situation where he was often alone for short periods of time. Almost invariably, he would finish his assigned work and head into the laboratory section.

After Robert had burned his eyebrows off for a third time while playing with the chemicals, Professor Brand decided that he had better start teaching the boy which chemicals might be dangerous. Dennis Brand found that Robert was very eager to learn everything possible about chemicals and chemistry in general. Thus it happened that the chemistry teacher supplemented Robert's science lessons for several years.

For Robert's sake, the teachers never told the cadre about the boy's mischievous adventures in the chemistry lab. They loved the cadet and would not give any reason for the cadre to consider mistreating him.

In his succeeding years at Waterline School, Robert continued his meteoric rise in academics. He learned everything he was allowed to learn. He read everything he was allowed to read—and some things he was not given permission to read. Principal Lawson taught him modern psychological principles personally. She wanted this cadet to learn *everything* that Waterline could possibly teach him long before his time was finished. She knew that he belonged elsewhere, and she intended to push the bureaucracy into action. She would not allow Gerralds, Snider, and their thugs to destroy her star pupil. Robert Crandon's welfare kept her at Waterline Academy long after she had originally decided to quit. Her only regret was that he had not yet been transferred to Bethesda Academy. Her mentor, Dr. Emma Wynn, seemed too preoccupied to have read her letters concerning Robert Joseph Crandon.

Another teacher with whom Robert met daily did not have him read any books or manuals. His third day at Waterline Academy, six-year-old Robert Crandon approached Sensei. The cadets had just completed their physical defense class. "Sir," Robert peeped in his high-pitched voice. "Sir, Cadet Crandon wishes to speak with Sensei." As the man turned, Robert remembered to bow.

Sensei Shuichi Wakahisa (Wakahisa Shuichi in his parents' homeland) turned and observed the child. The boy was wearing his white tee shirt and light-blue shorts with the Waterline Academy logo on the left leg section. He had large, blue eyes and very short, blond hair with traces of red showing. Shuichi sensed that the boy's hair was going to turn color—it had not been discolored due to blood. "What is it, cadet?"

"I … I … if it pleases the Sensei, I wish to … learn," the young boy finally managed.

"You have classes twice a week, cadet."

"Yes, sir, but I'm little." Robert meant much more than what he said, but he was young and could not express the fullness of his thoughts. It was clear from the boy's voice and the look in his eyes that he was desperate.

Shuichi understood the boy's fear. The boy in front of him was the youngest and smallest boy in the academy—probably in the history of the academy system! He had been sent to the toughest academy the United States academy system ran. Shuichi remembered times when he was younger and was picked on for his Asian heritage. Growing up Japanese in the United States was often not a pleasant experience just after World War II. It did not seem to matter to Shuichi's tormentors that he had been born after the war to loyal American citizens, one of whom had been unfairly incarcerated in a concentration camp for the duration of the war. The other had earned several medals fighting as a US Army soldier in Italy.

Shuichi addressed his young student. "I will show you the way to learning. You must accept it and embrace it." The smile on Robert Crandon's face told Shuichi all he needed to know.

"Successful warriors win first then go to battle. Defeated warriors go to battle first then seek to win," Sensei told his youngest student.

"How do I know what fight I'll be in, Sensei?"

"Think about it, cadet."

Robert thought long and hard. "I would need to plan every fight possible first?"

"The wise one anticipates."

During an Academy demonstration, Sensei addressed all the cadets, "Any fool can smash his head against a board or his foot against a cinder block. Only the one who concentrates can defeat the board and the rock." He then proceeded to break the board with his head and the cinder block with his foot.

"Wow!"

"Cool!"

"Awesome!" The boys cheered.

"Who will try it?" the master asked. Several of the older cadets took their turns breaking boards with their feet. Cadet Lieutenant Colonel Ted Washington broke one with his fist.

"Cadet Crandon!" Sensei demanded.

Robert popped up from his sitting position immediately. The seven-year-old had never tried breaking anything before. "Shuichi-sensei!" Robert responded automatically.

Shuichi smiled. He had been training the boy daily for over a year. He had taught Robert the basics of the Japanese language—as well as the lessons in hand-to-hand combat. The boy just automatically gave the honorific to his sensei—out of respect, not out of fear. "Those three boards need breaking, cadet," Sensei told the little boy.

Robert approached the three boards. They were spaced two centimeters apart from each other. He stopped to control his movements. He remembered Sensei's teaching, "You must concentrate on your movements. Know what you will hit before you strike it. Know what strength you need to break it. Plan your movements during your marching and chores. Win your battles first, then go to war.

"You must become one with your surroundings. Let others try to use their 'sixth sense.' We will use our five. See what is around you. Hear what noises there are; smell any odors that are out of place. Feel the wind and the ground for movement. Taste the world. With these mastered, you will be as the blind man in a darkened coal mine."

Shuichi approached his young apprentice. "You are ready." He said nothing further.

Robert bowed toward the boards, took in his breath, and unleashed his strength. His concentration was on the boards. He and the boards were one. He was the master; the boards were his tools. Robert's thoughts vanished. When he regained his thoughts, his right hand hurt a little. "Do not let pain be your master. Pain is a signal, but you must be its master," Sensei had instructed long before. Robert moved the pain to a side portion of his thoughts. He noticed the noise of clapping and cheering. It took him a while to understand that he had just accomplished a feat that even most of the cadet senior officers could not accomplish.

Sensei addressed his students. "You cannot defeat the three boards with strength. You can only defeat them with your mind."

PUNISHMENT AT
WATERLINE ACADEMY

Robert thought back again to his early time in Waterline Academy. His first Major penalty had come in the first week. He had not received one hundred gigs, only ninety-two, but he had separately received a minor penalty. Since ten minors got you a major, he was told to report for detail that Friday morning. He woke at 0430 and gobbled up as much food as he could before his detail; he had been warned that food breaks were not required for those serving on the *Battalion Death Squad.*

The cadets assembled next to Alpha Company's barracks and were told to strip down to skivvies and put on "field work" clothing. Robert followed the cadets who headed to a truck and began taking out rags. Robert took what he could find that seemed to fit—a torn shirt and a pair of cut-off shorts that had probably been parade dress uniform trousers at one time. He also scored a pair of old running shoes that had no shoelaces.

The cadets were marched about two kilometers to more waiting trucks. These trucks had buckets in the back. The trucks also had army personnel drivers. The cadets were driven out to a site that was, apparently, an army rifle range. When they arrived, Cadre Captain Summers told them to get off the trucks and take the buckets with them. There was a large liquid storage tank that had been parked near the latrine. The cadets were marched over there and told that they were to empty the latrine holding area into the tank.

There were more than a few groans. Robert Crandon worried that Captain Summers might punish all of them if the complaints got worse, so he spoke up, "Okay, guys. Let's form a bucket line—two of them, in fact."

"What's a bucket line?"

"Just stand in line with a bucket going all the way to the tank," Robert said. He made sure that everyone got placed and placed himself and another plebe into the toughest section—the *inside* of the latrine holding pit. He began filling up the buckets and pushing them out to the cadet waiting. Because of the assembly-line approach, the task went much, much faster than Captain Summers had anticipated. Each of the cadets took turns in each position along the line and worked in cooperation.

Although the work was hard, the sun was hot, and the stench was stifling, the cadets continued their task without further complaint. Captain Summers had expected to have to come back to repeat the detail at least three times before it was complete. Because of Robert's bucket brigade approach, the entire task was finished in twelve hours.

When they returned, they removed everything, including skivvies, and rinsed off under the spigot attached to the Quartermaster Building. The frigid water was both shocking and welcome after the day's excursion. Afterward they ran to their barracks, showered, got dressed, and made it in time for evening meal.

The second time that Robert Crandon had received a Major penalty was not due to any gigs. Cadet Crandon had seen two cadets fighting in the hallway of the school. He had been given permission to go to the latrine, and he simply came upon the scene. He sprung into action the way he had seen SFC Thompson do such things.

"Hey! Guys! Break it up!" Crandon ordered. "Do you want to get Majors for fighting? If you do, why not just go to Captain Gerralds and ask him?" Cadet Jenkins and Cadet Hamilton calmed down some. "What's this all about?" Crandon asked. That was a mistake.

"He called me a j*****!" Jenkins accused.

"You called me a turd!" Hamilton exclaimed.

Both cadets began their melee again. Robert tripped both of them and yelled, "Cut it out!" Both cadets again calmed down, now that they were on the floor. They had not expected the youngest and smallest cadet in Waterline to be able to take them down. Both were feeling a bit sheepish.

"What's going on here?!" Cadre Captain Lazo demanded.

"Martial arts training, sir!" Robert spoke up immediately. "I tripped both cadets."

"One Major for fooling around, cadet! The two of you get to your next classes. Crandon, write it up!" Robert wrote up the punishment and gave his gig book to Captain Lazo to initial. While the cadre officer was signing the book, Robert realized that his punishment could not have really been for "fooling around." If that were the case, then Hamilton and Jenkins would also have been punished. Robert made a mental note to never, ever attempt deception with a cadre officer again.

His punishment had been to stand at attention for sixteen hours straight, most of it in the hot, South Carolina sun. He was only permitted water once every two hours. He was not permitted a latrine break. Since it was such a long time, Robert had to wet his pants to relieve his bladder.

Minor penalties at Waterline Academy usually consisted of meaningless or mindless tasks. Some of the cadets were used as runners for the cadre. Others were given the jobs of cleaning windows, polishing door handles, sweeping hallways and cadre offices, and other such janitorial tasks. Once in a while, a cadre officer would intervene and take special delight in torturing a cadet.

Such was often the case with Cadre Captain Michael Pace. The man considered Waterline Cadets to be worse than murderers—or so one might believe. He often made cadets do brutal calisthenics for the entire hour of their minor punishment. Unfortunately for

Cadet Crandon, Captain Pace singled him out three times. The first time, Robert did jumping jacks for the entire time—vomiting several times before finishing. The second time, Robert was told to run in place, making his knees touch his hands. The third time, Captain Pace sent Robert onto the pull-up bar and made him hang there. Whenever the cadet lost his grip, Captain Pace ridiculed him and then pushed him right back onto the device.

No one liked Captain Pace, not even Cadre Captain Gerralds. Gerralds thought that Pace was a bragger and a bully. He eventually got the cadre officer fired and replaced with one of his own buddies, Cadre Captain Cloud, from Fort Dix. Both had served as drill sergeants together.

Penalties not given out for gigs were often immediate and painful. Cadre Captain Gerralds carried his metal stick. Other cadre officers had placed their handprints and boots prints on most of the cadets' backsides—and other parts of the cadets' bodies. Just being slow could cost a cadet. Cadre Captain Stretcher used to wait at assembly times to find out which cadet arrived last. He would punish that cadet if it was the second time in a row.

Using foul language within the hearing of a cadre officer or professor was a sure way to win a painful episode. Often a cadre officer would grab such an offender and twist his ear until the cadet was on his knees crying. Sometimes a quick backhand to the face would teach the cadet to watch his words—but that was rare. The cadre officers had been schooled on how to inflict pain without causing permanent damage. They were not there to injure the cadets; they were there to *alter* the cadets' behavior to socially acceptable levels.

Robert was almost never struck—except during common weeks. He saw from the very beginning that he needed to always "move like you have a purpose" and "watch your language." It sometimes amazed him that the other cadets often seemed to forget the obvious. Whenever they did, they learned a very harsh lesson.

Gigs were given out for uniform violations, room violations (such as having one's scissors pointing in the wrong direction), and giving the wrong answer for required knowledge questions. Each gig cost a cadet one credit. Each cadet earned one hundred credits per week. A reckoning of accounts was a weekly task that each cadet had to perform with the master of discipline.

It was a common claim that if a cadet had no credits left, he was almost certain to end up on the Death Squad—since he could not "buy" boot polish or brass cleaner. The reality was a bit different: cadets would share all of their resources and materials. The cadets always helped fellow cadets.

In his hospital bed, Robert thought of other punishments that had been meted out to the cadets by the cadre. He shuddered at the memory of what had been done to some of them by Captain Gerralds. As he shuddered, he felt stabbing pains throughout his body. He had already learned to not give in to those pains. That would only lead to yet more pain.

The cadet officers also punished cadets. Robert remembered the first time he had been ambushed. He never even saw the cadet who had done it. He was hit in the head from behind and then kicked several times. This taught him to always be aware of his surroundings. The second time he had been ambushed, he knew exactly who it had been. Cadet Mark Blanchard attacked him for no reason except that Blanchard was angry. Robert had learned a lot about self-defense, but he did not want to hurt Blanchard after the boy had just been hit by one of the cadre officers.

Lieutenant Harry Tromp came to Robert's rescue. He pounced on Blanchard, a much larger cadet than Robert, and gave him a severe beating. He then sent Blanchard on his way. "You should have been able to stop him, Robbie," Harry suggested. "Sensei taught you how to stop that kind of attack, didn't he?"

"I didn't want to hurt him," Robert answered. "He was just mad because Cadre Captain Trebor hit him."

Harry thought for a bit. "Look, kid, you and I are different from most of these creeps. We care about other guys; they don't! You may not want to hurt him, but he doesn't care one bit about hurting you. You can't hesitate in this place. If you stop yourself from acting, you're going to get pounded. Follow Sensei's teaching. These guys have to learn that they can't do that kind of stuff on the outside. They can't make it here if they keep attacking guys. You really aren't doing them any favors by holding back. They have to learn, usually the hard way."

NO PASS HOME

Robert thought about the passes he had not received. He wondered if Father Jeff would be able to find out why he had never gotten one. He desperately wanted to see his parents and his family. He wanted to apologize for all the nasty things he had thought about them earlier during his time at Waterline Academy.

All cadets had been drilled on the mantra that they were at the Academy due to their own faults. Anything that happened to them was their fault, because they were sent to the Academy in the first place.

At first, Robert had been so angry at all of his immediate family that he vowed that he would never want to see them again. That went double for Mrs. Rowell! Eventually he came to realize that the cadre was right. It was his fault that he was there. His parents were only doing what they were told was best for him. But what about Mrs. Rowell?

When talking over the situation with Father Jeff, Robert finally came to realize that Roger Granson was responsible for the mix-up of the letters. Robert did not know what was in his real letter, but that did not matter. He had misbehaved too many times at home. His parents saw the letter, checked with the school and believed that he had become a monster.

Robert then began thinking back to all the passes he had missed.

Robert was expecting that he would get to go see his family for Christmas, 1969. He had only three majors; it required four for a cadet to be banned for Christmas Common Week. When Lieutenant Marks came out to read the names of the cadets who had received passes, Robert did not hear his name. Lieutenant Marks did not have time to console those who were banned—he had to get those with passes to Cadre Captain Gerralds's instructions assembly. After the assembly, the cadets were loaded into buses and brought to Atlanta's Hartsfield/Jackson airport.

When Marks returned from pass, he remembered that his little protégé had not had his name called. He went to see him. "I don't understand it, Robbie. I thought for sure that you would get a pass. You're the first cadet in the history of this academy to ever earn a pass as a plebe."

"Maybe they just don't allow plebes to have passes, sir. Thanks for caring," Crandon responded despondently.

Marks was not satisfied. He went to the battalion adjutant demanding to know why his cadet had been banned. "How the hell would *I* know?" Cadet Major Dowdy asked. "A cad can ban a cadet just for the hell of it. They don't have to give any *reasons.*"

Darryl was still not finished. "You had better find out what's going on, Ted," he told his battalion commander. "That kid has opened up the vent system for us, reorganized the files, gotten all sorts of information for us, and what thanks did he get? He earned a pass at Christmas and was banned! He had better not get banned at Easter without you finding me a reason!"

Darryl recommended Crandon for promotion to Corporal Cadet. Ted had originally told the feisty platoon leader that he had to be crazy. "You can't possibly expect the cads to promote a *plebe.*"

Darryl insisted that he would not take any other cadet as his new fire team leader. He threatened to immediately demote any cadet that Ted sent his way. "The guy already has more medals than any fire team leader in the academy. Just what does it take to get promoted around here?"

On March 6, 1970, the order came that Crandon, Robert Joseph was to join the Cadet Officer Corps. He had been promoted to Corporal Cadet. On March 27, 1970, the list of those who had passes was read; Robert Crandon was not on the list. Once again, Darryl had no time to research the problem until *after* Common Week.

"I don't get it," Ted said to Darryl. "I personally asked each and every cadre officer—except Commandant Snider. There's no point in asking him; he wouldn't take the time to go through the paperwork to ban a cadet. Nobody banned him."

"He was banned!" Darryl insisted.

"I know, I know!" Ted said. "I just don't understand *how*. All the cadre officers sing the kid's praises—even Gerralds and Pace. None of them banned him. I'm sure of that. Maybe the computers just won't allow a plebe to get a pass."

"That's *not* what the law says. You know that as well as I do."

"I really don't understand. I can only tell you that nobody banned him," Ted said. That was the end of that.

Sergeant Cadet Robert Crandon was in his second year at Waterline Academy. Nobody had ever been promoted to squad leader in his second year, but that did not stop Darryl from insisting that Crandon was ready. Robert was assigned to Lieutenant Todd Harnon's platoon. This was Harnon's first year as a senior officer, and he was uncertain of his authority and leadership skills. Sergeant Crandon sensed that and made sure that all of his cadets followed their platoon leader's orders religiously.

In spite of having two transfers, Crandon's squad (B Company, 2nd Platoon, 4th Squad) passed the preliminary inspection. The platoon failed, but not Crandon's squad. Lieutenant Harnon had not sought any input from Crandon and had turned down Robert's offers for help. This cost the platoon a failing inspection grade at the end of October 1970.

After Preliminary Inspection, Darryl approached Lieutenant Harnon and "had it out with him." He told the newly promoted lieutenant that if the latter did not swallow his pride, the senior officer corps would shove that pride down his throat. Lieutenant Harnon swallowed his pride and began asking Sergeant Crandon for help. Once Crandon's suggestions were followed, the platoon's performance improved rapidly.

On November 25, 1970, Robert Crandon had already accumulated all five of his achievement medals and had been awarded three commendation medals. He had received only twelve gigs since September 1st, the least amount in the entire Academy—including the field grade officers. He was expecting to be on the pass list when Lieutenant Harnon read it aloud. Robert's hopes were crushed.

Christmas Common Week of 1970 came and went; Robert still had not received a pass. He had no idea if his family was alive. He had no knowledge of whether or not anybody in his family even *cared* about him. If he was banned, he could not leave the campus to go to the PX, and he could not send or receive mail.

By this time, Robert was taking out his anger and sadness on some of his squad mates. He did not mean to dog them during chores, but he started to become very picky about all the cleaning tasks. It got to the point where Lt. Harnon had to tell his best squad leader to "lighten up on them."

Robert's last hope was coming up on April 9, 1971. He knew that the law required *any* cadet to be given a pass after one and a half years. He also expected that something was wrong with the entire Waterline Academy Pass system and that the law might not be followed. Nevertheless, as the day approached, he got excited about the possibility of going to Massachusetts.

When that hope fell through, Robert Crandon was violently angry. After Easter Common Week, when the rest of the cadets had returned, he went to the academy gymnasium and began working out his anger on one of the punching bags. Robert had never used the "anger management" devices to take out his aggressions. He had practiced on them for karate and judo, but he had always contained his temper. As he continued to beat the device, some other cadets came into the gym—planning to do the same thing with some of the other punching bags.

Darryl had been given the duty of supervising the gym group. It was common for the cadets to show up and take out their aggressions, so the cadre insisted that one senior officer always accompany the group. As Darryl watched the line proceed, he noticed that Robert's line was stagnant. Robert had been kicking and punching for over forty minutes when the tiny cadet shouted out in frustration and kicked his foot into the bag one last time. Robert then gave another shout and punched his hand through the bag all the way up to his elbow.

Darryl went over to the device and led Robert Crandon away. He ordered Lieutenant Barry Smith, who had come to the gym to take out his own aggressions, to take command of the gym and led Robert outside. "Robbie, I've seen guys put their foot or hand all the way into one of those bags before. I have never seen anyone under the age of thirteen do it though! What's wrong?"

"I have never gotten a pass. I'm never going to get a pass. My family will be dead and gone, and I'll never even know it!" Robert cried.

As Robert had predicted, he was banned for the Fourth of July Common Week. He began the next academic year as a squad leader for Lieutenant Timothy Reynolds. Reynolds' platoon was assigned five plebes—a nearly unprecedented amount for Waterline Academy. Waterline was used to getting overflow from Boise, Leavenworth, and Baton Rouge. Whenever lots of boys were enlisted into the academy system, those academies unloaded their worst prospects on Waterline—albeit their worst who had not passed sixth grade. Very rarely had a platoon been assigned five plebes, because the amount of work required to transition those cadets was considered to be beyond a squad leader's capacity.

Although not every squad in the academy had a plebe, Robert Crandon's squad had two. The little cadet never missed a beat. He was already becoming a legend at Waterline Academy, and the senior officer Corps had even more ambitions for Robert. Since Reynolds' platoon had five plebes, they were exempted from Preliminary Inspection. That did not slow down Sergeant Cadet Robert Crandon, though. He pushed his squad to its limits. He went around his entire platoon (Lt. Reynolds had given his young sergeant full access) and helped everyone he could—once Lieutenant Reynolds gave the nod.

Robert knew that incoming cadets had to be punished into the realization that they needed others. He also knew that the cadet officer corps used nasty tricks to ensure that such cadets *would* be gigged. There seemed to be an unwritten agreement between the cadre and the senior officer corps that whenever a cadet was pegged for not cooperating, he received enormous quantities of scrutiny.

As the Thanksgiving Common Week of 1971 approached, Robert no longer expected a pass. He was resigned to the likelihood that no one who mattered cared about him. The list of those with passes included Crandon's entire squad except for him and his two plebes—and the two plebes had received four and five Major penalties already. Robert had received none since Fourth of July Common Week, when Cadre Captain Gerralds gave him a Major penalty because the cadre officer could not accept that a cadet with an unblemished record had been banned. When Robert showed the reason that Captain Gerralds had given him for the Major Penalty to Captain Sinclair, the latter could not believe the brazen and outlandish attitude of Captain Gerralds. At least Crandon had not had to serve the penalty; he was already on the Banned Squad and any Major Penalty would have been a break from that, not a punishment.

On March 31, 1972, Robert destroyed another punching bag. Once again, Darryl witnessed the event. This time, it took the cadet only two hits on the device. Robert continued hitting the bag until it could no longer put up any resistance—the stuffing falling out all over the floor. Robert then moved to the next bag and the next, destroying four of the items before he considered his aggression to have "subsided." Each bag had at least five holes in it.

"You know, we don't usually have to replace more than two or three of those in any single year," Darryl commented.

"Get ready to break open the piggy bank," Robert said between breaths. "I'm going to bankrupt the country if that's what it takes to get noticed. I don't want to have to wait until I'm dead for my family to see me!"

"What are you talking about?" Darryl asked.

"You've seen Captain Gerralds. He's not the same person who came in here five years ago. You guys had me log all the history. Just how long do you think it's going to take before he kills somebody? With my luck, that someone will be me!"

Darryl responded, "Rumor has it that Commandant Snider is retiring after this school year. I promise you, Robbie, I *will* get to the new commandant to bring up your passes. I will *not* let the system get you banned again. I can't do anything about Fourth of July, but either you go see your folks in November, or nobody does!"

Excerpts from "Letter to parents of prospective disciplinary academy cadets" by Jacob Williams, Director of Academies, August 3, 1954:

Please keep in mind that you are not at fault. You are doing the best thing you can for your son. His teacher's recommendation and his principal's approval ensure that you are not just acting in a fit of anger …

It will greatly facilitate your son's transition into the academy system if you display your *extreme* disappointment in his behavior … If he has any brothers and sisters, they should be made aware of why their brother is being sent away …

Your son becomes a ward of the federal government. This does not mean that you have no rights concerning your son; however, the commandant of the respective academy, or his designee, will have the primary role of guardian …

Do not believe everything your son tells you about the academy he is attending. It is common for the cadets to exaggerate the amount and type of discipline …

… your son to have the best chance possible of being capable of functioning in society. It has been shown that the rate of recidivism (turning to anti-social behavior again) out of disciplinary academies is very low. This statistic alone makes the action you have chosen to take for your son one of the most loving and self-sacrificing actions you could possibly make. I congratulate …

WOULD PRAYERS BE ANSWERED?

When Mrs. Crandon, Mrs. Rowell, and Principal Edwards, a tall, lanky man, had rushed onto the steps with the changed paperwork, they saw the van carrying Robert Crandon pull away. The two women collapsed into each other's arms, crying hysterically. Each woman tried to console the other that it had been, "my own fault, not yours," and neither was consolable. Principal Edwards had slumped to the stairs. He knew that he had just sentenced a child who would perhaps have been the next scientific genius of the world to the harshest fate that any boy in the United States could receive. He still recalled reading Mrs. Rowell's *real* letter to the Crandons.

Your son is the most gifted child I have ever heard of. I would have written sooner, but this is my first year as a teacher; I needed to confirm my suspicions with some of the more experienced teachers on the floor. I recommend that you begin paperwork immediately to send him to the gifted academy at Bethesda, MD. I realize that they usually won't take a child under the age of eight, but I honestly believe that his spectacular capacity for learning will convince them to make an exception.

If you are worried about the possible loneliness that your son might face, you can apply for a government package to relocate to Bethesda, and the country will pick up all reasonable expenses. I know that you have four other children and that such a burden is heavy, but the country needs to develop its most promising minds. Please con-

sider your son's options carefully. I look forward to meeting you and discussing your son's prospects, and I am hoping that it will be as soon as possible.

Mary-Ann K. Rowell

John Crandon was in a dismal mood. The ten-year-old boy blamed
himself for his brother's absence. John had lost his playmate, his
confidant, and his baby brother because he was too mean to say anything. When Robbie started getting spanked with the belt, John had
thought, "Cool, now he gets it too." John knew that his brother was
innocent. After all, he played in the same recess area as Robbie. He
was just so tired of his brother being right all the time. He was also
terrified of his father's temper and admitted to himself that he had
been afraid to interfere since his father might turn his attentions
on John. John hated that he had participated in chiding his little
brother; he, above all others, knew his brother was innocent, yet he
spat insults at Robbie anyways.

He waited for news, and he prayed for his little brother, Robert.

Kevin was sure that he had failed his parents. He prayed for forgiveness. He prayed that his little brother would be okay. It was his job
to look after Robbie and instead, Robbie turned into a bully and a
problem child. Kevin couldn't understand how such a nice kid at
home could be such a terror at school. It must have been so; his parents read the letter aloud to all of the children. Now his brother was
in the toughest academy in the country, probably getting beaten up
daily since Robbie was so small, even for his age.

Kevin knew, even though his parents had not said it, that Robbie
was hurt. It had been three years since any of them had seen Robbie. If
going to South Carolina meant that they could see their little brother,
his parents would have taken all of the children with them, unless ...

Marie was the most whimsical of the Crandon children. She played happily with dolls and then moved on to stuffed animals when she turned ten. She was a social butterfly and was very popular with all the boys. She was budding into a pretty young redhead with very little between the ears. Her siblings used to joke that what Robbie got extra in brains must have come at Marie's expense. She did not care; she just continued on her merry way.

At that time, though, Marie was deadly serious. Aunt Jen had never cried in Marie's presence. Marie had complained when her parents said they were going to South Carolina "for some important business," she wanted to go too. It was not until the next day that Nancy reminded her that Waterline Academy was in South Carolina and that their brother attended Waterline Academy. Marie knew that her mother and father would not have left her unless there was something they did not want her to see. She prayed that she would get to see Robbie again.

Nancy, although two years Marie's junior, was the leader of all the Crandon children. She took care of them, even Marie. She was the one who organized the Christmas plays that they put on for Mom and Dad each year. She was the one who decided when they could wake their parents on Christmas and Easter. She made sure that each of the children did his or her chores properly. Now, she was the one who cuddled Patrick and changed his diapers and sang him lullabies while his mother was away.

Nancy hated her failure. She swore that none of the others would ever get accused falsely again—not if she could help it. Marie knew all the gossip at South Side Elementary during Robbie's first year. Nancy should have grilled her to find out if the claims in the letter were true. Instead, she just took the word of the teacher and scolded her (then) youngest brother for being naughty. It was not until Nancy found her mother crying on the school steps that she realized that something was terribly, terribly wrong.

"What's wrong, Mommy?" the little girl had asked. "Why are you crying? Is it because we had to send our two-faced, little beast to the academy?" When her mother burst into another uncontrollable fit of hysterics, Nancy started to put two and two together. Nancy waited for her sister to come out to recess and took her away from their mother.

"Marie, I want you to think really hard. You got that?" The older girl nodded, somewhat bewildered. "Do you know who all the bullies in the school are and were, even the little kids?" Marie nodded again, this time with definite confidence. "Was Robbie one of those that the little kids complained about?"

Marie thought for a long while. "Actually, uh-uh. I never heard anything bad about him. He got beat up. I heard about that the day after it happened, but nobody ever told me he was so mean. Anyways"— the girl bubbled—"I have to go meet with Jan and Lisa. I'll see ya' around." Marie ran off to meet the other two girls in her clique.

That was when Nancy knew that her brother was innocent, that he had been telling the truth. "Why didn't I stick up for him? Why didn't I force Dad to go to the stupid school and check?" These were questions that haunted the child up to that very day in November when all of the family awaited news about Robbie.

Nancy prayed for her little brother, Robbie. She could not imagine how the small boy had managed in such a notorious academy. She pictured him getting attacked every day by the real hoodlums.

PAUL AND ROBERTA
MEET THEIR SON AGAIN

Mr. and Mrs. Crandon were *not* going to be put off again! They had endured three years of stalling, indifference, lies, stupidity, and outright bigotry toward their third son. Mrs. Crandon was especially emotional, having just delivered her fourth son less than one month earlier. Mr. Crandon was in his "violent temper" mood, so typical for his Irish heritage.

"I'm sorry, sir," the receptionist tried to explain again, "but the commandant of the academy has custody of all the cadets. Only he can authorize you to see Cadet Crandon. In order to do that, he must give express, *written* consent. I am not authorized to change that, sir." She was doing her best to try to keep an explosive situation from becoming an illegal one, with her being the victim.

"Then call the commandant, right now!" demanded Mr. Crandon. "I mean, *right now!*"

The receptionist considered this to be the most accomplishable request she had heard from this large, angry man since he entered the hospital, so she immediately grabbed her telephone receiver and punched in some numbers. "I need to speak to the commandant of Waterline Academy!" she pleaded. After a short while, the Crandons heard the one-sided telephone conversation.

"Sir, the *Crandons* are here. They are demanding to see their son, sir. They are very, *very* insistent." A pause. "Sir, the regulations require your express, written consent." Pause. "Yes, sir, I suppose I can do that." Pause. "You will be on your way right after this call?

Thank you very much, sir!" The last sentence was said with an emotion of such extreme relief that one might have assumed the woman had just heard the news that she had been taken off of death row.

"The commandant said that you can go right in. He said that he will be coming by with a letter giving you access to your son for your stay here, but that you don't have to wait. Hold on, I'll get a nurse to take you up to the ICU."

After being allowed to pass the armed military police guard, Mrs. Crandon looked at her son and was reminded of cartoons that her other children watched. Whenever a cartoon character seemingly took enormous damage, whether from being hit by a truck or falling off of a cliff, the character would be wrapped nearly from head to foot in bandages. Robbie had some parts of his body exposed, but she only saw all the white linen and cotton bandages. She rushed to her child's side, crying, "Robbie!" and began to weep. She remembered the last words she had said to her baby boy: "What did you do this time, you little beast?" She had wept over the memory of those words countless times, and she wept over that memory again.

Mr. Crandon was similarly taken aback. He had been a US Army Corpsman, trained as well as any paramedic; he knew what those bandages must mean underneath. The bandages, by and large, were not bloodstained. That meant internal bleeding, a lot of internal bleeding, and broken bones as well. He was haunted by his last words, "Get out of my face, you little beast. I don't want to see you anymore!" and wept profusely.

"Mr. Crandon?" a voice asked. Paul looked at the priest and nodded glumly. "I am Father Lions. I was the one who wrote you the letter."

"How?" was all that Paul could choke out. Once again, he tried to articulate, "H–How?" He gestured at his son.

"I would prefer to tell you away from Robbie's hearing—if you don't mind." The priest gestured outside the hospital room, and Paul nodded, solemnly. "Not immediately. Whenever the two of you are ready," Father Jeff added, reassuringly. "I won't be going anywhere anytime soon."

The Crandons waited at their son's side for nearly fifteen minutes when a weak voice came out of the bandaged head, "Mother? Father? I'm so sorry that I caused you to need to put me in Waterline. Will you please forgive me? Please?"

Thrilled at their son's resiliency and choked with guilt, the two nearly stumbled over each other's speaking trying to reassure their son that he had done nothing to deserve his fate. Robert began to weep in great distress and sorrow. Father Lions noticed the disappointment in the child's eyes; he was only just starting to understand the necessity of Robert holding on to the world that the small child perceived. He whispered into Mr. and Mrs. Crandon's ears, "It would be best to just offer him your forgiveness for now, I think. We can all work on the other part later."

Paul Crandon seemed to grasp the priest's intent and declared, "Robert, I forgive you. I take back my last words to you. You have done well and made the family proud of you." He quickly turned away, lest his son see the agony on his face from such a difficult set of statements. Robert's face brightened considerably. Roberta was taken aback at her husband's change of attitude, until she saw his face after he turned away. Then, Roberta finally understood what Father Lions was intimating.

"I forgive you too, Robbie. I forgive you anything you may have done. I love you, Robbie. I will always love you, no matter what." She put her head near his and did her best to try to think happier thoughts about her son. He was alive. He had the willingness to live, to continue breathing. She was grateful that she got the chance to see him at least once more before he died. At that last thought, she began weeping again, but silently this time.

"I'm kind of tired, Mother. Is it okay if I get some more sleep?" Robert asked.

"Of course it's okay, dear. You do whatever you need to do. We'll be fine, Robbie." Roberta's little boy smiled a peaceful smile. Roberta could see the peace in her third son's face. She wept lightly and thanked God that she got to speak to her son at least one more time.

WHAT IS WRONG WITH WATERLINE ACADEMY?

Right after Robert had passed out in front of the rectory where Father Lions lived, the priest immediately called for an ambulance, the military police, and the academy commandant. Commandant Leary had rushed over to see the broken body of one of his cadets. In his entire history with the academy system, he had never seen a boy beaten *that* badly. He asked the priest what had happened.

"Just what did you *expect* to happen?" the priest demanded sarcastically. "Did you think that these thugs and killers of yours would always get away with their heavy-handed tactics? Did you think the boys were made out of rubber and plastic? You let a madman like *Gerralds*"—the feisty priest spat on the ground—"you let a madman like that beat the living hell out of the kids with metal bars, and you think that the kids will always bounce back! You and yer kind ought to be the ones gettin' yer' brains beat in, not this little darlin' of a boy!" Father Jeff knelt down next to Robert and performed the rites for Anointing of the Sick. It was called "Last Rites" by some, and Father Jeff suspected that just might be the case of his young altar server.

"This," the commandant indicated the damage done to the cadet, "is not me, Father. This is patently illegal. I had no idea that things were this bad." Commandant Leary's salt-and-pepper eyebrows furrowed. He suspected there was much more than just a few beatings bothering the priest. He knew he had to proceed carefully.

"Well then, you shoulda'. Why didn't ya, huh?" the priest demanded. "Why go tell the boys that ye got an open door policy and then torture anybody tryin' to use it? Why hide yerself in yer office and let that maniac run the whole, God-forsaken place like he owns it, huh?"

Commandant Leary paused only shortly but began to discern much as he said, "I have been here just two months, Father. I agree. It is *my* responsibility. I am not offering excuses, only an explanation. I depend upon the other cadre in this academy. I did not actually *see* anything remiss. If I had, I would have investigated it. The boys must have found *some* way to adapt to what has been going on. As you have just informed me, apparently, the other cadre officers made sure that no cadets ever got to make any complaints to me.

"I don't consider myself innocent in this. I've been in the academy system for twelve years. I should have known that something was wrong when I received no complaints. In Boise, there were usually at least ten complaints a month. I just figured that since Waterline is a maximum-security facility, that things were different here. I was still trying to figure things out.

"I need your help, Padre. I need to know everything that's been going on under my nose. I promise you that I will do my absolute best to change everything wrong about this place. After I do that, if you want, I will personally hand you my resignation. Deal?" Commandant Leary was serious in his pledge, and Father Lions decided to trust him. Father Lions told the new commandant about all the physical attacks that were going on. He told him about the alleged child sexual abuse. He told him all the complaints that the boys had been building up for five long years.

Cadre Captain Gerralds arrived at the rectory a short time after the military police. "What's up, Joe? I heard that some kid got attacked?" Gerralds had been a drill sergeant in the army before taking a post at Waterline Academy. His youthful countenance showed in stark contrast to Commandant Leary's age. He had dark-blond hair and was perfectly clean-shaven. His hair was cut very short, nearly as short as that of the cadets he was placed in charge of. As Commandant Leary studied him, he could see no sign of nervousness.

He's playing it very cool, thought Commandant Leary. *Very smooth, very smart.* Out loud, Commandant Leary asked, "Where's your swagger stick, Tom?"

The master of discipline of Waterline Academy took an involuntary step backward. "I … I heard that you needed me right away, so I must have forgotten to grab it. I don't really need it anyways, right?" He laughed disarmingly. On a cool, November day, the master of discipline began to perspire.

You never failed to take it along before, the commandant thought. Out loud, he asked, "And why the change of clothes? You came in this morning in parade dress, now you're in Class A? You've changed your shoes, your socks. You've changed everything you're wearing." Joseph Leary had been a top interrogator for the air force before retiring and taking a job with the academy system. He could break lies in his sleep, and this man had not had nearly enough time to form a good alibi.

"I don't like your intonation, *sir,*" Captain Gerralds answered. "Just what's going on here? Am I under arrest for something?" Captain Gerralds motioned toward the military police officers who were waiting about twenty feet away. All cadre officers had been taught to closely guard their outward responses. As a consequence, Joseph Leary had learned to read a lot into the smallest twitches that any fellow cadre officer made. Captain Gerralds's quick eye movements back and forth from his commandant to the military police spoke volumes to the commandant of Waterline Academy.

Commandant Leary decided to push his emotional advantage. "Well, Tom. If there's nothing going on, then you won't mind these gentlemen searching your office, right?"

Gerralds's face showed panic (at least to a highly trained observer). "I … I think I mind that *very much,* as a matter of fact! I have personal items in there, and I see no reason why anyone should need to search me. If some cadet lieutenant has been sent to the hospital with broken ribs or broken legs, you should be questioning all the cadets, not the master of discipline! Give me five minutes with each cadet, and I *guarantee* you I'll get a confession for this crime!"

"I just bet you might, Tom. I bet you might. Of course, then we would have more crimes on our hands, wouldn't we? And tell me, Tom, how did you know it was a cadet lieutenant? I didn't even notice that before they took the boy off to the hospital. I've been here with Father Lions the whole time, and I didn't see him tell anyone else about *which* boy was injured." Father Lions shook his head, affirming that he had not told anyone about the boy's identification. "You also named injuries that I'm sure will prove to be accurate. I wasn't told by the paramedics which injuries the boy received, but you already know them—before the doctors? We don't need your permission to search your office. We'll just have these gentlemen hold you here until we get a warrant. We probably don't even need a warrant, since the office is academy property, but we'll get one, just to be certain."

The bloody metal stick, bloody boots, and blood-spattered clothes were found in Gerralds's office. The commandant had kept the cadets in lock-down in the school while the investigation proceeded. The cadet battalion commander and the cadet battalion executive officer had not been scheduled for class, so they were in their barracks. Commandant Leary ordered a head-count to be taken of all the cadets, and two came up missing: Cadet-Lieutenant Robert Crandon, who was accounted for since he was in the hospital, and Cadet John Freeman. Commandant Leary ordered the cadre to find the boy—wherever he was. The search went on for three hours before Commandant Leary gave it up as hopeless.

He ordered all the cadets back to the barracks area, got them fed, and then had them kept in their rooms until further notice. His fellow cadre officers were not pleased at the increased military police presence all over the academy grounds, but they kept their complaints down to silent glares. As Commandant Leary was about to call his superior, he heard a knock on his door. "Enter."

"Sir, Cadet Major Marks wishes to speak with the commandant!" Leary leaped to his door, calmed himself down, and opened the door. He ushered the gangly teen into his office. He noticed that only the secretaries were in the main office; the other cadre officers must all have retreated to their private offices.

"Go ahead, Marks. What concerns you?" the commandant asked in the formal voice he nearly always used with cadets.

Cadet Major Marks stared straight forward, at the position of attention. "Sir, it has come to my attention that you may be searching for one or more cadets. As the cadet adjutant, it is my responsibility to be able to locate any cadet as soon as the cadre requires it. If you can name the cadet or cadets in question, I will locate them as required, sir!"

This was more cooperation than Commandant Leary had expected, more than Father Lions had left him believing was even possible from the cadets. "Close the door, cadet." Cadet Major Marks closed the door quietly and turned back to the commandant. "I am not interested in punishing *any* cadet. Do you understand me? I am investigating a *very* serious incident. A cadet was nearly killed today. He is not expected to live through the night. I need to know if there were any witnesses to the attack.

"I am not one of *them*," Commandant Leary continued, moving his eyes toward the area where many of the individual cadre offices were located. "I should have found out about this place sooner, and that is for me to correct, but I am not one of *them*. I need a witness, if there is one. I need to have other witnesses about other crimes that have been occurring in this academy. Pass the word that I will take any statements from any cadet who wishes to make them. No repercussions will come from any accusations. All, and I mean *all* accusations will be investigated with diligence and honesty. Tell the cadets that they can come to me anytime, day or night, for the next few days and tell me what they know. I will not allow any backlash, punishments or harm come to anyone who tells me anything."

Cadet Major Marks was nodding his head, contemplating. *He's wondering if he can trust me,* thought Commandant Leary. Out loud, Leary said, "Please send Cadet Freeman to me. If he has not eaten, then have a tray of food brought here. I swear to you, cadet, there will be no negative repercussions for any cadet concerning this."

"What do you think?" Cadet Lieutenant Colonel Perry Temple asked. He looked at his two fellow field-grade officers.

Cadet Major Peter Lee, the battalion executive officer, looked toward Major Marks. "You're the one who talked to him."

"Robert Crandon may have given his life to give us this chance! We can't pass it up!" Darryl insisted. "I say we take him at his word."

"We haven't checked out his file yet, though," Perry reminded them.

" … And we won't for a long time! Robbie's in the hospital!" Darryl whispered intently.

"Yeah, that's gonna be a problem," Peter agreed.

Perry Temple took a deep breath and let it out. "I'll go talk to Freeman. I'll offer to go with him—if he wants. If the commandant is serious, he'll let me stay with Freeman."

"We've got to give him up soon anyways," Peter stated. "After six hours his name will be all over the country—armed and dangerous!"

Perry nodded. "Darryl, get Freeman's dinner. Peter, go get an MP to take us to the cadre office."

For the next several days, Commandant Leary heard tales of beatings, rapes, terror, and cover-ups that he thought were nearly impossible. He tracked the stories the best that he could while the academy chaplain, Father Lions, kept a lonely watch next to the bed of a nine-year-old boy whose body had been shattered by a sadistic maniac.

Four days after Cadet Crandon had been attacked, Father Lions came into Commandant Leary's office in frenzy. "If you want that boy to live, you gotta give me all the help ye can!" The priest was desperate.

"Of course, Padre. Just what is it that you need?"

"That cadet has the most stellar record in the history of the academy, I'd be willin' to bet. Yet he's never gotten a pass for Common Week in all his three years! He wants to know why, and he wants to know in two days. If he doesn't find out, I don't think he'll have the will to live!"

"Three years!" the commandant shouted. "That's illegal! How did he even manage to remain sane after all this time?"

The commandant worked on the problem all that day and long into the night. He questioned the cadre officers who were still at the academy (several had already been placed on administrative leave pending further investigation). He checked the cadet's records, gig books and academic records, but he could not come up with any reason whatever why Cadet Robert Crandon had not gotten a pass. In fact, Cadet Crandon should have set a record in Waterline Academy, having earned a pass by Christmas Common Week of his first year in the academy system, but he had been banned out of principle by Gerralds. None of the cadre officers had banned Cadet Crandon after that. Even Gerralds's records showed a deep respect for the young cadet. It just made no sense.

Commandant Leary visited Tom Gerralds in prison. "Did you ban Crandon from getting passes?" he asked.

Gerralds's Lawyer, Joseph Hamilton, whispered into his client's ear. Tom answered his lawyer, "No, there's nothing there that he's looking for." Hamilton nodded. Tom Gerralds looked at his former superior. "I only banned him for his first Christmas. Now that I recall, I wish I hadn't. Old Sourpuss kept bothering me about that … something about him not getting a pass—ever?" Joseph Leary nodded. "I don't know what happened. I didn't ban him after that. The kid was the best of the bunch … best we've ever had." Commandant Leary returned to his office to search some more.

Finally, when searching through the computer records of all the cadets, Commandant Leary typed in Crandon's identification number as 0245637. The record for "Anderson, Paul Charles" came up, so Commandant Leary immediately typed in the correct number O245637. No name came up. He typed in the identification number again, and still no name came up. He scrolled down the database and came to "Crandon, Robert Joseph." The identification number next to the name had a zero, not a capital O. The cadet officers had all been identified with capital Os to show them apart from the rest of the cadets.

Commandant Leary created a new database with just the two cadets, Crandon and Anderson. He identified both with the zero number instead of using the capital O. He then put in passes for both cadets. The first name showed Ps, the second one showed Bs. He changed the ID number for Crandon to reflect the capital O and input the passes again. This time, both names had Ps in the slots. A typographical error and a similar identification number had kept Cadet Crandon from receiving passes for nearly three years!

The evidence was clear. Once Cadet Crandon became Corporal Cadet Crandon, he was assigned a new identification number. That had occurred in March of 1970. Starting Easter Common Week, 1970, a freshly promoted fire team leader with the fewest gigs in the history of the academy for a plebe had been let down by the system not just in spite of his success, but *because* of it. Had Crandon never been promoted, he would have been allowed to go home for Easter Common Week—the first plebe to ever accomplish such a feat. Instead, the secretarial staff had simply entered the data and never double-checked the entries. Commandant Leary informed the chaplain of the error that had kept Robert prisoner to Waterline Academy for a longer time than any previous cadet in academy history.

Two days after his discovery of the clerical lunacy, Commandant Leary received an urgent phone call from the hospital. It was the receptionist at the front, "Sir, the *Crandons* are here. They are demanding to see their son, sir. They are very, *very* insistent."

"Then, by all means, let them in."

"Sir, the regulations require your express, written consent."

"If I come there immediately, do you suppose you can let them in now?"

"Yes, sir, I suppose I can do that."

"Then do that! I am on my way with a letter."

"You will be on your way right after this call? *Thank you very much, Sir!*"

WATERLINE FROM A CADET'S POINT OF VIEW

Robert thought back on his first Thanksgiving at Waterline Academy as he lay in his hospital bed alone.

Over half the academy cadets had been banned from common week. Cadre Captain Gerralds was in charge of the punishments. He decided to have the cadets scrub the walkways and roads with toothbrushes. Robert had remembered something that Cadet Lieutenant Marks had told him, so Robert was scrubbing away fiercely. One of the cadet company commanders came over to him. In a *very* soft voice, Cadet Captain Sealer asked Robert, "What's up, cadet? Why are you so gung-ho about this?"

Robert explained it. "Well, sir," he began, looking around to ensure that no cadre officer was in listening distance. "All the toothbrushes have *Waterline Academy* written on them."

"Okay. So what?"

"Well, sir, according to Lieutenant Darryl, we can sign for one toothbrush at a time. The cadre can also have these toothbrushes, but they have to *pay* for them."

"Yeah, they get paid, so they have to pay for certain items. I still don't *quite* get you." Cadet Captain Sealer was starting to realize that he may have a great opportunity for revenge against Cadre Captain Gerralds, but he needed to understand fully. Captain Gerralds had banned Sealer because his company had the lowest grades.

Robert put his head down and scrubbed more furiously. Sealer, being attuned to such signals, did the same. As Captain Gerralds passed the two boys who were scrubbing vigorously on the sidewalk, Robert held up the remains of the toothbrush he was using. "Sir, this toothbrush has had it. May I have another, please?" The six-year-old smiled and blinked in an impish way.

"That's the third one today, cadet. I may have to put you in for a *merit* for this." Captain Gerralds suggested. He took a new toothbrush out of the box he was carrying and handed it to Robert. "Keep up the good work, cadet."

After the cadre officer had moved a safe distance away, Robert continued to explain his plan. "Anyways, sir, if Cadre Captain Gerralds has to pay for *each and every* toothbrush that I use up, then I figure that the more I use up, the better. Then I win, and *he* loses." Cadet Captain Sealer now knew why a rival company with the youngest plebe in the history of the academy was sporting more merits than his own company. He smiled and then moved down the line of cadets. He told each and every cadet the means toward *out-cadding the cad.*

Although Robert had not known it at that time, he soon learned that all punishment details were logged into a book. Once a cadre officer logged a punishment into the book, he could not rescind the order. Thus, once Captain Gerralds had used the idea of having the sidewalks and roads scrubbed with toothbrushes, he was stuck for it; even though he was paying a fortune to replace destroyed toothbrushes. Captain Gerralds did not even know that his paycheck was being automatically deducted for the cost of the items. For eleven days, the academy cadets worked more diligently at scrubbing the sidewalks and roads than they had ever worked on any other project.

During Christmas of 1969, the cadets had been set to washing the windows in the school building. Once again, Cadre Captain Gerralds was supervising the work. Once again, the cadets relied on their youngest, smallest member to help them gain an element of revenge. "We know how to make the windows look perfectly clean yet have letters show up at a distance. The only problem is that *everybody* can see them, the cads included. Any ideas, Robbie?"

Cadet Johnson had been told to rely on this young, gifted cadet. Robert was the new "vent rat" and was to be completely trusted. Harry Johnson had been in the academy for seven years and knew that he was stuck there until he was finished with his schooling. He had little ambition concerning officer ranks, but he was the oldest cadet assigned to this detail, so the cadet officer corps had put him partially in charge.

"Well, we could always put up a message in code," Robbie suggested.

"Code?" Harry asked, dumbly.

"Yes. We could code the message so that the cads can't read it. Well, they might be able to read it if they break the code, but they won't be able to *prove* it."

"Okay, but how do we win with that?" Harry asked.

"Well, we make the code easy to understand if you *know* the code, but hard to get if you don't have the translation."

Captain Gerralds is a weenie! Please smile when you understand! The windows of the school screamed out the message to each and every cadet in the academy. Smiles went on for months, and the cadre showed no signs of having broken the code. Apparently, the military personnel on the military base *had* broken the code, because there were laughs, horns honking, and some good-natured praises for the cadets whenever military personnel drove by the school building. The cadets got their revenge once again.

Cadre Captain Gerralds was in a particularly mean mood by the time Easter of 1970 came around. He planned to work the cadets at his most meaningless task yet. Robert had been promoted to fire team leader, had expected a pass, and had *not* received it. Robert assumed that since he was in his first year, he must have been ineligible to earn a pass, in spite of the fact that he was earning credits at the PX at unprecedented levels. Captain Gerralds sent the *Banneds*, as they were called, out into the parade field to cut the grass with nose hair clippers. Robert, when he heard this, was thrilled beyond any reasonable measure any other cadet could imagine, especially upon hearing such dire news. The boys were each given nose-hair clippers and told to begin cutting.

Corporal Cadet Crandon organized all the cadets in work groups. He made sure that each cadet was cutting to his *exact* specifications. By this time, none of the cadets questioned having a six-year-old in charge. They knew his prowess at sneaking through the vents, picking locks, and creating the code that had gone unbroken. They worked as diligently as they could, figuring that they would be given the *good news* about their work after the common week was over.

Captain Gerralds is an idiot! Please send him postcards to let him know this! The message in the grass was unmistakable from the air. The pilots, who were constantly in flight over Fort Waterline, had passed the message on to the other military personnel. Gerralds became the laughing stock of the military base. He was inundated with postcards from the entire base. He heard snickers and mumbling whenever he was anywhere near the military personnel. He was, of course, never told about the messages the cadets were leaving. As far as the military personnel were concerned, if the boys at the academy could leave the messages, the academy cadre officers needed to find the messages themselves.

Cadre Captain Gerralds *always* supervised common week punishments. He began carrying a leather strap and routinely hit cadets. His claim, each time, was that the cadets were lollygagging, but the evidence showed otherwise. Some of the time, he used the punishment on boys who were not working as hard as they could, but he never failed to strike each and every one of them at least once a day.

Robert continued his creativity. When all the metal garbage cans in Fort Waterline were sent to the academy for cleaning, Robert scrubbed them as hard as he could, destroying at least one third of those he scrubbed. When the cadets were forced to strip the wax off of the floors of C Company's barracks and rewax them, he also had the boys wash the windows. In a new code, the message was, "Captain Gerralds has no brains!" The code was simple; one only had to follow the letters from one side of the building to the other in alternating fashion. If any cadre member deciphered it, the cadets never heard about it. Captain Gerralds had not learned his lesson with the parade grounds, and leaving messages via nose-hair clippers became one of Robert's great specialties. Captain Gerralds also spent a small fortune on toothbrushes, since he had also failed to learn that lesson.

The biggest problem, from Robert's point of view, had been passes in general. He just had no idea what he needed to do to get the cadre to allow him to visit his family.

Another budding specialty of Robert Crandon was his uncanny capacity to find his way to places. Each June, before Fourth of July Common Week, the cadets were sent on a "Land Navigation Course." This usually consisted of cadets being given maps and compasses, one fifteen-minute period of instructions, and a lot of points on the map where they needed to go to get their meals for the next several weeks. They crisscrossed back and forth over the training course as per instructions left to them. Often a group would stop at a point only to discover that it was actually another group's meal location.

During the June 1970 course, most of the cadets were assigned to groups of five cadets each. Although Robert Crandon was a member of the Cadet Officer Corps, he was not the ranking member in his group. That position belonged to Sergeant Cadet Anthony Fernandez. Sergeant Fernandez, Corporal Crandon, Cadet Peters, Cadet Jackson, and Cadet Murray were put together. Each of the other cadets—besides Robert Crandon—was eleven or twelve years old. They assigned the "water fetching" duty to Corporal Crandon.

The cadets had been closely instructed to use their water purification tablets a half hour before drinking any water. Robert had to keep track of his own and each of the other boy's canteens. Each cadet had three of them. Robert simply made sure that the cadets used their canteens from left to rear to right. That allowed him to keep track of which canteens needed to wait for more time before they were safe.

For their part, the other boys taught Robert how to start fires using flint rocks, how to track animals, how to dig fire pits and other useful outdoor tasks. Robert had first grumped about having to serve all the other boys—after all, he outranked all but one of them. In the end, he decided that he would just put up with having to do tasks for everyone else.

Sergeant Fernandez was not good with maps. He had been given the location to each of their destinations and had failed to arrive at any destination on time. Robert Crandon had tried to suggest alternate routes, but Fernandez always replied, "I've got it, small fry. Butt out!" The penalty for not arriving early enough was that the cadre took your food back to have the cookware washed. Those who had not completed their journey on time also did not get a morning meal, sunscreen, or bug repellant.

By the fourth day out, Peters, Jackson, and Murray were ready to start a mutiny. While Robert Crandon was filling canteens, Peters gave an ultimatum to Sergeant Cadet Tony Fernandez. "Either you give the map and compass to Crandon, or we leave your shattered body here and give the map to him ourselves!"

When Robert returned with the water, Sergeant Fernandez announced, "I think that the new guy should get some practice at following maps." He quite unnecessarily explained to Robert how to use a map and compass. Robert looked at their next destination and the penciled route that Fernandez planned to take. The route would have followed a ridge and then a stream. That might have delayed the group until midnight—trying to remain on top of a ridge and then slogging through a swamp.

Robert changed the course immediately. He led the team into an open area and crossed along to the end. He then shot an azimuth straight to their destination through overgrowth and forest. He had Jackson break up any big brush in the way and had Peters go as far as he could see him. He adjusted Peters until the cadet was at the correct azimuth and then paced out one hundred seventy steps for each one hundred meters.

Although Robert's course took them away from a direct line to their destination, it cut the time so quickly that the cadets arrived at the destination hut before Cadre Captain Sinclair had reached it. Captain Sinclair had been dropping off food for other cadets and had not really expected to see this team anyways. He was pleasantly surprised when he came driving down the pathway and found the cadets waiting for him.

"You finally made it to one of your objectives! Well, congratulations, cadets." He had the cadets help him unload their meals and—thank goodness—bug repellant and sun screen. Robert was the navigator for the rest of the two weeks.

In June of 1971, the cadets were allowed to separate themselves into teams of five members each. Robert fell into a line randomly and then twenty cadets began pushing and shoving to get into line behind him. Darryl Marks, soon to be the battalion adjutant, had to come over and break up the potential melee. Cadre Captain Cloud noticed the group and asked what the problem was. Darryl tried to side step the question, but since he was a *senior* cadet officer, he was not supposed to be with that group anyways. The senior cadet officers had a more challenging course that they had to follow.

Captain Cloud decided that since the cadets had not separated themselves, that he would assign them to teams. He looked up the notes he had about the cadets and assigned three plebes and a transfer to go with Sergeant Cadet Crandon. The note next to Crandon had said, "Could find a needle in a jungle and would probably find extras while on the way."

Sergeant Crandon's team was initially given a *typical* course to follow. After he had achieved the first nine objectives, the cadre decided to test their youngest, and presumably, most capable (as far as land navigation was concerned) cadet to his absolute limits. Cadre Captain Sinclair had been assigned Robert's team, so he brought the next day's objective. When he came to give Robert their tenth objective, he took the map away.

"You will follow these dogleg instructions, cadet. There are two sets, one for tomorrow and one for the following day. If you get lost, shoot a 315-degree azimuth and follow that until you come to a black-topped road." That was it.

Robert calculated the instructions and figured their trip to be about twelve kilometers—all of it without a map. The next morning, he assigned duties to his teammates. One would be "brush breaker" for a while, another would be "azimuth point," and the other two would fetch water and help the brush breaker. The course set was not easy going because the cadets had little choice about which terrain to cover. They either had to follow their instructions, or Robert would have to recalculate new ones. Although he knew how to calculate where their final destination would be, Robert did not know if there were impassable barriers in between; he chose to go through whatever terrain they came along.

When Crandon's team arrived near the end of the last dogleg, Robert was relieved to see that it was an open area—the group had left the trees about three hundred meters before the objective. That did not mean the objective would be right where they expected it—the difficulty of following such a long route made it all but impossible for the group to arrive directly at their destination. Robert had his team fan out and walk along until one of the team members spotted the cottage. The other cadets began to run, but Robert told them all to stop.

"You've never been here before. If you go hopping around like that, you're liable to break a leg or twist an ankle," Robert cautioned. His team slowed to a steady walk and arrived at the objective hut. There was food already waiting for the cadets—for that evening and the next morning. There were also snack items and some packaged, dry noodles. Sergeant Crandon would not permit any of the cadets to eat any of the snack items—none of them asked for the noodles.

The next day, Robert found flint rock and put it into one of his field uniform pockets. He had a feeling that the cadre had not finished "testing" him just yet. He had his team store all the candy bars and high-sugar items in their packs for later. He did not define to them just what "later" would mean. Robert stored all the soup noodles in his own pack.

Just as on the previous day, Robert led his group to the objective hut, arriving just as the darkness began to settle in. Given the fourteen kilometers they had to cross, Robert considered the march to be a success. He also noted that they were on the extreme edge of the military grounds. Captain Sinclair arrived and proclaimed the dogleg crossings to be, "adequate." From Captain Sinclair, that was usually considered very high praise indeed.

The next morning Captain Sinclair took Robert Crandon away from the hearing of the other cadets and gave him the final instructions. "You have to make your way along 315 degrees until you come to a blacktopped highway. The highway has call boxes along it about every three to five kilometers. When you arrive at a call box, tell the operator that you are ready to be picked up, which group you are, and which call box you are at. Any questions?"

"Yes, sir. How far is the highway?" Robert asked.

"That depends upon how accurate you are with your direction, cadet," Captain Sinclair replied cryptically.

"May I ask, sir, how far a bird would fly in order to reach the highway directly?" Robert asked.

"Okay," Captain Sinclair allowed. Since the boy had come up with a question whose answer could not be obscured, and since Captain Sinclair happened to like Robert anyways, he chose to give a straight answer. "The highway is about thirty-five kilometers away—and there's a river in the way, cadet."

"Captain Sinclair, do all of my team members know how to swim?" Robert asked.

"I doubt it. You'll have to find a ford, or you'll have to think of something else. Don't risk their lives, Robbie. I'm depending on you. I've got a bet going with five other cadre officers, and if you keep up the good work, I'll make five times my next month's salary." Captain Sinclair smiled—actually smiled (something no other cadet had ever seen him do)—at Robert Crandon.

"I won't let you down, sir. I'll be there in two days," Sergeant Crandon said.

Two members of Crandon's team could not swim. They had some capacity to remain afloat, but they would never be able to cross a river. That meant that Robert would have to find the river, find a means across that was safe, and keep in mind which way 315 degrees was. Captain Sinclair had been ordered to take Robert's compass away, after allowing the cadet to make mental notes after his morning meal.

Robert checked the alignment of the sun and how the shadows moved. He spent two hours watching the shadows before letting Captain Sinclair leave with the compass. "How much farther do we have to go?" Cadet Mills asked.

"Over thirty-five kilometers." Robert said.

"Thirty-five!" all the cadets exclaimed.

"Why did you waste so much time this morning if we have so far to go?" Mills demanded to know.

"Because I don't have a map or a compass anymore! We have to navigate by the sun. I wanted to be sure that we would not be walking in circles or in the wrong direction, cadet. If we do that, we'll be out here until the cadre decides to send the helicopters looking for us!" Crandon explained—a bit harshly.

The other four cadets were dumbstruck. How could the cadre expect them to cross open terrain for thirty-five kilometers without a map or compass? That was idiotic. Nevertheless, Sergeant Crandon seemed confident, so when he said it was time to go and led the way, all the cadets followed, trusting their tiny leader.

Crandon's team found the river on the first day. Robert had the boys pull down some vines along the way in case they needed them to safely cross. The river was too wide and deep to cross where they arrived, so Crandon had his team follow the river, checking for a place to cross. Eventually the team came to a rocky ledge that would afford a crossing—provided that nobody slipped. The water was about three feet deep at its deepest, and the bottom was filled with slippery rocks.

Robert Crandon swam across the river with Cadet Kevin Michaels. Michaels was a good swimmer and helped Robert along the swift-flowing current. When they arrived downstream with the vines, Robert and Kevin made their way back up stream to where their companions were. Robert and Kevin tied the makeshift vine rope to a tree. Robert waded back to the other three cadets, holding on to the vine rope as he crossed. He tied the other end of the vine to a tree on the side with the waiting cadets. Having seen their leader accomplish the task, the other three cadets were willing to take their chances.

Robert had to cross *with* Cadet Mills, who was just too shaky about the endeavor. Robert kept soothing Mills's nerves along the way. "Don't worry, Bobby. You're taller than me, and I'm right here. Just hold onto the vine and take little steps to your right. Don't look over. Just look straight ahead. You can do it!" Mills was immensely grateful to his young leader for the words of encouragement and the willingness Crandon had shown to help the cadet if he had fallen.

When all the team members were across, Kevin Michaels brought up a point that had been on everyone's mind. "How are we going to dry our boots?"

"With this," Sergeant Crandon answered.

"How do we dry our boots with a rock?" Cadet LaPorte asked.

Robert unfastened his belt to strike against the flint. "It hasn't rained here in days and days. Go gather all the really dry grass and tree bark you can find," Robert Crandon ordered. The team moved out and brought what they could. Robert dug a fire pit with a stick and cleared all the loose brush out of the way. Robert took the flint and belt buckle and began striking pieces off the former into the kindling that the team had collected. Eventually the sparks took flame on the dry kindling, and a fire started. Robert carefully fed fuel to the fire, ordering the others to get larger—but already fallen—pieces of fuel. When the fire was roaring, Robert set up some tall sticks where they could put their inverted boots to dry.

Next, Sergeant Crandon ordered the cadets to remove all the goodies that he had had them store. He took out the noodle packets and some canned meats that Captain Sinclair had given to him. The team made soup in their canteen cups and had a hearty meal of meat and noodle soup along with some of the treats.

"How much farther do we have to go?" one of the team members asked.

"I'm not sure. Finding the river crossing took us off course. I would guess about twenty kilometers," Sergeant Crandon answered.

"That's a long way!" Bobby Mills exclaimed.

"Not necessarily," Robert corrected. "It's only a little over twelve miles. Of course, we don't know what's ahead of us, so we might get slowed down some. I think we'll make the highway before nightfall tomorrow."

Sergeant Cadet Robert Crandon was uncannily accurate. He had, without realizing it, given nearly the exact distance that the cadets needed to travel. Robert had not calculated anything—he just *felt* that that was the likely distance. The terrain ahead of them consisted of some dense foliage and hills, but Robert guided them accurately. They reached a blacktopped road at about 1600 hours.

Along the way, the team munched on candy bars, pastry treats and other high-energy items that Sergeant Crandon had made them save. The food lifted their spirits as well as their energy level and kept them going even though their legs were feeling the strain of all the walking they had done in the past two weeks.

Once on the road, Crandon's team walked along the hard surface until they reached Call Box 1175. Robert took down the receiver and passed on the information to the operator. Within an hour, Captain Sinclair arrived with a pickup truck to take the cadets to the bivouac holding area. Robert Crandon had won Captain Sinclair's bet with the other cadre officers.

Robert came out of his reverie when he heard loud voices in an adjoining area. "…could you have…to my son?"

"…swear to you that heads will…"

"…never…such a thing! …"

"…already changing…"

He concentrated on his injuries, telling his body to repair bones and replace tissue. He did not know if this would work, but he tried it anyways. After a short while, he heard footsteps and opened his eyes.

Standing just a few feet from his bed, Robert could make out the stern face of Commandant Leary. His first reaction was to jerk to an upright position of attention. His training had overcome his common sense. That attempt earned him pain shooting throughout his body, causing him to immediately lose consciousness. When Robert woke again, he heard a man's sturdy, calm voice declare, "Don't worry about me, son. I don't need you to show me respect. You have already shown me more respect than I ever earned from you."

Robert opened his eyes again and placed the commandant's face to his voice. "Okay, sir. I don't mind if you don't," Robert said in his high-pitched, child's voice. He smiled weakly and batted his eyelashes in his cute, impish manner. Commandant Leary laughed in spite of himself. He had come to see this cadet when the latter was hurt beyond measure, and the cadet still had enough humor to play little games with him.

"Cadet, my name is Commandant Joseph Leary. Do you recognize me, Robert?"

"Yes, sir."

"As soon as you feel able, I need to have you give a statement called a *deposition* to a military police interrogator."

"Is the MP here now, sir?"

"Oh, you should gather your strength first, cadet!" the commandant suggested.

"Permission to give more input, sir?" Robert requested. Robert never contradicted a cadre officer, but he found that they would often allow him to "give more input."

"Of course."

"I believe that I have enough strength to give a … what was it, sir… deposition?" Robert pronounced the word syllable by syllable.

"If you *really* feel up to it, son. I don't want you to think you have to push yourself in this."

Robert took a deep breath—for him. He had learned in the past few days that he had to take very easy, slow breaths or his entire chest would feel like it was on fire. "I believe that I can do it, sir. If you wish me to give the MP information, I will do my best."

Commandant Leary left the room. He returned a few hours later with a female military police officer. Robert saw the familiar three-angled stripes of a sergeant and assumed that she must be of that rank. The sergeant MP was crisp and matter-of-fact, "Cadet, where were you at ten hundred hours on November 1, 1972?"

"I don't know the exact times of events, ma'am. Waterline cadets do not possess nor carry personal time pieces." Robert recited the mantra in the formalistic style he had been drilled in so many times.

"Cadet, give me a synopsis of the events that occurred on the morning of the day in question, please."

"I'm sorry, ma'am, but I don't understand the question."

"It is my *understanding*, cadet, that you attended Roman Catholic Religious Services on November 1, 1972. Is that correct?"

Robert mused the statement partially aloud, "Roman ... Catholic ... Religious Services? Oh! You mean Mass. Yes, I went to Mass. It was All Saint's Day." Robert smiled, happy that he could finally answer at least one question that this police officer had asked.

"What occurred after the Mass was over?" The officer continued.

"Um ... well ... Johnny and I—that is, Cadet Freeman and I, we led Father Jeff out of the main church area. He was called to take a telephone call and told us to clear the altar and go to class." Robert stopped abruptly at that point. He was not about to volunteer any information at that point.

"Did you and Cadet Freeman clear the altar?" the woman asked.

"Yes, ma'am. Well, to be more accurate, we took off the things we were *supposed* to take off the altar and put them all away as we had been shown."

Commandant Leary had twelve years experience as a cadre officer in the academy system. He could sense when a cadet was being evasive. He could also usually sense when a cadet was not going to cooperate willingly. He became more and more frustrated as the police interrogator continued to learn that Robert had put away this piece, Johnny had put away that piece, the robes had been folded in such and such a manner. "Hold on a minute, Officer!" Commandant Leary demanded of the interrogator. "Officer, may I have a *private* word with my cadet?" Commandant Leary asked the question but his manner said that there was no room for dissent. The police interrogator left the room with as much pride as she could muster after having been summarily dismissed by the imposing man.

Commandant Joseph Leary had retired from the US Air Force as a colonel thirteen years earlier. He had entered the US academy system as a cadre member. Due to his military training, he was immediately assigned as a cadre officer to Boise Academy. Boise was a medium-security academy—only Waterline was considered maximum security—but Boise was the academy where the hardest cases were sent, unless the cadets had been sent to Waterline. He had spent the last twelve years learning how to pick out nuances and intonations that even some of the most prolific special interrogation units of the military might miss. He knew how his cadets thought, and he knew how they could evade questions they would rather not answer. Given the disaster that faced the new commandant, he could not afford to have stupid MPs wasting his and his cadets' time.

Commandant Leary took a long look at the shattered body of the cadet in front of him. *I wouldn't trust me, if I were him,* he thought. *Why should he trust anyone? I have to win his confidence first or at least get him to give me the benefit of having his cooperation.* The man did his best to reduce his imposing demeanor and give a caring touch to his voice. The touch was not overwhelming, as he did not want to sound phony. It was simply his way of saying to this cadet, *I'm not one of them. I really want to help you.*

"Cadet, I need your help. What happened to you was abominable, but I can't fix the problem if I can't learn the entire problem. I need you to trust me. Nothing you say in this room can get you into trouble. I promise you that. You can tell us that you murdered half of the people in Riverton, and the information will not leave this room if you say so. Do you understand?"

"I think so, sir."

"Would you be willing to tell the MP what happened that day?"

"No, sir. I don't like her. She doesn't seem to … well … *care.* I don't want to sound mean, sir, but I don't think that I trust her. I mean, with some things that I might say, that is, sir." Commandant Leary could see sadness and a sense of betrayal in the young boy's face.

Commandant Leary considered. "I'll get you a different interrogator, one you can trust." He left the room, presumably, Robert thought, to get a new interrogator. When he returned a short time later, he was alone. "The police will send a new officer up to take your statement. If you don't mind, I thought you might want to tell me first, just in case you wanted to add things that you don't want to tell the MPs. I promise you again, Robert, nothing you say to me will shock me, and nothing, absolutely *nothing* that you tell me will go beyond these walls, if you say so."

Robert decided to take a chance. It had been over three years since he had arrived at the academy. He had learned how to survive by following *the rules.* Cadets don't turn in cadets; cadets help cadets. You never badmouth a cadre officer. Anything that happened to you was your fault because you were sent to Waterline in the first place. You never attack a cadre officer. The cadre was there for your benefit; nothing they did was wrong. You never earn anything; you are a Waterline Cadet so anything you get was *given* to you. You never give up cadet secrets. These rules had allowed the young boy to survive in spite of setbacks, hardships, punishment, and pain. Nevertheless, it took all his courage to finally *trust.*

"Okay, sir. I'll trust you. I'll tell you *everything*, but you have to keep your promise and not tell any other cadre officer or staff member. You have to allow things to go on, even though they may affect you as well. I won't ask you to allow anything dangerous or stupid, I promise, but I will be telling you all sorts of secrets that we have. I will trust you to keep them as secret, as we have."

Commandant Leary nodded solemnly. Inside he was rejoicing. This was far more than he had expected, far more, he told himself, than he deserved. "Any secrets told in this room stay in this room," he stated. That was all Robert needed to hear.

Robert told Commandant Leary all about the cadet side of Waterline Academy.

"Sir, have you been with the academy system for a while?"

"A little over twelve years."

"Have you heard about the *Game*, sir?"

"A little, but why don't you explain it in your words?"

"Yes, sir. Each cadet who enters into Waterline Academy eventually learns to play the Game, or he fails. That's just the way it is, no exceptions. In the Game, the stakes are us against you, that is, the cadets against the cads—oops! I mean cadre, sir."

Commandant Leary thought about the mistake and smiled a large, friendly, warm smile. "Have you guys been calling us cads behind our backs all these years, cadet?" Leary asked.

"Yes, sir," Robert peeped. "Remember, sir… " Robert continued sheepishly, "… anything heard here … um … stays here?"

Commandant Leary laughed. He held up three fingers of his right hand, "Scout's honor, Cadet. The name is rather poetically fitting, considering what happened a few days ago." When Robert looked at him quizzically, he realized that the boy had likely never been *in* the Boy Scouts and may never even have *heard* of them. *What have we done to this child?* he thought. To Robert, he said, "It means, yes, I will keep my promise, no matter what, cadet," and he smiled again.

"Well, sir," Robert continued, "The Game is cadets against cadre. As cadets, we win if we can accept what happens without whining or complaining or anything of that sort. Also, we can win if we can outdo the cadre officers in their own requirements. This is how it goes: for instance, if you tell me to cut the parade field lawn with nose hair clippers, I win if I go through that silly task without crying or complaining or moaning about it to anybody. If I go to my platoon leader or company commander and start talking about how stupid and horrible and yucky it is, then you win because you got me to think that this place is all other than it really is. If I come to think that this place is supposed to do things to us in a *nice* way or a *fair* way, then I haven't really figured this place out. I'm not here for fairness. I'm here to learn to be a 'productive citizen of the state,' as our required knowledge likes to put it.

"Now, in addition to winning by putting up with all the tasks, punishments, pain, and silliness, I can win by outdoing the cadre at their own tasks. Once again, if you make me cut the parade field with nose hair clippers, I win extra big-time if I can find a way to cut a message about you into the grass. It only counts if somebody from the outside world can see the message, though. If, for instance, you have me scrub garbage cans, well … to be honest, sir, that seems rather pointless. Why scrub something shiny-clean that you plan to put garbage into in the next minute? I mean really? Well, if I can scrub *so* hard that I scrub right through that garbage can, then I win big time again! I have made the task even more useless ... and you're out one garbage can, at that!" Robert's eyes were eager at his telling of the Game. His eyelids fluttered in his impish way whenever he described how cadets could win "big-time."

"There has never been a graduate from Waterline who did not understand and play the game, sir. Not in its whole history. I know, because I read the archives," Robert stated.

"The *archives*, cadet?" the commandant asked, truly bewildered.

"Oh! Yes, sir! The secret cadet records, sir. The Waterline cadet senior officer corps has been keeping records since 1947, sir, about two years after the academy was founded. Since I was so small when I came here, I was given the task of straightening them all out and adding the years 1967 and 1968. They always use the smaller guys because it's a lot easier for us little guys to get into the cadre offices, sir."

"The *cadre* offices?"

"Yes, sir. That's where we keep the records, sir."

"How? How is that even possible, Robert?"

"Well, sir ... I suppose the better question might be to ask, 'Where else could we *possibly* keep them,' sir? I mean, you strip-search us four times each year. You search our quarters when we are in classes. You inspect us any time of the day or night. We couldn't *possibly* keep them on *us!*" Robert explained.

Robert thought back to his first treks through each of the barracks' ventilation systems. His first one went without a single negative incident. The senior officers of Alpha Company and the field grade officers were running maximum interference. Robert moved through the vents fairly easily; he was, after all, a small, six-year-old boy. When Robert got to the fans, he found that all of them had been repaired. He worked for two hours realigning the cadre office fans (so that only cadets who knew how could put them on). He then returned to his floor and got some much needed sleep.

It was a cold December night. Robert was painted black with a rough polish mixture that did not shine in light. His next assignment had been Bravo Company. Since he had to cross the Company B assembly area to do that, every cadet in the company—and the battalion—had been told to keep quiet. That worked about as well as a balloon made out of lead. It was 2240 hours, long after lights out, and no sooner had Robert exited the door to the second floor of Company A and taken his first few steps when a commotion alerted all of the police guards and those cadre officers who had not gone home. Robert hit the ground, rolled about ten meters, and kept his head down.

Lights popped up in the Bravo Company barracks. Robert had been told by his platoon leader to "play it cool" in such circumstances. "Don't run. Don't even move. If the cadre can see you, then they'll come to you. So long as they aren't picking you up off the ground, you're probably safe," Lieutenant Darryl Marks had cautioned. So, Robert waited, and he waited, and he waited. After nearly two hours, the armed police guards and the cadre officers vacated the Company B assembly area.

Robert crawled back to the doorway to the second floor of Alpha Company's barracks and opened it very, very quietly. He went up the steps as softly as he could. He needed to get to the third floor, where his platoon, A-1, was housed; that stairway was on the opposite side of the building. He crept into the A-2 platoon leader's room and saw Cadet Lieutenant Jack Howard, who was still awake. "I can't believe you didn't get caught!" Jack whispered.

Robert just stared.

"Okay, Crandon, just go through the vent to Lieutenant Marks's room. Do you remember the way?" Robert nodded. Jack opened his ventilation screen and sent the tiny cadet on his way. Robert later learned that David Gendron had been the cause of the commotion. The senior officer Corps began keeping tabs on that cadet from that time onwards.

Eventually, Robert Crandon became spectacularly efficient at crawling through the vents, and from building to building along the ground, and had the "listening posts" all in working order.

His next task was to find and arrange the cadet archives. The task was more than just difficult; it was monumental. Five cadre officers had come and gone since the files had last been adjusted. That meant that much of the previous work would have to be found and cataloged—in Robert's head! He began with Commandant Snider's office since that changed the least. He went on to each and every individual cadre office in the academy. It took him two years, but he finally straightened out their archives, added the histories for 1967 and 1968, and began updating events that had occurred since he had arrived. *Very few* cadets were surprised by Robert's meteoric rise in the cadet ranks. He was a lifesaver as far as the cadets were concerned.

Robert continued his explanation to Commandant Leary. "Back in 1946, one of the senior officers decided that we needed to keep our own records. The cadre kept all sorts of detailed records on *us*, so why shouldn't we keep records for ourselves? If the cadre believed they could learn from past mistakes, well then, so could we. Then the senior officer corps sat down and tried to figure out where to keep them. They decided that the only *logical* place to keep the records was in the filing cabinets in the cadre offices.

"Since there is nearly always at least one cadre officer in the main office, the secretary files are not a great place to keep hidden records. We can get into those files, but it would take too long to decipher the contents. What they figured, back in 1947, and it still works today, is that no cadre officer is going to stay in his office 24/7. That gives us the chance to go into the office, open the filing cabinet and add stuff and read the stuff that's already there."

"But how do you get into their locked offices?" the commandant wanted to know.

"Oh! That's easy, sir. We just crawl through the vents. That's why we need small guys to learn the codes. Once you have a small guy, like me, able to move through the vents without making noise, it's just a matter of teaching him how to pick the locks and decipher the codes. Since we're always having to memorize stuff anyways, it's not too, too hard to find a guy who has his head screwed on right. The biggest problem they had—before I came, that is—was getting the guys to remember what they had *read*. I mean, it doesn't do much good to send a guy out to get info on 1964 and then have him gum up the translation. Also, they had to use guys who were not dumb enough to get caught."

The commandant was dumbfounded. "So … you've actually *read* these records, cadet?"

"Oh! Yes, sir! They pegged me for a vent rat the moment I came into the academy. Lieutenant Darryl, that is, then Cadet Lieutenant Marks, sir, started having me trained as a vent rat less than a month after I was here. The senior officer corps had been waiting for somebody like me, sir. They hadn't had a smart, small guy for some years and were actually thinking of trying to send one of the bigger guys into the offices—just to update the records! It was getting really bad.

"Anyways, I came in and they taught me how to pick locks, lift keys, move really silently, and move on just toes and fingers—all sorts of things like that. Then, they taught me the codes and sent me to read the files. Some of the records had been moved, but we kind of expected that. I created the historical records for 1967 through, well … through 1972 … now, that is, sir."

"And you can just go in and read the records any time you want?"

"Oh! No, sir. There are only a few times that we can actually pull something like that off. I just happen to have been able to do enough of it in the past three years that all of our records are up to date … well … more or less. I don't suppose anything about Cadre Captain Gerralds attacking me is in the records yet, sir." Robert's eyes fluttered again, as if suggesting to the cadre commandant, *Go ahead and challenge me on that one.* The commandant was not going to take up that challenge.

"*Mister* Gerralds is no longer a cadre officer … and he never will be again, Robert. I promise you that! However, speaking of Mr. Gerralds, what do you remember about November 1?" Commandant Leary was eager to hear this cadet's telling of the story. He already had interviewed Cadet John Freeman and had pretty much learned all he needed to know soon after the incident had taken place.

Robert Crandon described his ordeal to Commandant Leary the same as he had described it to Father Lions. He emphasized that he had never intended to hurt Cadre Captain Gerralds and that if his tripping the man caused the cadre officer any harm, then Robert was prepared to take the consequences.

"Why are you worried about possibly causing the slightest harm to that … monster?" the commandant wanted to know.

"Sir, the cadre officers are our only means of life. Without you, we couldn't live, or if we could, we would not really want to. The cadre is our last, best hope of redemption, sir. Without you we don't eat, we don't have clothes, and we don't have guidance in how to straighten out our lives. We would be totally lost without the cadre, sir." Robert seemed to be truly puzzled by the commandant's initial lack of understanding.

"Mr. Gerralds almost killed you, cadet! Yet, here you are defending him?"

"I'm not trying to defend his … unlawful … acts, sir. I am only saying that without the cadre, Waterline cadets would be lost. We accept whatever happens to us because … well … because we are in Waterline Academy. We all had to do *something* to get put in here, sir. Society would like us to be useful. We want to be useful to society. This is our last hope, sir.

"Guys who leave this academy generally leave in one of three ways, sir. I know this because I've also read the cadre officers' records. One way is that a guy can't take it, loses all will to go on, and is sent to the loony bin. A second way is that a guy never straightens out and goes into reform school, and later prison, for the rest of his life. The third way, and it is by far the most likely, sir, is that he graduates or finishes his time and becomes a productive citizen of the United States. According to the Waterline Cadre Records, graduates of Waterline Academy have the second lowest crime rate of any group—the lowest group is Roman Catholic nuns and monks.

"Anyways, sir, that is why we never attack a member of the cadre. It would be like … well … killing ourselves. It just wouldn't make any sense, sir." Robert finished and looked at the white-haired man standing near him. "Was there anything else you wanted to know, sir?"

"Actually, there is, cadet. You said that you called Mr. Gerralds a sadistic creep. Why did you use those words?"

"Well, sir, I read a book that said there was this guy named the Marquis de Sade. He was in the Bastille at the start of the French Revolution, in 1791, I think. *Anyways*, the Marquis seemed to like causing other people pain. That's how they got the word "sadistic' … or so I'm told." Robert finished his history lecture.

"Very good, cadet, but I was actually wondering if you knew of the *other* implications," the commandant said, hoping for more input.

Robert remembered back to when he had first asked Cadet Lieutenant Marks about one of the cadets who had returned from the master of discipline's office. Cadet Murphy had returned from receiving his punishment for waxing the windshield of a cadre officer's car. He had gone into the latrine, vomited up his evening meal, and then rushed into his quarters. Robbie saw him grab a towel and head to the showers.

Since Robbie was Murphy's fire team leader, he followed him back into the latrine to see if the cadet was sick. He saw Murphy bleeding, and when Murphy saw Robbie, he turned his head away. Robbie knew that the boy wanted privacy, so he simply said to him, "If you need anything at all, just let me know." Murphy nodded, and Robbie went to Lieutenant Darryl's room.

"Sir, would you please explain something to me?" Robbie asked his platoon leader.

"Sure, sport, shoot. What's on your mind?"

"Sir, I just saw Cadet Murphy return from getting a punishment. He looked kind of hurt. I mean, like, maybe he needed to go to the clinic. His injuries, though, they didn't look like a beating or anything. I don't understand, sir…"

Darryl Marks took a very deep breath. He was unsure of how much he should divulge to this brilliant but *very* young cadet. "Close the door, sport." Robbie complied. "Okay, what I'm going to tell you has to stay in this room, got it?" Robbie nodded. "How much do you know about where babies come from? I mean human babies."

"Well … they come out of their mommies—I mean, mothers, sir. That's about all I know, I guess." Robbie waited for his platoon leader's explanation.

Darryl explained the very basics of human sexuality to the six-year-old child. He explained what the male and female organs were used for and how males had to have their part enter the female in order to "maybe make" a baby. He explained that grown-ups did this all the time, especially if they were married. Robbie seemed to understand perfectly well.

"But, sir, what has that got to do with Cadet Murphy's punishment?" Robbie asked.

"I'm getting to that. Now, can you understand that a man who does his part in trying to make a baby it feels really good? I mean, it's like an explosion of feeling good!" Darryl continued. Robbie took a few seconds and nodded his understanding.

Darryl told Robert the truth.

"Why wouldn't he just do that with his wife?" Robbie asked.

"That's getting to a part that I can't really explain," Darryl said. "I guess sometimes a man wants to do things to somebody because it makes him feel powerful, or dangerous, or … who knows? I just know that sometimes it happens." Here, Darryl motioned Robbie closer. He whispered, "It's also against the law to do that to kids!"

Robbie's eyes widened. "You mean," Robbie whispered, "that Captain Gerralds is *not supposed to do that?*" Robbie had never expected to hear that any cadre member would actually knowingly break the law. Darryl nodded his head glumly. "Did he ever do that to you, sir?" Robbie had tears coming to his eyes.

"No. He only does that to guys who get sent to his office. Also, I guess he never does it to guys until they're a bit older, like maybe twelve or thirteen. So you don't need to worry that it will happen to you. At least … *probably* it won't, and I hope it doesn't. Okay?"

Darryl talked to Robbie about the youngster's lessons in picking locks and lifting wallets. He then asked about Robbie's academic studies and continued to distract the young boy until he figured that Robbie would not be traumatized by the information he had just learned. Darryl did not put his thoughts into those words; he just knew that he had to clear the kid's mind.

Robert was considering how to approach the subject. He had looked up the word *sadist* in the dictionary. He knew that his biology lessons had included human sexuality, so the commandant would probably not be surprised at his knowledge in that respect, but how was he going to explain how he learned about what Mr. Gerralds had done?

"Sir, it is not very hard to guess what's going on. You see a cadet come from the master of discipline's office, and he is walking kind of funny. The cadet grabs a towel and goes into the latrine at twenty hundred hours to take a shower even though he's going to take one the next morning after PT. He vomits his guts out in one of the toilets, so you go to see if you can help." Robert faltered for a while. "In the end, I asked one of the cadets. He told me sir."

"Did this ever happen to you, cadet?" the commandant asked.

"No, sir. Mr. Gerralds seemed to only pick on the older cadets, those who were twelve or more. He never did those things to us younger guys. I'm pretty certain of that, sir."

"Because you are the one who logged in all the names of the cadets who had this happen to them?" asked Commandant Leary.

Robert made a mental note: Commandant Leary was very perceptive. "Yes, sir. I logged in the names of all fifty cadets who had this happen to them in the last five years, sir. I also logged in the dates and whether or not the cadets went to sick call the next morning. Seven of the fifty went to sick call, sir. I don't know for certain what happened with all of them, but I guess that since all complaints would go to either the master of discipline or the commandant of Waterline Academy, the complaints never really got anywhere."

Robert again thought back: he had been assigned to "sweep the cadre office" by his field grade officers. He was in his second year at the academy. They wanted to check the secretary files, and Robert Crandon had the most nimble fingers in the academy. As Robert swept, he kept his eye on the two cadre officers who were pulling night duty. There were three other cadets who were serving Majors by having to stay up all night as runners. They were the diversion.

The cadre never allowed cadets to just lollygag around. The runners were told to polish the handles to the doors of the individual cadre officers' offices. At a designated time, one of them "accidentally" overturned his bottle of brass cleaner.

"You jerk!" Tim Hyder yelled. "You got it everywhere!"

"Aw, shut your trap, you!" Tom Norton yelled back. Soon both boys were yelling cuss words at each other.

The "fix" was on. Robert knew he had only moments before the cadre might turn their attention back to the main lobby. As both cadre officers entered the corridor to "prevent the fight," Robert opened up the secretary files and checked all the logged entries for work orders and complaints. He had already checked Commandant Snider's office for complaints and had found none.

Robert found all five complaints in a double-locked file drawer. He knew that he could not possibly copy them on the Xerox machine, so he simply read the files as quickly as he could (his speed reading classes really came in handy) and put them back. By the time the two cadets had received "correction" (in the form of forty pushups each), Robert had accomplished his mission. He knew that the complaints from the medical staff had been routed through Commandant Snider directly to Captain Gerralds. Robert never got the chance to check the "last two" complaints that were likely filed. He was scheduled to do that November 6, 1972, a mission that would go unaccomplished.

Commandant Leary nodded his head sadly. At least he knew of one *more* conspirator he would have the federal agents investigate: former Commandant Maxwell Snider. "Robert, when this is all through, I'll be handing in my resignation. I need to know who else needs to be booted from my staff. Cadre officers, teachers, anybody you name I'll have investigated." Leary saw a strange look on the young cadet's face. It was a sense of sadness and betrayal. "You don't approve?"

"Sir, it is not my pos—"

"I don't care if it's your position, cadet. You are the one person most capable of determining who's good and who's bad. You said yourself that you logged things into your secret archives." Commandant Leary wondered if he had gone too far. The look of betrayal had not left the boy's face. "Is there ... something else, besides your naming a few bad cadre officers, that's bothering you, cadet?"

Robert took some time before he answered. "Sir, it's very ... difficult for me to ... voice disagreement with a cadre officer."

"Go on, Robert, I'm listening. I outrank the other cadre, so you can feel free to speak."

"I believe, sir, that you don't outrank yourself?" Robert blinked his impish blink and smiled.

"Aha! I think I understand." Leary thought for a few moments and came up with an idea. "Let's play a little game. Let's pretend that we are talking about a business, a *theoretical* business. If this were a company, what would you have to say about my plans?"

Robert thought about that for a moment and then said, "If this were a business and the president of the company had told me those plans, I would tell him that he was a coward, sir! I would say to him that getting rid of all the...bad...employees...well, that only makes sense. Giving up, though, that would be the act of a coward.

"I guess the president of the company would be sort of at fault, but if all his employees were holding stuff back, that's not his fault—especially if his... um... customers... never got to talk to him. Even still, he's supposed to fix the problems! He shouldn't just quit and leave it to the next guy!

"I would tell that president that he has to make everything better! I would say that he has to be *fair*. All of his customers are counting on him. They had to put up with yucky, horrible...um...*people?*... for so long. He owes them!" Robert paused, blushed, and then continued much more meekly. "Anyways, sir ... that's what I would tell the president, *theoretically*." The last word sounded much more like a question than a statement.

Commandant Joseph Leary, former Colonel of the US Air Force, stood up on his feet at the position of attention. The act was unconscious, but it was also unmistakable. "Cadet, this is the first time that I have ever been lectured on duty and responsibility when I actually needed it. You are absolutely right. If I resign, I simply pass on the responsibility to someone else. I'll make you a different pledge, Cadet Lieutenant Crandon. I, Joseph Donovan Leary, promise that as long as my superiors allow me to do so, I will make Waterline Academy function the best that I can. I won't allow it to lose its capacity to do its job. I won't allow it to go overboard. I will make sure that as many cadets as possible will either graduate or leave with honor, dignity, and the capacity to make it in the world.

"Now, cadet, let's get to the business of who's complicit, who's guilty, and who just needs to get a breather at another academy, shall we?" Robert outlined what he knew of each of the cadre officers. He assured the commandant that none of the teachers were part of the problem, at least none that he knew of or had been told of. The commandant wrote down every word, read it again and again, and prepared to leave.

"Sir?"

"Yes, cadet?"

"How do you plan to replace thirteen cadre officers?"

"I don't know, yet. I just don't know. Leave that to me. That's my problem. You just get better and come back to us, okay?" Robert nodded and soon fell asleep.

Robert continued to dwell on other events that had shaped his time in Waterline Academy. He had been caught going from barracks to barracks—after hours—only once. As luck would have it, his own cadre officer, Cadre Captain Sinclair found him just as he got to the bottom of A-1's stairwell.

"It's after hours, cadet. Just what do you think you are doing?" Captain Sinclair demanded in his deep, bass voice.

"No excuse, sir," Robert said. He had learned his lesson about deceit.

"I asked you why you were out of bed and moving around, cadet," Captain Sinclair said ominously.

"I couldn't sleep, sir," Robert answered. That was true. He could not sleep because he had a mission, but he could not sleep.

Captain Sinclair ordered him to write down one major and sent him back to his room. As punishment for "not being able to sleep," Captain Sinclair ordered Robert Crandon to spend twenty-four hours (starting at 1700 the next day) as a runner in the cadre office. All in all, Robert considered himself very lucky to have gotten off so easy.

Another time that Robert *almost* got caught was when he *repaired* Company B's vent system. He had been crawling through the vents for several hours when Captain Sinclair went to Lieutenant Marks asking for him. "He's over in Bravo, sir, actually the company commanders' quarters. He is practicing required knowledge, sir. I'll go get him for you," Darryl offered.

"That's all right, cadet. I can walk," Captain Sinclair answered and headed to find Robert. Darryl put up a warning signal, and Cadet Captain Peter Lush saw it. He could not yell into the vents since the cadre officers who had offices in the building might also hear. He tapped three times on the vent—hard. That was the cadet universal signal for danger.

Robert could not make it back to the first floor (where the company commanders' quarters were located), so he came out on the third floor. He went into the latrine and relieved himself. Next, he rushed down the steps and over to the "marching band" to rejoin the "required knowledge" session. He found Cadre Captain Sinclair already waiting for him.

"Where were you, cadet?" Cadre Captain Sinclair demanded.

"I was in the latrine, sir," Robert answered.

"Why didn't you use the one right over there?" Captain Sinclair asked. He pointed to the smaller latrine that the cadet company commanders used.

"The company commanders' latrine, sir?" Robert exclaimed. "I thought that was for the company commanders, sir." Robert sounded almost scandalized.

"Well … it *is* for their use … but that doesn't mean *you* can't use it," Captain Sinclair explained.

"Oh! Okay, sir, I'll remember that!" Robert said exuberantly. He smiled and blinked his cute, impish blink unconsciously.

Captain Sinclair had come to find the cadet in order to bring him his permission slip allowing him to take books along. Robert could read the books nearly anywhere provided that they did not interfere with his assigned tasks. Captain Sinclair then handed the cadet a copy of *Charlie and the Chocolate Factory*, by Roald Dahl. Robert continued to carry that permission slip with him whenever he had a book that he could carry.

A PARTIAL SOLUTION

"Joe, what the hell's going on down there?" The voice in the receiver was not happy, to say the least. "The press is all over me! My staff is threatening to call in sick for a week, all twelve of them! I thought you said you were going to handle this!"

Joseph Leary took a long, slow breath to settle his nerves. "Matt, it's a lot worse than we initially thought. I've got over a hundred complaints of abuse, and a kid who is still just clinging to life. I need more *authority*. If I don't have the power to deal with the problems, I can't deal with them. I told you that *the first time*. You have got to get Congress to hold a joint committee hearing and empower us to *act;* we don't need to suggest—we need to act!" Commandant Leary thought he would try just one more time with the director and then give up on him.

"All right, Joe, I'll ask for the committee hearing. In the mean time, can you do *something* to deflect the heat? The Secretary of Defense was over here, in *my* office, telling me *he's* catching hell from reporters—and he's only got to deal with this for another two months before the new administration takes over! Have you got any ideas, *any ideas at all*, on how we can cool this powder keg down?"

"I just got through talking to the cadet in the hospital. The kid is a genius. I'm for real on this. I think he should be in one of the gifted academies. He pegged all the bad apples and gave me suggestions on what to do with the three who aren't bad. He told me that I've got only one who I can safely keep. Amazingly enough, the kid said that old Sourpuss Sinclair is the only completely innocent one of the bunch!"

"What do you need from the committee, Joe?"

"I need all the best and brightest cadre officers in the system. That means that I need to be able to coax them in here. I need the committee to kick in the cash, Matt, and a lot of it. I want to double the pay of any cadre officer at Waterline. Hell, I don't see the rationality behind them getting the same pay while working at a maximum-security facility anyways! Also, I want full reign on who comes in here this time. No *political* appointees. I've got a mess on my hands, and I don't need weenies throwing more sand into the machinery."

"Okay. I'll get with the committee chairs and let them know. After what's been happening here and in DC, they'll probably jump at the chance to throw more money at the place. It's a lot easier to throw money at a problem than it is to figure out how to fix it. Besides, if they can announce that Waterline is getting *elite* cadre from now on, that just may be what they need to calm down the press." The director actually had a hint of hope in his voice. Leary prayed that the director's hope was not unfounded. They still had a *long* way to go.

Paul and Roberta Crandon had to leave. They desperately wanted to stay with their injured son, but Roberta's parents, the McPhees, could only watch the other children for another day or two, and her sister had to care for her own children. In addition, Roberta needed to get back to her baby boy, Patrick. "Here is a picture of Patrick for you." Roberta told her son, joyfully. "You can keep that one, we have lots more. We'll send you more as we take them. That way, you can watch him grow up." She smiled.

Robert did not smile. He looked solemn. Paul asked him, "What's wrong, Robbie. Don't you like your little brother?"

"Oh! He's great!" Robert exclaimed. Then the excitement left him. "It's just that, well … here." He handed the picture back to his mother.

"It's okay, Robbie. The commandant assured us that you can receive mail from now on … " Mrs. Crandon told her son.

"Oh, yeah. He told me that too. But I'm still in the academy, Mom … Mother. We're not allowed to keep *anything*, not even mail. When the cadre officers distribute the mail—at least, so I've been told; I haven't really had the chance to find out *firsthand*—anyways when they give guys mail, they take them to the gymnasium in their PT outfits—just the shorts and tee shirts, no sweats. The guys have to open the mail in front of the cadre officers and some police guards. Then they have to give all the mail to the cadre. All the cadets are searched before leaving the gym. I can't have any pictures. Those are the rules, no exceptions, no … excuses," Robert's voice trailed off at the end of the mantra, "No exceptions, no excuses." He was so used to saying that that he had forgotten that his father would remember using those exact same words.

"Sorry, Father. I didn't mean to bring up bad memories. Really, I didn't. It's just that we say that so many times … " Robert was nearly in tears.

"It's okay, Robbie. I'll get over it. I should never have said those words to you. I should have listened to you. I won't make that mistake again as long as I live. I promise." Paul hugged his son. Robert used his good arm, his left one, to hug his father back. He then hugged and kissed his mother good-bye.

An idea suddenly popped into Robert's mind. "Anyways, if you send me pictures I can look at them in the gym and then send them back to you!" Robert suggested. Mrs. Crandon agreed that she would do that.

"We'll be here to pick you up for Christmas. You have a pass for Thanksgiving, but your doctors tell us that you won't be able to travel. Grandma and Grandpa McPhee said that they'll come visit you over the Thanksgiving Normal Week," Roberta told her son.

"Actually, ma'am, it's called Common Week, but I know what you mean. I'll try to write you as often as I can. Father Jeff said he would get me some forms to sign for stamps. I can't really walk down the PX to get them just yet." Robert giggled.

The Crandons waved good-bye to their son and headed back to Massachusetts.

Robert's recovery was remarkable. By any measures that Doctor Todd Salwart had ever seen, the child should be in recovery for at least a year. By most measures, the child should not even have been alive. Instead, the damage to the boy's body was visibly healing. The broken bones in both his legs had begun to fuse back together although he would still need to be cautious. His ribs were similarly on the mend, although they appeared to be taking more time. His right arm was already out of a cast, and he was able to use it, although sparingly. His kidney had full function, which was, perhaps, the greatest miracle of them all. Even his broken collar bone was mending well. The only serious limitation Robert had was his numerous headaches.

"May I go back, yet?" Doctor Salwart heard the familiar voice asking the same familiar phrase. "Please? Please may I go back yet?" Robert was persistent, if nothing else.

"How do you plan to get around, young man?" Dr. Salwart asked. "Are you planning to hobble on your two broken legs?"

"I bet I could..." Robert offered. "If I can prove to you that I can hobble on them, will you let me go back?" he added, hopefully.

Dr. Salwart sighed. It was Tuesday before Thanksgiving, and he knew what this young boy wanted. "All right, Robert," he agreed. "If you can hobble down the corridor, then I'll clear you to go back to your academy." He was really clearing the cadet to visit family in Massachusetts. He expected that the pins in Robert's legs and the healing might just be enough to allow the boy to walk. It would be painful, but the boy could do it without reinjuring the bones. He believed in finding out everything he could about his patients. Robert's file was enormous, but Dr. Salwart had read enough to know this boy's most ardent wish. Robert wanted to see his family. He wanted it so much that he would try to walk on legs that were still in casts.

Robert bent over immediately and stood on his legs. The casts had been altered to allow his knees to bend slightly. Walking on his bare feet, he managed to move to the doorway of his hospital room. Balancing himself with his left arm on the wall, not too much so as not to harm his shattered shoulders, he winced with pain and made his way down the corridor. The rest of the medical personnel in the ward watched in shock as the little boy took step after step all the way to the end. "Do I need to prove that I can walk back, also?" he asked. Dr. Salwart shook his head no, and immediately a nurse brought a wheelchair over to the injured boy.

Dr. Salwart began writing an extensive profile—a list of restrictions—for this unstoppable cadet. "Why don't you just have him move around in a chair?" asked one of the nurses.

"His shoulders are too damaged. He can't push the wheels. The chair won't get up and down the stairs of the school, either. They do not have elevators. Besides, the gravel in some of their areas is too thick to even push a wheelchair. If he can't walk, he can't really stay at the academy," Dr. Salwart explained.

"Okay, cadet. You can leave just as soon as one of your cadre officers brings you a uniform and accompanies you. This profile lists the medication you are to take for pain—" Dr. Salwart told Robert.

"Oh, I won't need *that*, sir." Robert interrupted.

" … And lists the restrictions you have. You will be housed on the first floor and have a shower and facilities close to you. Don't argue with me, you either accept the restrictions or you stay here." Dr. Salwart was adamant. Robert nodded his agreement. "In addition, you won't be doing any physical training with your fellow cadets." Robert frowned but said nothing. "You will, instead, report to the physical therapist each day, over in the academy gymnasium. He will give you all sorts of help in recovering.

"If you promise me that you will not violate this profile, then I'll have one of the nursing staff call over to your academy." Dr. Salwart waited for the words he *knew* he was going to hear.

"I promise to follow my profile, *to the letter, sir!* I'm from Waterline, sir. I always keep my promises!" Robert gave a huge smile and blinked his eyes in his signature, impish way.

Dr. Salwart knew that such a promise was only as good as his writing of the profile limits. Enough cadets had made their way through his office for him to realize by now that "to the letter" meant that the cadet would find all sorts of ways around his intent. In spite of this, he smiled at the injured boy. He truly wanted Robert to get some joy, and going home for Thanksgiving when he had been scheduled for the hospital just might be the happiest moment of this child's life. That kind of physical therapy would heal wounds much, much faster.

The next day, a cadre officer entered the hospital ward. He was carrying a hangar with some clothing on it. Robert recognized the insignia of the dress blues, Class-A uniform, but he did not recognize the uniform. The jacket resembled a bathrobe, and the trousers and shirt resembled pajamas. Robert had snapped to the position of attention the minute that the cadre officer entered the room.

"That's another one I have to add," Dr. Salwart said as he scribbled on Robert's profile. "No snapping to attention ... and no *standing* at attention for more than twenty seconds, cadet—for that matter, no standing for more than a few minutes, either. By a few, I mean that you can use your own judgment, but it had better not be for ten minutes and most of the time it had better not be for more than thirty seconds! Got that?"

"Yes, sir!" Robert answered crisply.

"Cadet Crandon?" the new cadre officer said. "I'm Cadre Captain Peter Toole. I am your new platoon cadre officer. I have a uniform here for you. Do you need help getting it on?"

"Probably, sir." Robert admitted.

Cadre Captain Toole helped Robert take off his hospital clothes, put on underwear, and then put on the uniform. "Sir, Cadet Crandon requests permission to ask a question," Robert said formally.

"Go ahead, cadet."

"Sir, just what kind of uniform *is this*?"

"This, cadet, is *your* new convalescent, dress blues uniform. You have an entire wardrobe of convalescent uniforms already hanging up in your new quarters. They don't have quite as many pockets as you cadets seem to like, but then, you can't be gigged for the condition of your uniforms nearly as much as you could for the standard uniforms. The battalion is waiting for you for an assembly. That's why it's Class A."

Robert finished getting dressed, wrapping the housecoat/Class-A jacket around himself. He cinched the loose, cloth belt at his waist. "Am I acceptable, sir?" he asked, turning completely around so Cadre Captain Toole could evaluate him.

"You'll pass, cadet." Captain Toole said in a serious tone. He then smiled at the nine-year-old boy in front of him. "You need something on your feet, cadet."

Robert looked up at his cadre officer, astonished at his own lack at noticing the deficiency. "Sir?" he asked. Cadre Captain Toole handed him a pair of fuzzy, black slippers. The bottoms were sturdy enough for walking outside, but the footwear was clearly designed for light use. Robert pushed his bare feet into the slippers and asked, "No socks, sir?"

"We'll worry about those later, cadet, after you can actually put those things on without wincing." Robert nodded. "Are you ready to go back to your platoon, cadet-lieutenant?" Captain Toole asked, smiling. Robert began hobbling out of the hospital room, taking the question as rhetorical. "Hold on there, cadet. In this thing," Captain Toole indicated a wheelchair.

Robert obediently sat down in the chair, and Captain Toole pushed him to the elevators. The cadre captain signed his charge out of Ft. Waterline Hospital and pushed him to a waiting car. He helped Robert get into the passenger seat and then got in on the other side. "I'll be parking near your company's staging area. If you feel up to it, I think your platoon would like you to take command and inspect them. I'll make sure that you have a chair around to rest, if you want. Not a wheelchair, of course, but just something for you to rest on."

"Thank you, sir."

The car pulled into the Company-A parking lot, and Robert opened his door to get out. He hobbled over to A Company's staging area and saw the cadets getting ready for their march to the assembly field. Robert went up to his platoon sergeant and told him, in a whispered voice, "I'll take charge for now, sergeant. When the company moves out, I'll call for you to post, okay?" Captain Toole had preceded Robert over to the sergeant and handed a chair to SFC Cadet Dickey.

"Yes, sir." Dickey answered. "Welcome back, sir."

Dickey smiled, and Cadet Lieutenant Crandon smiled back as he intoned, "Second platoon, inspection ranks, march!" The cadets separated for inspection, and Robert checked out each one of his cadets. SFC Dickey carried the folding chair with him and followed his platoon leader just behind and to Robert's right. Whenever the platoon leader became tired, he would sit in the chair to rest. After Robert finished his inspection, he ordered the platoon to close ranks, counted the number of boys in his platoon, and looked at his platoon sergeant. The sergeant was standing behind the rest of the platoon, so they did not see him flash his hands, showing four fingers in his left and one in his right. Robert nodded; he now knew that his platoon consisted of forty-one members, including himself and his platoon sergeant.

Robert waited on his folding chair until Cadet Captain Falmer called the company to attention. "First platoon report!"

"First platoon all present, sir!"

"Second platoon report!"

"Second platoon all present, sir!" Robert called out. The entire company cheered wildly. Those words had not been heard in Alpha Company since November 1. After the noise calmed down, Cadet Captain Falmer continued, "Third platoon report!"

"Third platoon, one cadet on telephone detail, all others present, sir!"

"Company!" the company commander shouted.

"Platoon!" each platoon leader answered.

"Right face!" The entire company conducted the maneuver as one.

"Platoon sergeant post!" Robert called out. SFC Dickey came running around the platoon and saluted his platoon leader. Robert pushed his right arm up with his left and saluted back, made an "about-face" maneuver and headed toward the assembly field. The field was nearly four hundred meters away, and Robert used every last bit of his energy to reach the battalion, which had easily beaten him to the assembly. He then walked up to Dickey, who saluted him and promptly vacated his post at the head of the platoon. Robert turned around. He was unsure why the battalion had assembled, but he noticed a lot of people around the grand stands and podium.

As he took in the sights, he also noticed that there were some army and air force units assembled in formation on the field as well. He had never seen the military form up with Waterline Cadets. He knew that *technically* the two were related to each other. His chain of command included the chairman of the Joint Chiefs of Staff, the secretary of defense, and the president of the United States. The same was true for each soldier, sailor, and airman in the military, but he had never been in an assembly with any of them in his three years at Waterline Academy.

A general called the entire formation to parade rest. Robert could not go to "parade rest" due to his injuries, so he just spread his legs some and bent his elbows to give the best semblance of the ordered stance that he could.

"Cadet Lieutenant Robert Crandon post!" the general ordered. Robert came to the position of attention then made his way to the podium. When he got there, he saw several cadre officers flinch as if to help him up the podium. Each one of the cadre officers, however, held his ground. Robert made his way up the stairs the best that he could. All the people on the podium seemed content to wait as long as Robert needed to take.

When Robert finally reached Major General Bernard Rogers, he used his left hand once again to help him salute with his right. The general saluted Robert back, both dropping their hands about the same time. The general took a step back and a man stepped forward. Robert thought that he might be hallucinating. He recognized the man's face. Every cadet at Waterline Academy would recognize the man's face. Robert had seen his photograph many times in each of the barracks. The photograph always had the title, *The Honorable Melvin Laird, Secretary of Defense*, written under it.

As Secretary Laird approached the microphone, a voice ordered, "Formation! Attention!" Robert heard the soldiers, airmen, and cadets move their feet as one.

Secretary Laird began reading, "On November 1, 1972, Cadet Lieutenant Robert Joseph Crandon of Waterline Academy was confronted by a dangerous assailant. Cadet Crandon willingly placed himself in the path of the assailant, disregarding any personal injuries and danger, in order to save his fellow cadet from grievous bodily harm. In spite of taking numerous blows with a metal weapon and having his chest caved in, causing his right lung to collapse, Cadet Crandon continued to impede the attacker in order to permit more time for his fellow cadet to escape. Cadet Crandon then managed, in spite of grievous and life-threatening injuries, to crawl over seventy meters to notify staff members of the dangerous situation. Cadet Lieutenant Robert Crandon's actions and bravery were above and beyond the call of duty and in keeping with the highest traditions of the United States Academy System and the United States Military in general. For his heroism in the face of danger, Cadet Lieutenant Robert Joseph Crandon is hereby awarded the Medal of Freedom, signed this 22nd of November, 1972, by order of Richard M. Nixon, President of the United States."

Secretary Laird pinned the medal onto Robert's outer jacket, the one Robert thought of as his "housecoat," and shook his hand. "Well done, cadet."

"Thank you, Mr. Secretary," Robert managed to croak out. As Robert was gently turned around to face the formation, a cheer went up from all of the academy cadets. That was soon added to by the army and air force personnel who were there for the presentation. Light bulbs were flashing all around the podium and some murmuring was going on from the spectators seated on the grandstands and standing on and around the podium.

General Rogers, who had called the formation to attention, approached the microphone. All the cadets and service men and women in the formations immediately quieted down and came to the position of attention. "Battalion commanders take charge of your battalions." The general ordered. Each of the groups was marched off the field toward their respective destinations.

Robert was in shock. He had medals. He had received all five Cadet achievement medals he could. Technically, each subsequent achievement medal was called, "achievement medal 1st or 2nd or 3rd or 4th Oak Leaf Cluster." After he had gotten all five of those, he had begun receiving commendation medals, with oak leaf clusters. Since he excelled in academics and in behavior, he had even started receiving commendation medals with silver bars—after all, only so many oak leaf pins could fit on one tiny stretch of ribbon. In spite of the acclamations he had received previously, he had never expected what had just happened. He had expected that the achievement and commendation medals were the only "carrots" in the "carrot and stick" approach of the cadre officers. The Medal of Freedom was the highest honor the Academy System could bestow. In the entire history of the Academy System, Robert knew that he was only the fourth cadet ever to receive the honor, and all the others were from the *gifted* academies.

Robert made his way down the podium steps, very slowly and methodically. He was about to head to his academy grounds when

Commandant Leary stopped him. "Hold on there, cadet. You're not getting away from me *this time*." Robert stood his ground and waited for the head of his academy. Commandant Leary pointed to an odd-looking scooter. "You get to travel around on this until your physical therapist says otherwise."

Leary brought Robert over to the machine and showed him how to operate the joystick. There were two buttons, forward and reverse, and a joystick that could easily be operated with one hand. "You should have no trouble with this. It doesn't go fast, that way it won't give you a bumpy ride. You are *not* to worry about being *on time* for anything. You are also not to eat in the mess hall until your physical therapist clears you for that.

"He was very specific about his instructions. He doesn't want you taking stairs unnecessarily. He also said that you are ordered, and I quote, 'ordered to take his pain medication. I need him to heal up and get better, so he had better use the meds.' I think that about covers it, cadet. Any questions?"

"Sir, if I get *carried* up the stairs, will that be okay?" Robert asked.

"I suppose that would still fit into the instructions. What are you thinking, cadet? Your quarters are on the first floor now, and your meals are going to be brought to you ... " Commandant Leary asked.

"Yes, sir, but my *platoon* is on the third floor. I can't help them out very much if I can't be *with* them. I'll just have them carry me up. Thank you, sir," Robert added as he hobbled onto the scooter. Robert assumed that the engine must be powered by battery, since it was so quiet and he saw no exhaust ports. The wheels were very wide, allowing the scooter to travel over nearly any terrain.

As Robert was adjusting to his perch atop the scooter, Justin and Alice McPhee made their way over to their grandson. "We are so proud of you, Robbie!" Alice told her grandson. Justin congratulated his grandson as well. They told Robert that they would be waiting for him after he got his uniforms together. They would accompany him to Coventry, so that he could spend Thanksgiving with his entire family.

"Just pick out any cadet on the banned list to help you gather uniforms, cadet. You can't possibly lift them yet. Some of those cadets happen to be lounging around my cadre office, if I don't miss my guess," Commandant Leary suggested. Robert was thrilled. He had assumed that since he needed to go to physical therapy that he was stuck at the academy. Robert was going on his first pass since he had come to Waterline Academy over three years earlier.

Robert made his way back to the barracks atop his scooter and stopped at the bottom of his platoon's stairs. He hobbled over to the open door and banged on the metal railing three times. Three cadets came rushing down the stairs. "Okay, guys, time to take your platoon leader up to the billeting area." The cadets understood immediately. They formed a moving human chair for their platoon leader and listened carefully to his instructions on how to lift him just so and support him without his needing to hold onto them with his arms.

Robert inspected the rooms, checked the roster to see who had passes and who was banned and made sure that necessary repairs had been filed. He greeted all of his platoon members warmly and promised to "take it easy." He also reminded them that their First Inspection would come just after common week. He then had three cadets carry him down the stairs to his scooter. He also had one of his banned cadets go get his uniforms.

He was on a plane out of Atlanta before 1500 hours that afternoon, one of his grandparents sitting on either side of him. For the first time in over three years, he had left Waterline Academy.

While Robert was visiting his family for the first time in over three years, he knew he had a mission to accomplish. "If this is your first visit, you need to apologize to all those you have hurt and to make amends if possible." Robert could hear the voice of Cadre Captain Newman giving him and the other cadets their departing instructions.

He began with Marie, his oldest sister. "Marie, I need to talk with you alone," He begged.

"Of course Robbie! How are you feeling, anyways. Oh, probably terrible, so never mind. Did I tell you about this boy, Dean, that I'm dating? He is so dreamy!"

Robert interrupted, "I meant that I need to tell you something." He smiled and blinked his impish blink.

"Oh! Of course. Listen to me just going on and on. You wanted to tell me something and here I am rambling. Well, okay, you go ahead first."

"I was really mad at you and called you some mean things. I'm sorry. I was wrong to do that. I hope that you will forgive me."

"Oh of course I forgive you," Marie said in a matter-of-fact way. "You're my little brother. Of course, now you're not my youngest brother. Isn't Patrick so cute? I just love holding him and rocking him to sleep. Mom says that he should be able to support his head soon and everything. Nancy is the one who changes his diapers when Mom's not around. I kind of like that. I'm not really into changing dirty diapers. I get to feed him sometimes though." Marie continued on for nearly half an hour before she decided to head off with her friends.

The next one Robert talked to was his brother, Kevin. Robert insisted that Kevin had done no wrong in having "failed to stop you from getting in trouble." As far as Robert was concerned, Kevin had been a wonderful protector and a good brother. He apologized to Kevin for calling him names and cursing him.

By this time, Robert was used to the idea that his siblings had not been told about the letter mix up. As a consequence, he never even brought up the subject with Nancy and John. Both of them knew that Robert had been sent to Waterline Academy by mistake, but Robert did not know that they knew.

The day before Robert was to head back to South Carolina his parents confronted him about the mix up. Roberta took the letter that Mrs. Rowell had written about Robert and handed it to him. "This is the letter your teacher meant for us to read, Robbie."

Robert read through it in just a few seconds, his speed-reading skills being nearly automatic at this point. After he read it he wiped a tear from his eye. "I kind of suspected," he admitted to them.

"We are so sorry!" Paul said apologetically.

"You don't need to be sorry, Father! You did what you thought was best for me! I'm the one who is sorry. I did things that made you think I was awful. No matter what Mrs. Rowell's letter said, you believed that I could have done those things! If I ever do anything to make you think I'm bad, will you please tell me? I promise to do my best to change—really!"

Paul and Roberta decided to allow Robert his coping mechanism. He was just too vulnerable to accept any possibility other than that he had done something to cause them to send him to Waterline Academy.

Dear Mother and Father,

This letter is for you alone. I have been thinking about my recent trip to Massachusetts. It was really, really great to see everyone again. I really loved it! I also noticed something that I need you to help me with.

Christmas is coming. My platoon had the highest marks for First Inspection. Unless something really ridiculous happens, they will almost certainly pass Second Inspection. So, unless a cadre officer really has it out for me, I will likely be given a pass for Christmas Common Week. I am scared of what I need to tell you. Please try to understand that I do not mean to cause you any sadness.

Waterline cadets are not allowed to have anything that is not issued from the academy. My first year here, they took away our pencils whenever we sharpened them past the Waterline mark. We cannot have notebooks, pens, pencils, or even paper that does not have the Waterline mark (the paper has a Waterline Academy symbol watermark on each page)! When I first arrived, as you may remember from my telling you, they had me burn all of my clothes in the Civvies Pit (civilian clothes). All of this is for the best. We have a lot (and I mean A LOT) of former thieves here. Since they are not allowed to own anything, they get in the habit of not taking things.

This brings me to the problem. I cannot have anything from outside of the academy. I remember our Christmas traditions. We used to go to Grandmother and Grandfather McPhee's on Christmas Eve. That night Grandmother and Grandfather McPhee would give us presents. In addition, Aunt Jenna and Uncle Jim would give us something (usually with Sally's and Jessie's names added on). Uncle Dennis would give us something as well. You two would give presents to Grandmother and Grandfather, and Mother's siblings and nieces. On Christmas Day, we would visit Great-Grandfather Lowry and Grandmother Crandon. They would also give us gifts. In addition, we always started Christmas Day by opening lots and lots of presents that were under our Christmas tree (going to Mass after that).

I have really, really happy memories of Christmas. I do not want to lose those. At the same time, I know that I cannot accept presents from ANYONE! I cannot accept them from my grandparents, my aunts, my uncles, my siblings, my cousins, or my parents. I do not mean that they cannot be given (at least legally); I mean that it would kill me to have to refuse! Nevertheless, I would and will refuse to accept them.

I do not think that I could easily handle the pain involved in having to refuse gifts from my family. I think it would make everyone sad to see me do this. I am pretty sure that I would start crying—both because of the memories of my Christmases spent at the academy and that I would be making everyone else sad. I do not want to cause Christmas 1972 to be sad for everyone. That is, I think, the last thing I would ever want to do.

I noticed when I visited a few weeks ago that many of my relatives were very happy to see me. They had big smiles on their faces. They spoke to me as if I had simply been on a long trip. They wanted to be with me, to be happy with me. I want that as well. I also felt that they were looking forward to this Christmas. That scares me.

I guess that I have put it off long enough. The only two solutions I can think of are first: I could remain at Waterline Academy for Christmas Common Week. It is not as if I would be facing the same treatment as the other times that I was here during common weeks. When a cadet is on pass, but stays at the academy, he only has to do a few of the things that the others have to do. Usually this means I would have to show up to physical training, keep my room clean, and show up to each meal. I would also usually have to remain on the academy grounds unless I was given permission to go to the PX. In my case, I would not even have to go to physical training, since I am convalescent—I would go to physical therapy instead.

As for meals, I would not have to eat them in the mess hall, since I have not been cleared by Captain Green (my physical therapist) to do that anyways. This means that I would probably eat most of my meals in Commandant Leary's office. That is how we do things right now, anyways. Commandant Leary and I eat in his office for every meal—at least whenever he is here. When he is home, I eat in his office with Cadre Captain Newman (he is our new master of discipline). I am learning all sorts of cool stuff from them! Commandant Leary was a top interrogator for the Air Force. He is teaching me all sorts of stuff from his work in Africa!

The second possibility is that you could tell everyone to not give me presents. I would need to know that this would be followed. You could try to figure out if someone was going to cheat. If that was going to happen, you could leave me in Coventry for that particular get-together. If it would be too embarrassing or too upsetting for you to do this, then I would rather stay here. Also, if it would be too upsetting for you to not give me presents I would rather stay here.

I am currently in Commandant Leary's office and he made a suggestion. I could hold my baby brother and open any gifts given to him! This would be really, really great! Even in later years, I could keep him with me and watch him open presents! This would make me really happy! If this is okay with everyone, then I would love to do it. If not, that is okay too.

Please let me know what to expect. I will be waiting for your letter. I will tell my cadre (well, really Commandant Leary) to hold off on reserving plane tickets until I get the letter. I am counting on you to tell me the truth. I love you and trust you.

Your loving son,
Robert J. Crandon
Cadet Lieutenant, USAS
Waterline Academy

PART II: RANK HAS ITS RESPONSIBILITIES

★★★★

FIELD DUTY

Eight months later, some of the cadet senior officers stood looking at a bleak landscape. There were leaves on the soggy, black mud. The trees stood at varying intervals—some thick, some thin. They didn't have many branches. Puddles of murky water could be seen everywhere, going until the trees finally blocked one from seeing further.

"We have to do *what* with this?" Cadet Captain Reynolds asked for a third time.

Cadet Lieutenant Colonel Darryl Marks was starting to become annoyed with this freshly promoted cadet. "We have to muck it out and make it safe for military training maneuvers."

"Well, what's that supposed to *mean?*" asked the cadet adjutant, Cadet Major Stevens.

"It means we get to dig until September, wait until next June and then dig some more," Cadet Major Tromp, the XO, answered.

"Hold on. Let me go ask Robbie what he's got. Maybe our resident genius can get us some sort of … of … synergy." Darryl Marks had enormous respect for the young cadet he had taken under his wing nearly four years ago. Cadet Lieutenant Robert Crandon had helped them get other jobs done more quickly than the cadre had expected; maybe he could come up with another miracle. Marks headed toward the section of the woods where Alpha Company was making lean-tos.

"Cadet Lieutenant Crandon *post!*" Marks shouted out. In a short while he saw a nine-year-old boy running across the hill in his rags and flip-flops. It was still hard for Marks to think of this little boy as the platoon leader who led his platoon to the top ranks of Waterline Academy. *He shouldn't even be a squad leader yet, by age…* Darryl thought.

"Cadet Crandon reports as ordered," Robbie called as he slid to a halt. He saluted his newly promoted battalion commander as he caught his balance. "What's up, sir?"

"We've been ordered to make this swamp a safe training area for the military. They expect us to muck it out, I guess. I'd like you to take a look at it and see what ideas you can come up with."

"What have we got for equipment?" Robbie asked.

"Right now," Darryl answered, "we've got shovels, buckets, and any light items we want to ask for. No axes, saws, or sharp instruments. I guess they don't trust us with those."

Robbie nodded and headed out with Darryl to the edge of the territory to be worked. Harry Tromp handed Robbie a map of the area. "We have to try to clear out this area," he explained, while pointing on the map to a region about two and a half square kilometers. "They expect us to take at least three summers to clear it out. They want us to make it *safe*."

"Safe from what?" Robbie asked

"Don't know," Marks added unhelpfully. "That's part of what we have to figure out."

Robbie nodded and began tromping into the swamp. His foot dropped into a sinkhole and when he pulled it out, he saw a leech on him. He squealed in alarm and ran back to the other boys. "Get him off of me!" he squealed. "Get him off! Get him off!"

"How?"

"Use some salt!" Robbie cried. "Hurry!" The boys reached into a supply of pretzels they had sitting in an olive-green pack. They grabbed one of the pretzels and began rubbing it onto the leech. The animal let go of its perch and squiggled away.

"First thing we need is about … let me think," Robbie said. "Two hundred and fifty kilograms of salt!"

"Anything else?" Darryl asked.

"I won't know until you get the salt!" Robbie said, definitively. "I *hate* those things. They're filthy, bloodsucking beasts! I'm not going back in there until I have salt to get rid of them!"

Lt. Colonel Marks submitted his request for Robbie's salt. The Quartermaster Officer, Jim Thomas, looked askew at the cadet battalion commander, but initialed the request and drove off in a truck to fill the request. The next day, Darryl called Alpha Company's 2nd platoon to perform a work detail.

Robbie got his platoon moving immediately and led his platoon moving bags and bags of salt. They placed the commodity under a tarp to keep it dry. Robbie took a small bag of the salt and tied it around his neck.

"The stuff's not wolves' bane, you know," Darryl said as he followed the cadet toward the swamp. "It's not leech bane either," he added, half-jokingly.

"Yeah, but it gets rid of leeches that are sticking on me. That's all I care about!" Robbie continued to trudge through the light forest.

When he got to the edge of the soggy region, he asked, "Okay, who's coming with me?" He got no volunteers out of any of the cadet senior officer corps. "I get it!" he exclaimed sarcastically. "Send the little guy in by himself to face all the big, bad leeches. Thanks a lot!" He trudged off into the muck.

The other cadet senior officers watched as he made his way through the area. He disappeared beyond the tree line at times, but would reemerge soon after. As he headed southeast, he appeared to crouch over. He reached out and grabbed at something on the surface. The other boys could see something moving in his left hand. It looked, initially, like a wide stick, but they began to dread what it probably was. A short while later, Robbie grabbed at the surface again. Now the boy had something in each hand. Seemingly not deterred, Robbie continued southeast, out of sight. When he returned, about a half hour later, his hands were empty. He rubbed some salt on his body, apparently to rid himself of leeches. When he reached the group of senior officers, he spoke to them, "Okay, I need to do some calculations and drawings. We'll need to dig some, so we had better get organized with that. We'll also need snake guards, so go bash some branches off the trees to use as bats. The snakes don't want to eat us, so we just need to scare them away."

Most of the boys' faces were ashen. Darryl took charge, "You heard the lieutenant, get moving and organizing." To Robbie he asked, "How many snake guards do you need?"

"Don't know yet," Robbie answered. "Two or three at least for each detail, but I haven't calculated how many spots to do, yet."

"Why not have all the guys working in the same spot?" Stevens asked.

"We might," Robbie continued, "but like I said, *I don't know yet!*"

Stevens handed Robbie a pencil and some paper. As the cadet Adjutant, John Stevens had to keep a role of all the cadets. Due to that requirement, he was given a waterproof container in which he kept all the paperwork while the cadets were out in the field.

Robert Crandon sat down and began to scribble calculations on the paper. Occasionally, he would look up, orient himself to the map of the region, and draw a close-up map of a specific area. He would then furiously scribble more equations. After he had filled up the fronts and backs of twelve pages, he looked up at Cadet Colonel Marks, Cadet Major Stevens, and Cadet Major Tromp and began to explain, "According to my calculations, if we dig out a region I saw over there"—he pointed beyond the trees in the northwest—"muck out three areas over there"—he pointed generally west—"and clear out the muck and vegetation over there"—he pointed to the southwest—"then we should be all set. I'll show you where, exactly, we need to dig and then we can get everybody to work."

"We're going to need about three hundred meters of *really* strong rope and six pulleys, sir," Robbie said as he looked at Darryl. "We will also need anti-venom for copperheads and water moccasins. I'm not sure about other things. We'll just have to deal with them when they come up."

The older three boys nodded as if approving, but each one knew that if he asked for a detailed explanation of how things were supposed to work, he would get it. The explanation would likely take eight hours, cause their brains to freeze up, and they would understand little more than when they started. They just accepted that this nine-year-old genius must know what he was up to.

Most of the work was drudgery. The cadre officers were in very bad moods. The commandant had been sent off to a class for the summer, ostensibly to help him learn to control his academy better. The cadre adjutant had resigned for, "personal reasons." Those reasons were that his wife hated South Carolina and insisted that they move back to Buffalo. Without either of those two cadre members, there was no one left to request a different assignment for Waterline Academy. The cadre officers did not mean to do it, and probably did not realize that they *were* doing it, but they blamed the cadets for their being stuck out in a bug-, snake-, and leech-infested swamp in the hot July heat of South Carolina.

The first order of business the cadets accomplished was building lean-tos to sleep under. The next job was setting up tents for the Medical aid station and the cadre. After those jobs were accomplished, the cadet senior officers came to the cadre with their plan. They had outlined five areas in which to work. They needed ropes, pulleys, and anti-venom for snakes. That final request had not gone over well with any cadre member. Even still, they made the requests, obtained the items, and got the cadets working. They also ordered a full-time doctor and two full-time nurses to be assigned to the aid station—if there were dangerous vipers around then the military could darn well provide them with medical personnel.

Darryl Marks rotated the work crews from station to station, just to give the cadets a change of scenery and the chance to work at the "clean water". The portion that Robbie had marked for digging in the northwest was near a river that ran into the swamp. There was a section right near the digging area where the boys could wade in and clean off the muck from the other areas. Darryl did not understand why his little protégé wanted to dig out an area that was dry, but he trusted the little guy.

Robert Crandon was everywhere. He carried his shovel around from site to site. He helped dig out the toughest areas and kept putting salt on the leeches. All the boys carried salt bags after the first two days. The leeches seemed to be all over the swamp and there was no way to get to a digging site without picking up at least one of them. Cadet Crandon also monitored the progress of each site. Each night, he would go over the progress with the cadet adjutant and suggest what the distribution of workers should be for the following day.

The work was not without its hazards. The senior officer corps set up snake guards with sticks. That particular job was always changing hands. Whenever a guard freaked out about a snake wriggling through the water, one of the senior officers would randomly assign another cadet to take his place. The senior officers were not very lenient, though. They could tell when a snake guard was truly panicked or simply faking. In addition, the region was hazardous due to disease. The cadets had to wash their hands and faces each night when the light became so low that no digging could readily be accomplished. There was a potable water tank brought onto the area each day. The cadets were given soap and told to wash, but inevitably some would not wash well enough and would come down with fevers. Additionally, the leeches carried disease. Some of the fevers were not fought off easily. The medical staff was passing out antibiotic pills like candy.

After two weeks of toil and drudgery, Robbie announced to Darryl that it was time to use the ropes and pulleys. "What are we going to *do* with them?" Darryl asked.

"We're going to move really heavy rocks and trees," Robbie answered.

"Tempers are flaring, Robbie. Are you sure this is necessary?"

"Yep. The digging and the moving of these rocks and trees should just about finish it all up." Robbie answered. Marks was skeptical, but the alternative was dredging the *entire* swamp, and that would take years.

Lt. Crandon was assigned to hook up the ropes and pulleys. He created harnesses and had the work crews try to pull one way, would adjust his harnesses and have the work crews try pulling in another direction. All the while, the digging was continuing as well. Only Robbie could see the finished product about to come about. Nevertheless, whenever Robbie yelled, "heave" and some cadet would yell back at him, "You heave!" there was always a platoon sergeant around to pop the malcontent on the head. Invariably, the malcontent would soon correct himself, saying, "Yes, sir! I'm heaving!"

After nearly three weeks, the weather changed and a storm front was moving in. Robbie was pushing the cadets to their absolute limits. Stevens had informed his battalion commander that the academy had lost nearly forty percent of their strength due to dysentery, diarrhea, and fevers. There were no malingerers. There was little point in trying to get out of work by making yourself sick. The benefits of the aid station did not outweigh the pain of the fevers. The doctor gave out "light-work profiles" for those with gastrointestinal problems. Whenever a cadet was placed on "profile," he would be handed a stick with which to scare snakes away. As a consequence, there were an awful lot of snake guards.

"Rob, we've just about pushed these guys to their limit, don't you think?" Darryl warned Robert.

"We can't stop *now!*" Robert pleaded. "We don't want to miss the *rains!*"

"Well, I agree that we can't muck out the swamp while it's raining, but ... " Darryl answered in confusion.

"No, no! We need the rains to clear the swamp out!" Robbie added. "We have *got* to move the last rocks and vegetation before the rains begin. Otherwise, we'll be stuck out here digging just because the work won't *look* done."

Darryl nodded his head, partially understanding. "Okay, we'll work on into the night if need be. We'll get it done." He and his protégé pushed the cadets who could work to move the largest obstacles to date. No amount of pushing and pulling would get the largest rock moved. Finally, Robbie sat down dejectedly, defeated. "We just can't move the thing." Darryl gasped.

"I know it," Robbie sniffled out. "If we just had something to use as a fulcrum for a counterweight." He sighed.

"A what for a who?" Harry Tromp asked.

"In order to use a counterweight, I have to have something to loop the rope over," Robbie explained.

"Why?" Harry asked.

"Well, if we had the fulcrum, then we could attach the rope at *both* ends to heavy items, kind of like a seesaw. The items would then balance each other out and when we applied lift, the heavy item at our end would add its weight," Robbie explained some more. He used hand gestures to try to show his intent.

As Darryl sat thinking about the explanation that his "resident genius" had just given, he looked off to the west. "What about using the cliff?" he asked.

Robbie looked up. He started looking through his hands while holding his fingers in odd ways. "Hey, Harry, go on over to that set of trees over there," he asked.

"That's *sir* to you, cadet," Harry chided.

"Okay. Sir, Harry, please go over there so I can look at the ground correctly," Robbie giggled.

"That's better!" Harry agreed. "I hear and obey!" He walked over to the trees Robbie had indicated. As Harry stood there, Robbie grabbed up a pencil and paper and began doing more calculations. He erased things furiously, and then he wrote more equations.

"I think we can pull this off!" the little boy exclaimed. He bounded up, ran over to the site with the huge rock, and began pulling one end of the rope over toward the small hill that the boys called "the cliff." He called over for some cadets to bring him all the extra rope. He hooked up pulleys onto the sturdiest trees he could find, ran around to the bottom of the small hill, and found a large tree trunk. He created a harness and called the work crew to come and lift the trunk.

There was a universal moan as the little cadet lieutenant called for the boys to get moving. Darryl took charge again and got everyone moving as Robbie directed. Robbie had the crews move a trunk to the base of the hill, then move another one on top of the first trunk. He then tied the end of the rope still attached to the carefully balancing trunk to the rope that was attached to the harnessed rock. As he finished he told Darryl to start taking guys off of the rope detail *one at a time.*

As the cadets let go, the rope pulled taught and held. The pulleys strained to their limits, but they also held. Robbie went over to the rock and pulled on the rope. He seemed satisfied. He called for the work crews to reorganize themselves. He sent most of the cadets around the hill to the precariously perched tree trunk. He kept only enough with him at the monstrous rock to guide the thing to its destination. He called for the larger crew to pull the trunk off and pull it toward them. The rock began pulling out of the muck and finally was lifted off the ground. The guiding crew moved it to the destination Robbie had previously designated and then Robbie ordered the other crew to let go.

The rock moved down to the ground slowly as the counter-weighted log rose up. Robbie had the large work crew return up the hill, untied the knot holding the rock and trunk together, and the trunk crashed down to the ground. "Okay, now all we have to do is move the one tree at the other end of the swamp, and we're done," Robbie announced.

The cadets all staggered to the fallen tree Robbie had indicated. Robbie supervised some digging under the tree and toward his intended destination for the log. Once again, Robbie harnessed the object. Once again the boys pulled with all their might. The fallen tree pivoted as Robbie had intended and moved away from an increasingly deepening region of water.

The entire work crew then staggered back to their bivouac area, washed up, grabbed some food, and collapsed under their lean-tos. Darryl Marks asked the cadre for a rest day. The next day was Sunday, and the cadre officers all agreed that the cadets needed a break. Everyone went to Catholic Mass. Father Jeff was the only chaplain who had come out there, so it was Mass or nothing. The rain started about noontime, and Robbie was jumping for joy.

"I realize that we can't very well be in the deep water during the rain, but why so happy?" Cadet Captain Tim Reynolds asked.

"We won't have to dig *anything* anymore!" Robbie exclaimed. "You'll see! Just give it a few hours. Then give it a few days!"

On Monday morning, Cadre Captain McClay approached the lean-to that Cadet Lieutenant Colonel Darryl Marks lay in. Marks was trying to avoid the rain drops that kept slipping through his lean-to. "Don't you think it's about time to get to work, cadet?" Captain McClay asked.

"Attention!" Marks called out. All the cadets within hearing stood up and got into the ordered stance.

"Well, cadet?" Captain McClay prodded.

"Sir, according to our resident genius, the work is done," Cadet Marks answered.

"Well, let's go see your resident genius, then."

The two made their way over to Company A's bivouac area and found Cadet Lieutenant Crandon. "I hear that you claim the work is all done, Crandon," Captain McClay started.

"Yes, sir. Well, sir, that is, the work that *needs to be done* is all done."

"How do you figure that, cadet?"

"I would need Cadet Major Stevens to show you that, sir," Robbie stated.

"Then let's go find him, shall we?" Captain McClay suggested, rather sarcastically.

The trio went back to the field grade officers' bivouac area and found John Stevens. "I need the paperwork, Major Stevens," Robbie announced. Cadet Stevens looked through his waterproof bag and took out the roster.

"Here you go, Rob. That's a list of all the guys on sick call, on profile, or in the aid station—too sick to work."

"Oh ... *that's* not what I need. I need all the calculations I gave you," Robbie said.

John Stevens looked at him quizzically, but with a cadre officer standing right there, he did not hesitate to get all the calculations out of his bag. He handed them to Robbie, who in turn handed them to Captain McClay. "That's how I figured it, sir," Robbie explained, indicating the paperwork.

Captain McClay was no engineer. He had taken some advanced mathematics classes in college, but he could not understand the work on the pages he held. "I need to take these with me, cadet. I'll be sure to return them to you as soon as possible, okay?" Captain McClay said dazedly. Robbie nodded, dumbly. No cadre officer had ever *asked* him for something.

"Of ... course ... sir." Robbie answered.

Captain McClay walked off with the papers to the cadre tent.

"Is everything cool?" asked Harry Tromp, who had made his way over to the gathering.

"Oh, sure," Robbie said, mechanically. "I'll show you, if you'd like." He pointed over toward the work areas.

"That's okay, Robbie. I'll just wait for the movie to come out."

Cadre Captain McClay was no engineer, but Cadre Captain Peter Toole was. He had worked with the Army Corps of Engineers in Laos and Cambodia. When McClay handed him the calculations, Captain Toole was astonished. He looked through mathematical proofs for complex mathematical functions. He saw the different symbols that Robert Crandon had used for the same items that he, Captain Toole, would have used. Robert had reinvented many of the mathematical formulas that civil engineers around the world were using. Robert may have used stars and birds where tradition used Greek letters, but the calculations were still the same.

"I think he's right." Peter Toole told his fellow cadre officers. "The rain going through this area ought to clear out the river pathway that he has shown here," Toole indicated the paperwork he was holding, "and the swamp will dry itself out with a running stream through the area. I can't be sure until I look at the work, of course, but it all looks sound to me."

That afternoon, Cadre Captain Toole found Cadet Lieutenant Crandon and asked for a tour of the work areas. Robert took the man to the five work sites. Robert explained that the initial site was prepared to make the river run faster into the marshy area. The various dig sites were cleared to keep the water flowing. As the two approached the final work area, Robert told the cadre officer to stand still. Robert waited a few moments and then reached out and grabbed a water moccasin just behind its head.

"This guy just doesn't get it!" Robert said. "He just doesn't want to admit that he's beat." Robert then talked to the snake in a soft voice and began stroking it. "Don't worry, little guy. I'm not going to hurt you. I'm just going to send you on your way to another home. This place is no good for you anymore. At least, in a few days, it won't be."

Peter Toole was no fan of snakes. He kept his distance from the young cadet as the three made their way to the final work site—cadre officer, cadet, and water moccasin. When they arrived at the site, Robert carefully swung the snake out to arm's length and threw it about twenty meters. The snake landed in deeper water and swam away. Robert shivered. "Sorry, sir, but those things give me the creeps!" Cadre Captain Toole's eyes widened in amazement as he heard this news. He and Robert continued into the muck up to Robert's chest. Robert showed Captain Toole the final area. It was already draining out, now that the debris that had blocked the easiest water route had been cleared. "I'm thinking that most of this will clear out in about two to three weeks, sir," Robert explained. "After that, the entire region will shift from wetlands to a soggy, river-edge kind of region."

"Where did you learn to do this?" Captain Toole asked.

"I'm sorry, sir? I don't think I understand the question."

"All of these calculations, the plans for the river gouging, the draining system, those sorts of things—where did you learn these things?"

"Well … sir … I didn't exactly *learn* them. I … it just … *seemed* like it should work, sir."

Captain Toole agreed that the plans would probably work.

He and Robert made their way back to the bivouac area, and Robert applied salt to the leech that had attached to him. "I hate, hate, hate, hate, *hate* these things!" Robert yelled. "Get away, you slimy, filthy, creepy thing!" he shouted at the squirming leech. Robert kicked the thing as far as he could. "You had better let me check *you* out, sir," Robert offered. Captain Toole took off his shirt and trousers, and Robert applied salt to the three leeches that had attached themselves to the cadre officer.

"Thanks, cadet," Captain Toole said. "I haven't had to deal with these things in four years. By the way, where did you guys learn to use salt on them?" he asked.

"I read it in a biology book, sir." Robert answered.

Remembering the encounter in the now-draining swamp, Captain Toole then asked, "Where did you learn to grab water moccasins?"

"Oh. Well, I watched a film one time and saw a guy doing that. When I went out into the muck to see if there was some way to do things faster, a copperhead and a water moccasin decided to join me. Since we didn't have any anti-venom with us at the time, I figured that I might as well take my chances. If I just left them alone, they would probably bite me anyways."

Captain Toole just walked away, shaking his head.

The next morning, the rain had finally lifted. Darryl Marks got the word that one of his worst fears had come true: Robert Crandon was not moving. He appeared to be sick. Darryl ran over to Robert's lean-to and saw the boy shivering in the warm, morning air. He picked the boy up and could feel the red-hot skin indicative of the fever his little genius had contracted. "That last stupid leech," Robert murmured. "It just wouldn't give up without a fight, Daddy ... " Robert continued.

Darryl Marks was no longer gangly. He was sixteen years old and had filled out well. He was six feet one inch tall and weighed two hundred ten pounds. He lifted the tiny frame of his sick cadet with ease. He carried Robert to the medical aid tent and looked around.

"Another one with fever?" asked the nurse.

"I think so, ma'am. He seems to be confused, too," Darryl answered.

"Doctor!" the nurse yelled. "Doctor! This one may be serious. Like the others you said must have gotten fever from the leeches!" She then told Darryl, "Just put him down here," indicating a cot, "and go on back to your friends."

"Yes, ma'am," Darryl said mechanically. He placed the boy on the cot and left the tent.

As he made his way back to his lean-to, he saw Cadre Captain Toole come out of the cadre tent. Darryl saluted and said, "Good morning, sir."

"What brings you around here, cadet?"

"Sick cadet, sir. He couldn't make his own way to the medics."

"Who was it this time, Darryl?"

"Cadet Crandon, sir."

Cadre Captain Toole stopped short, "Is it serious? I can't imagine Crandon ever taking time off. He practically pushed his way out of the hospital when he was injured last November."

"I don't know for certain, sir, but the nurse seemed to be very concerned."

"Okay. Well, don't worry about it too much Darryl. I'm sure that Doctor Silver will be able to handle things. By the way, I'm off to the Army Corps of Engineers to tell them that the work is done. The rain seems to have caused the river to rise, and all the muck is flowing out of the area. Once the corps clears the work, we can go back to the barracks and let you guys have the rest of the time for battalion details."

"That's great, sir!" Darryl exclaimed. "I've got to go tell all the guys!"

"Well, why don't you wait until the Corps clears it? I wouldn't want them all to get disappointed," Captain Toole advised. Darryl agreed and waited for the good news to be official. That occurred the next day. Without Cadet Crandon to show the Army Engineer around, the man had to rework the details for himself. Eventually, Captain Toole noticed him moving around and brought Crandon's calculations to the army officer.

"The kid did this by *himself?*" asked the army major.

"He's probably one of the gifted," Captain Toole offered as an explanation.

"What's he doing in *Waterline?* Shouldn't he be in Bethesda or Berkeley?" the major commented.

"It's a very long story. To put it simply, the paperwork got messed up, and it's too late to fix it," Captain Toole said.

The army major declared the site as finished and agreed that the cadets could head back to the academy. He estimated that the area would be useable by the Basic Training battalions within two months.

Captain Toole informed the rest of the cadre and then went to tell Cadet Marks. He found Darryl Marks in the first-aid station, near Crandon's cot. "The site has been cleared, Darryl. We'll send for the trucks to take us home tomorrow." Marks never even left his seat; he just nodded. Captain Toole did not take offense at the breach of protocol; he knew that Marks had a close relationship to Crandon, like a big brother to a little brother.

Captain Toole went over to Darryl and put his hand on the boy's shoulder, "He'll be all right, Darryl. It will probably take him less time than any of the others to recover. Look at what happened last winter. The doctors couldn't believe how fast he healed."

Darryl looked up and began to stand up, finally realizing that a cadre officer was addressing him. Captain Toole held him down by the shoulder. "Don't worry about me, son. You're worried about Crandon. There's no harm done."

"He just lies there shivering, sir," Darryl said. "He's shivering while everyone else is sweating up a storm!"

"Have you asked the doctor about him?" Captain Toole suggested.

"I haven't seen her yet, sir."

"Why don't we go find her then?" Captain Toole said. Darryl got up and the two moved around the barriers that provided some semblance of privacy for patients. The first woman they encountered was one of the nurses. She provided directions to Dr. Silver's office area. When they found Dr. Silver, she was busy checking paperwork.

"Ma'am?" Darryl said. "Are we bothering you?" he asked.

"Oh, no, come on in," the doctor offered.

Captain Toole took over the speaking, as Darryl seemed too shy or too worried to ask the questions. "We were wondering about the prognosis for Cadet Crandon, Doctor. Is he going to get well, and if so, when?"

"Crandon? Let me see…" She looked at her paperwork. "Oh, one of the *leech* cases. Well, I can't say that I'm thrilled with keeping all the sick cadets out *here*." She waved her hand, indicating the general area. "The fever that the boys have gotten from the leeches should have been enough to put them into an air-conditioned environment," she chided. "Nevertheless, *most* of those cases have cleared up in about a week."

"One week!" Darryl looked crushed.

"Well, that's not too bad considering the *conditions*," the doctor added, somewhat apologetically.

"But … he'll miss everything. He won't get to see the burning. He won't get to enjoy the hot meal out here," Darryl continued.

"It'll be all right, son." Captain Toole tried to soothe the boy's nerves. "Robbie will be okay. Anyway, he may get to see some of those things yet," Captain Toole added.

The next day, the army sent out a convoy of five-ton trucks and three very large tents. The cadets enthusiastically put up the tents, since they were going to sleep under them that night. The trucks and their drivers stayed out with the academy personnel, set to bring them in the next day. The rain had stopped in the middle of the night and the sun quickly dried up the ground around the tents. The mess hall personnel brought out a hot breakfast for the cadets' morning meal.

As Darryl Marks, John Stevens, and Harry Tromp got into the line for morning meal, they were surprised to see Robert Crandon heading toward them out of the first-aid station. "Are you *supposed* to be out here?" Harry asked.

"I just got cleared by the doctor," Robert answered. "She was kind of surprised that I was up and moving, but she said I looked okay and that my temp had broken."

The four cadet officers were the last to get their meals. It was a tradition that cadet officers would wait for their command to eat before them. This was not required and often circumstances demanded otherwise, but at that morning meal, there were no pressing issues.

After they had eaten, the four cadets went to relax on a hill overlooking the swampy region. Already, the ground appeared to be drying out. As they lounged, awaiting orders to board the trucks, Robert looked over toward the site where the cadre tent had been set up. "Is that a new cadre officer?" Robert asked.

"I suppose." Darryl answered, looking over at the area.

"He's got oak leaves," Robert commented. "That means discipline or adjutant."

"Good!" said John. "I could use my advisor."

"Well, you'd better go introduce yourself, Darryl." Robert suggested. "You might want to go too," he added to John. "Either he's adjutant, or Captain Newman is. Either way, you'll get to know who's going to throw the darts." Robert was referring to the means by which the cadre adjutant assigned the boys to their platoons. It always seemed so random that the cadets joked that the adjutant simply threw darts with names on them and assigned the cadets wherever the darts landed.

Darryl and John went over to the cadre and waited about fifteen minutes before getting a word in. The new cadre officer did not seem very friendly, as far as Robert could see, but the boy *was* looking from a distance. As the two field-grade officers returned, Robert asked, "Is he any good?"

"Don't know," Darryl answered.

"Where's he from?" Harry asked.

"Don't know," John answered.

"Adjutant or discipline?" Robert asked.

"Adjutant," John and Darryl answered together.

"How long has he been a cadre officer?" Robert asked.

"Don't know," John and Darryl answered together.

"How can you not know?" Robert asked. "Cadre officers always tell you where they've worked before, how long they've been cadre officers … "

"Not this one," Darryl answered. "I have a bad feeling about this."

"But he's the guy who's going to assign all the troops … " Harry said. "What if he screws up?"

All three other boys looked at Harry. "That's why you're in Waterline, cadet," Darryl answered. That ended the discussion about the new cadre officer.

The four cadet officers sat back down on the small hill. "When are we going to burn it?" Harry asked.

"Burn what?" Robert asked.

"The stuff ... " Harry pointed out to the mounds of muck and vegetation that the academy cadets had moved. "You know ... everything," he added.

"Just *how* do you plan to burn logs that have been soaking in swamp water for the last five years?" Darryl asked.

"We could douse it with gasoline ... " Harry suggested.

"Yeah!" Robert said, only partially enthusiastically. "Or we could ask the army for a flame thrower, or better yet, ask the air force to drop napalm on the stuff. But really, cadet, why bother? We'll just burn our rags in the civvies pit back home. That should be enough to satisfy your incendiary tendencies for a year."

Harry nodded glumly as the other two cadets seemed to agree with the young platoon leader.

Later that morning, the word was given for the cadets to load onto the trucks. Darryl called the cadets into formation and told them to throw their rags into the pit where civilian clothes were burned, then go into their barracks and shower until their platoon leaders passed them as clean. This order applied to all of the gastrointestinal cases as well. Only those with fevers were exempted. Those were on their way to Ft. Waterline Hospital for the rest of their treatment. He then passed control over to the respective platoon leaders who got the cadets into trucks in an organized fashion.

A NEW CADRE ADJUTANT

The "End of Summer" tradition of burning the rags was the high-light of the evening. All the cadets who had been sent to Waterline Academy for pyromania were kept near the back of the circle surrounding the pit. Cadet Marks, the battalion commander, set fire to the rags, which seemed to have been doused with even more gasoline than was typical for the cadre. The flames were a symbol that the summer hard work was over. All the cadets cheered as the fire consumed the rags they had been wearing.

The next several days were filled up with physical training, random chores, and more physical training. The cadre of Waterline Academy never let the cadets have too long a break. Such a thing would never be tolerated, and, in most peoples' minds, probably would be extraordinarily dangerous. Each evening, the platoon leaders and company commanders would go into the field grade officers' section of the barracks looking for the new roster assignments. Each day, they were told that the roster had not been assigned yet.

"What the hell is he waiting for?" Darryl rhetorically asked, one hot evening. "What's he planning to do, wait until August fifteenth?"

"Could be," John answered gloomily. "I've been trying to get something out of him, but he just brushes me off like so much dust."

So the cadets waited, and the August 15 deadline came without any assignments. Late that evening, Cadet John Stevens was ordered to report to Cadre Major Sooner, the cadre Adjutant. Cadet Major Stevens came back with ten rosters. Nine of the rosters were for the platoons and the tenth page had the names of the company commanders and field grade officers. "Where are the *copies?*" his battalion commander asked.

"There are no copies, sir," John answered. "He said I only needed one copy of each … " he added in a stunned manner.

"How are the platoon leaders supposed to know who they've got?" Darryl asked.

"I get to *tell* them, sir. If they don't memorize it the first time, they can come ask me again … or so my adviser has informed me, sir."

The next morning after physical training, Cadet Lieutenant Colonel Marks called the academy to formation and had the cadet adjutant pass out the rosters. He told the platoon leaders to return the rosters after they had all their cadets in the correct barracks. The cadets were told to pack all of their uniforms and move them to the formation regions. After this had been done, each platoon leader walked around and found his cadets, telling them which barracks and floor they needed to move to.

After all the shuffling was done, Cadet Lieutenant Crandon came into the field grade officers section and gloomily handed his roster back to John Stevens. "What's wrong?" Cadet Major Stevens asked. "Another headache, Robbie?" Robert had been suffering severe headaches since the previous year, sometimes breaking into open crying. They had started with his long convalescence. John, Darryl Marks and Harry Tromp all helped Robert to cope with the pain, comforting him and letting him know that they still had respect for him.

"Look at my roster, sir," Crandon suggested.

"Not many guys in it. I don't see where that's a problem," Stevens said. At that time, Marks walked in.

"What's up, Robbie?" he asked.

"Twenty open slots," Crandon answered.

"Oh my God!" Darryl Marks exclaimed. "You aren't kidding me, are you?" he added hopefully.

Stevens still didn't understand. "What's wrong with twenty open slots, sir?"

"How many open slots are there in the rest of the platoons?" Darryl asked, hurriedly.

Stevens looked through all the roster sheets. All the other rosters had already been returned before Crandon arrived. "None," he said. "They all have exactly forty-two."

"Has this ever been done?" Darryl asked.

"I think so … " Robert answered. "I'd like permission to go check tonight, sir."

"Okay. It's your platoon. Go ahead. We'll run cover for you if needed," Darryl agreed.

"What's wrong with twenty open slots in a platoon? I mean, I guess that platoon chores will be a little heavy, but other than that … I don't get it," John asked again.

"We haven't gotten any plebes, yet," Darryl explained. "How many transfers are we supposed to get from other academies?" he asked.

"None," John answered. He paused for a short while. "*Now* I get it! He put every single plebe into the same platoon." John's eyes bulged out.

"Not just that," Robert suggested. "I checked with my junior officers. No one has ever served in his current position. I have four new fire team leaders, four freshly promoted squad leaders and a freshly promoted platoon sergeant. I kind of wish he'd thrown darts."

Darryl Marks was stunned. The plebes had always been split up amongst all the platoons. Newly promoted officers were always assigned with some veterans. Their new Cadre Adjutant had just changed "always" to "always before 1973".

Robert Crandon was still small. He navigated through the ventilation system with ease. He entered the private office of the commandant and read the historical records the Waterline Cadre of past years had left. He then looked up the secret records of the cadets for the 1953-1954 school year.

The next morning, Darryl Marks asked his young platoon leader about the previous night's excursion. Robert answered, "They tried it before. Nineteen fifty-three has been labeled 'the year we put all the eggs in one basket,' by the cadre. The cadets have added, 'and then roller-skated on ice.' It wasn't pretty.

"Actually, the cadre Historical Records book lists the 1953-1954 school year as a 'disaster that must never be repeated.' It's pretty clear about what happened. By December of 1953, the cadre determined that the experiment was a failure and reassigned the platoons. It didn't help much. By the time the 4th of July came, only fifteen cadets were allowed to leave for Common Week."

"Maybe he'll change his mind," Darryl suggested. "I mean, if it's all clear in the Cadre Histories, shouldn't he just have to read that and switch it all back?"

"He was supposed to read the Cadre Historical Records within the first week of entering Waterline," Robert answered. "I also looked up his dossier. He's never been a cad. He's a political appointee; he worked as the campaign finance chief for some senator last year. That's how he got the job, and at top pay, too. Apparently, the commandant got approval for double pay for Waterline Cadre after he cleaned house last November. Since this guy is a major, he gets that much more."

"Then I'm going to go tell the commandant," Darryl decided. "This can't go on."

Darryl went to the commandant and explained the problem. He told the commandant about the disaster of the 1953-1954 school year at Waterline Academy. He pleaded with the commandant, but to no avail. The commandant himself had told Cadre Major Sooner that such an experiment was unwise. Sooner had brushed off Commandant Leary and done things his own way. When Leary had complained to the Director of Academies, he was told that Major Sooner was "protected" and that there was little anyone could do about the possible problems.

Cadre Major Aldus Sooner was not finished with his changes. He ordered all the uniforms and boots to be exchanged for new uniforms and boots. Major Sooner ordered all of the desk protocols to be switched. Each cadet had always had to have his pencil, ruler, pen, etc. facing in an exact direction. Major Sooner changed the directions and locations. On this particular point, Major Sooner was overruled. It fell to the master of discipline to decide such things, and the rest of the cadre officers were thrilled when Commandant Leary declared this to Major Sooner.

The other cadre officers were worried. *They* had all read the histories. They knew what to expect from Sooner's "great experiment." The previous time all plebes had been put into one platoon, at least the platoon officers had been veterans. Each night, several of the cadre officers would gather at the Ft. Waterline Officers' Club and grumble about their new adjutant.

It was not long before Cadet Lieutenant Robert Crandon's platoon, C Company 3rd Platoon, or Charlie-3, began to fill up. The plebes ranged from ages eight to eleven. Each night, he drilled his platoon on "required knowledge," Waterline Academy standards, and the need for each and every platoon member to be a team player. "Cadets help cadets. Cadets don't turn in cadets. You never attack a cadre officer. You never steal anything. You never play pranks without tacit approval from your Cadet Officer Corps. If you need help, *ask me!*" In addition, he began taking his entire platoon to the gymnasium for "anger management" classes. These consisted of punching the punching bags until all the aggressions of the cadet were calmed down.

As September moved into October, Charlie-3 began to act like a team. There were still some plebes coming in, but with all the Charlie-3 officers helping each boy transition to life at Waterline Academy, the discipline problems were minimal. Charlie-3 filled up completely on October 20, 1973. Four days later, a Thursday, Crandon went to Cadet Major Stevens, the battalion adjutant, to get his daily bulletins for the next week. As Crandon looked through the bulletins, he commented, "I think you gave me someone else's Monday."

"What's that, Rob?" John Stevens asked.

Robert Crandon held out the bulletin for October 29. "This one. There must have been a mistake—maybe a computer glitch or something."

John looked at the bulletin and nodded. "Wait here and I'll go get another one." After about ten minutes, John came back into the field grade officers' section with a sad look on his face.

Cadet Crandon's eyes opened wide and bulged out. At that time, the battalion commander, Darryl Marks came in. "What's the matter, Robbie?" he asked. "You look like you've seen a ghost."

"Ghosts would be more fun!" Robert answered and pointed to the Monday bulletin in John's hand. Darryl took the bulletin, looked at the top three times, and sat down on the floor where he had been standing.

"He *can't*," Darryl pleaded. "He *just can't*. I'm going to see Captain Newman." Darryl got up and left the corridor. Robert and John went into Darryl's room and listened at the wall. Since the office of the master of discipline shared a wall with the cadet Battalion Commander, there was no need to listen at the vents.

"Ridiculous. Begging your pardon sir, but, what's he trying to do? Get my platoon leader three *Majors*? Plebes average fifty gigs in the prelim, and that's when there's only two or three per platoon. Rob's got twenty of them. No platoon has ever gone through prelim with more than four!"

"I understand the dilemma, Darryl. I just don't have the authority to change this. I can only guarantee you that I'll try to be lenient on his guys."

"It's bad enough that six gigs will fail the inspection, sir! He gets one percent of those gigs! Even if his guys can make the average, Rob would get a *Major*! I don't see how they can even pull off the average. One of his guys came in just *five days ago*. How the hell is *he* supposed to learn seventeen pages of required knowledge in just one week?"

"I know, I know … Look, I'll go talk to the commandant. Maybe, just maybe he can find some way to stop this disaster before it happens."

Robert knew that the commandant would *not* find a way. He walked back to his barracks and gathered his platoon together in the common room. "We have a preliminary inspection on Monday," he told them. "That means that a cadre officer will come in and try everything he can to gig you. You have to have all your uniforms perfect. You have to know all of your required knowledge. You have to have the barracks spotless. You have to have your boots and shoes spit-shined.

"I know that this seems like a lot, but I'm not going to let you down. I will do everything I can to help you guys. We *must* work as a team! Shoes and boots that have the beginnings of being shiny enough will pass. I'll show you all how to polish your brass so that it passes and doesn't tarnish easily. We're going to clean this place from top to bottom, and we're going to sing our required knowledge while we're doing it.

"Nobody is going to do any homework before Tuesday. Usually, the teachers don't assign it during this time, and if they do, take the gig for it. We have more important things to do. Any questions?" Nobody asked any.

For four days, Cadet Lieutenant Robert Crandon drilled his platoon on everything. He made up songs for required knowledge and had his platoon sing them. He showed them how to use clear boot polish to get the floors shinier than the floor wax could accomplish. He filled out forms for repairs, this time keeping carbon copies, and submitted them to the secretarial staff. He gave away nearly all of his "secrets" to his platoon, hoping that they would be able to survive the preliminary inspection without too many punishments.

On Monday, October 29th, Charlie-3 was the second platoon to be inspected. Cadre Captain Sinclair, of Alpha-2 had been assigned to conduct the preliminary inspection. As he approached the doorway that led to the stairs, Cadet Crandon crisply saluted him and stated, "Third platoon, Charlie Company, awaiting inspection, sir."

"Awaiting inspection, cadet? Isn't it usually 'ready for inspection?'" Captain Sinclair asked.

"I'm not quite that arrogant, sir," Robert explained. "With twenty plebes, 'awaiting inspection' seemed a more appropriate comment, sir."

Captain Sinclair nodded. He was not about to argue with that reasoning. In spite of his desire to give Charlie-3 leniency, Captain Sinclair was a professional. He inspected the barracks and questioned the cadets as diligently as he did for any other platoon. As he went from room to room and cadet to cadet, he marked down all the deficiencies. When he was finished, he checked Robert's room—there were no deficiencies there. He then checked the common areas: the latrine and common room. Again, there were no deficiencies. He asked about broken furniture and windows and Robert showed him the work order requests.

That day, the secretarial staff was working as hard as it ever had. The secretaries had to enter each gig into a database, assigning the gigs to the respective cadets. At 1700 hours (five p.m.) John Stevens was given the results of the prelim to pass out to the platoon leaders. It was required of the cadets to show up to the master of discipline if they had ten or more gigs, since ten gigs equaled one minor penalty.

Cadet Lieutenant Robert Crandon arrived at the door of Cadre Captain Newman. He knocked crisply and was told to come in. "Cadet Crandon to report two hundred gigs, sir," he stated.

"That bad?" Captain Newman asked.

"Yes, sir. Two hundred gigs, sir."

"Okay, Crandon. Show up tomorrow at the Battalion Penal Squad at 0500 hours. If you want to eat, eat before then. Wear extended PT uniform."

"Yes, sir!" Crandon saluted, turned about face and left.

Soon after that encounter, Darryl Marks, the cadet battalion commander, entered the office of Captain Newman enthusiastically. "Did you see it, sir?" he asked hurriedly. "Did you see how well Charlie-3 did? He beat out the entire academy! I can't believe it, but he beat out the entire academy!"

"What are you talking about, Darryl?" Newman asked. "Crandon was just in here. His platoon must have had twenty thousand gigs."

"Twenty thousand?!" exclaimed Darryl. "They had a hundred ninety-eight, sir. It says it right here!" He showed the master of discipline the results for the academy.

Captain Newman thought for a while. "I don't believe he *did* that!" Newman shouted. "That kid took all the gigs for his platoon *plus* the extra two added for the one percent. He took every gig for his platoon ... " he trailed off.

"*Can* he do that, sir?" Darryl asked, astonished.

"Well, according to the rules, a cadet officer can take the gig for any cadet under him if he feels that he had not trained that cadet adequately for the offense. He can't do that for penalties, but he can for gigs. I've just never heard of any platoon leader doing that for every gig in an *inspection* before. Usually it's something like tying his boots improperly or not having seen the daily bulletin."

"Why would he take all two hundred, sir?"

"So that his guys don't get the extra gigs added on to them, Darryl. He doesn't want them to lose heart, just because that idi... I—" here, he interrupted himself. "—because they had to undergo a prelim too early."

SOONER GOES TOO FAR

Cadre Captain Peter Toole was livid. He had put his platoon's leader in for a commendation, and that same platoon leader was serving two Major punishments for the *same thing* the commendation *cited.* He was not about to let the stupidity of a politically appointed Cadre Adjutant ruin his star cadet-lieutenant.

Sergeant First-Class Cadet Donald Lorte had been at Waterline Academy for six years. He had been promoted to Platoon Sergeant just that year and was still trying to understand his duties and responsibilities. His platoon leader, a young kid named Crandon, was the best he had ever seen. The kid might be young, but he was good. Crandon had shown him lots of ways to keep his boots, brass, and uniforms ungiggable. He had explained many of the ins and outs of the academy Cadet hierarchy. When Cadet Lieutenant Crandon had told Donald to be ready to run the platoon for two days, the platoon sergeant nearly choked.

"What's up, sir?" Donald had asked Cadet Lieutenant Crandon.

"I have to serve two Majors. I should be back after that," Crandon had answered. That was that. Cadet senior officers usually did not share why they had received punishments, especially Major punishments. Donald was stuck running the platoon for the two days that his lieutenant was gone.

When Cadre Captain Toole called for him, Donald ran to the end of the hall to address the cadre officer. "Sir, Sergeant Cadet Lorte reports as ordered."

"You will inform the platoon that they will be conducting the first part of PT over near the mess hall, cadet." Captain Toole was short and to the point.

Donald informed all the other junior officers of Charlie-3 to assemble near the mess hall as indicated. When he arrived, he noticed that there was a detail of cadets unloading a truck trailer. The bags looked heavy; Donald figured that they must weigh at least forty or forty-five kilograms. He noticed that one of the cadets carrying the heavy loads was not nearly as tall as the rest. That cadet was his platoon leader, Crandon. All the others were older cadets, all of high school age.

As Cadre Captain Toole approached, Donald called the platoon to attention. The platoon was facing the road, away from the mess hall back entrance. Captain Toole took command of the platoon and turned them all about face. He waited until Cadet Lieutenant Crandon appeared and then pointed to him. "Do you see that cadet?" he asked rhetorically.

Donald was crushed. His platoon leader had gone through great pains to hide that he was serving a Major and now Charlie-3's cadre officer was pointing him out. "Take a good look at that cadet," Captain Toole continued. "He's serving two days, *two days* of Major punishment for two hundred gigs during the preliminary inspection." Donald was shocked. He had seen his platoon leader's room; it was immaculate!

Captain Toole continued. "Your platoon leader took all the gigs— *all the gigs*—for you guys! He only had two coming to him, and that's because he gets one gig for every one *hundred* that you guys earn! You *owe* him. He saved you from punishments *you* earned. I looked up the results and not a single one of you passed through the inspection without a gig, not *one*! It takes ten deficiencies to get a gig and not one of you could keep the number down to nine!"

Captain Toole worked the platoon very hard that morning. He then took the entire platoon on a three mile run; the slower runners could only barely keep up. While on the run, Captain Toole kept on the Charlie-3 cadets. "Remember this. I'm going to work you so hard that you'll be wishing that you had received those minor punishments. Don't think Lieutenant Crandon will let you take them. He'll probably take all your gigs for First Inspection as well. You had better not put him into the Battalion Death Squad by *your* failures!"

When the platoon was dismissed for showers and morning meal, all the junior officers of Charlie-3 gathered around Sergeant Cadet Lorte. "He's gonna kill us," exclaimed Corporal Cadet Coelho, one of the fire team leaders.

"What are we gonna do?" Sergeant Cadet Cripps asked.

"What are we going to do?" Donald responded. "We're going to make certain that we *learn*! Lieutenant Crandon said he wouldn't let us down—and he didn't! It's up to *us* to make sure that the rest of the platoon takes up his suggestions. He's only one guy. He can only do so much. You guys," here he pointed at the squad leaders and fire team leaders, "are going to *inform* your cadets that gigs and punishments are in the past! The next guy who gets a Major is going to get a major *beating* from me!

"Our platoon leader has worked his tail off. He gave us the means to pass that inspection; we just didn't *take* it! That's not gonna happen again on *my* watch! You all got that?" Heads nodded. "Good! Because if you have a guy getting a Major, you'll be hearing from my fists too. I don't care if I have to make the whole platoon 'slip on bars of soap.' I'm not going to let my platoon leader down *ever* again!"

Cadre Major Sooner was in a foul mood. "Can't those idiots see that it worked?" he thought, grumpily. "First they say, 'Don't put all your eggs in *one* basket.'" Then they say, "Don't make that platoon face prelim. No platoon has ever had to do that with five plebes, and Charlie-3 has twenty! Can't they see that it was *the best* way to do things? Charlie-3 got the highest scores in the academy. Why can't those jerks realize that I was right?

"Meanwhile, what do I do about that young whippersnapper? He cut the balls out of my plans. Taking all the gigs for his platoon! How dare he? I don't care if he *is* their golden child; he's got some nerve taking away his cadets' due punishments. The cadets are here to be punished! That's certain; as certain as death and taxes! How *dare* he?"

Cadre Major Sooner looked at the cadre duty roster. As the cadre adjutant, it fell to him to assign which cadre officer would conduct the oversight of the Battalion Penal Squad. Captain Newman, the master of discipline, was usually assigned the task. That morning, Major Sooner had been unable to change the assignment—for the day. Instead, he demanded a detail to unload potatoes and other vegetables from a delivery truck. He *insisted* on picking his own cadets for the detail. "That's not enough!" he thought to himself. "I know just how to deal with malcontents … "

The next day, Tuesday, October 30, Major Sooner was assigned to deal with the Battalion Penal Squad. He had a large box of rubber scissors that he brought out with him to meet the cadets on punishment detail. He held up the box in front of the formation and said, "Today, you weasels are going to cut my parade grounds!"

Cadet Lieutenant Robert J. Crandon was smiling from ear to ear upon hearing this news. He was careful to keep the cadre officer from seeing his face. Some of the other cadets on the Battalion Penal Squad were also smiling. They knew the prowess of the cadet senior officer. "Crandon!" Major Sooner snarled. Robert was afraid he had been spotted smiling but dutifully fell out of formation and ran up to the cadre officer.

Saluting, Robert said, "Cadet Crandon reporting as ordered, sir!"

Major Sooner did not return the salute. He simply ordered, "Crandon, take this detail out to the parade field and get my grass cut for the end of the growing season! You are to make *certain* that no one uses anything except one of these pairs of scissors! Just because you're an officer does not exempt you from work. You will cut the grass along with them!" Major Sooner shoved the box into Robert's left hand. "You will cut the parade field until it has all been cut! I don't care if it takes you until Sunday. Is that clear, cadet?"

"Yes, sir!" Robert answered, still saluting. "Will the cadre officer be assigning another detail to bring out water or should I see to that, sir?" he asked.

"What? Water?" Major Sooner asked. "Oh, um … you see to that also, cadet. You should have *known that*!"

Robert waited for the cadre officer to leave and then dropped his salute. He turned to the Penal Squad, ordered them to march to the field and then set them up with *very* detailed instructions. Robert Crandon estimated that the entire job would take about nineteen hours. That was patently illegal as of last November. Nevertheless, he intended to make sure the job got done—to his own specifications. He knew that the grass would continue to grow despite what Major Sooner ordered. They were in South Carolina. The western part of the state, to be sure, but the grass-growing season did not end at the beginning of November. Even still, Robert hoped that the grass would *not* be cut again until next March.

> Major Sooner needs help with his reading lessons. Please
> send Dr. Seuss or *Fun with Dick and Jane* immediately.
> –The cadets of Waterline Academy

The message could not have been clearer. All the rest of the cadre officers had clandestinely made their separate ways to the top of the school building. They had heard that their top platoon leader was an expert at coded messages and cutting messages for helicopters into the parade field. When they saw the Battalion Penal Squad, often known as the Battalion Death Squad, over in the parade field with scissors, they *knew* that something was going to be written.

Captain Toole was the first to check out his platoon leader's handiwork. He could just barely make out the lettering that was forming, but it was enough. He pumped his fist into the air in a motion of triumph. Cadet Robert Crandon had beaten Major Sooner. Captain Toole could hardly wait for the response from the Army helicopter pilots.

The response was overwhelming! Starting on Thursday morning and continuing for nearly two weeks, special deliveries began coming into the Waterline Cadre Office. Each one was *special delivery* for Major Aldus Sooner. Sometimes a card was attached reading, "Hope this helps you learn to read," or, "I won't use big words. This book is to help you read. Ask your Mommy to read it to you." The books were *Fox in Socks, Green Eggs and Ham, The Cat in the Hat, Fun with Dick and Jane, Dick, Jane and Spot*, and other children's primers.

Major Sooner could not walk around Ft. Waterline without hearing snickering. Soon, the snickers extended into Riverton, South Carolina as well.

On Wednesday morning, Major Sooner approached Cadet Lieutenant Crandon during PT. "You owe me twenty minors, lieutenant. Be in my office right after morning meal."

"Yes, sir!" Robert responded crisply. He wondered if the cadre officer had actually figured out that there was a message on the field. Then he reasoned that had Major Sooner known, he would certainly have assigned Major punishment. The only reason that Robert could think of for twenty minor punishments was that he took two hundred gigs. It was traditional that if a cadet served a Major punishment, he would not also be assigned any additional minor punishments for the gigs, but that was not an absolute requirement.

After morning meal, Robert reported to the cadre adjutant's office. The room was dark and no one was inside. He waited for forty-five minutes for Major Sooner to show up. "Crandon? Oh yes, your twenty minors … " Major Sooner intoned.

Robert then asked, "Sir, what should I put down for the reason for the minors? My cadre officer will question me on that, sir."

"You got two hundred gigs. That equals twenty minor penalties."

Robert wrote the reason into his gig book. "Sir, I need you to initial this, please." He handed his book to the cadre officer.

"Why do you need me to initial it, cadet?" Major Sooner asked.

"Sir, a cadet must have a cadre officer initial any penalties assigned when there are no gigs shown on the day of the penalty assignment," Robert intoned in a formal manner. Major Sooner took the book and initialed the reason for twenty minor penalties.

"Follow me, cadet," Major Sooner commanded. He led the cadet to a stack of filthy, moldy, maggot-infested, metal garbage cans. There was a pail of soapy water near the pile and a water hose leading to the side of the Quartermaster Storage Building. Major Sooner pulled out a toothbrush. "You will scrub each of these *twenty* garbage cans until it is shiny clean. You will use a toothbrush to do the scrubbing. Is that clear, maggot?!"

"Sir? What do I do if the tooth brush runs out of bristles, sir?" Robert asked.

"I'll be coming around periodically. I'll get you new toothbrushes."

"Yes, sir!" Robert exclaimed enthusiastically.

Robert had never been able to match up two of his "comeback" specialties before. He went to work on the garbage cans with a gusto and energy he had not felt for months. He scrubbed as hard as he could, applied soap powder directly to the rusty bottoms, and generally amazed the cadre Adjutant with his enthusiasm over this odious detail. By the time Robert Crandon had finished with the twenty garbage cans, fifteen were totally unusable. In addition, Robert had used three hundred fifty toothbrushes, wearing each one down to nubs.

The Cadre Adjutant had not allowed Cadet Lieutenant Crandon to attend the noon meal. This was illegal; only those on Major punishment could be denied meals, but Major Sooner did not know that. Cadet Lieutenant Crandon was not about to tell the man about that particular rule; he simply requested his meals and was denied. When Robert finally finished all twenty cans, the evening meal had also ended. Major Sooner dismissed him to his barracks. Robert immediately took a shower, changed his uniform, and went to Cadre Captain Newman to report that he had been denied two meals while serving minor punishments.

"What do you mean, he wouldn't let you go?" Captain Newman asked.

"Just that, sir. I informed him each time that each meal was beginning, and he told me to continue scrubbing until I was finished. It is not my position to question a cadre officer's instructions sir. I am simply asking if I may be permitted to get one meal. Since you are the master of discipline, I believe that such a request falls to you. I was serving minor punishments, sir," Robert said.

Captain Newman looked at his watch. "The mess hall is closed for business, Rob. They might be cleaning up, but there are regulations about when they can serve food."

"Yes, sir. That is my understanding, sir," Robert answered.

"Do you happen to have any understanding about *how* a meal is to be given to a cadet *after hours?*" Captain Newman asked, hopefully.

"Sir, I believe that if you look in your *Manual of Academy Rules, Volume Three*, you will discover under the punishment section that any cadre officer who, by neglect or intent, fails to allow a cadet to eat, when that cadet is entitled to food, must provide for any meal that has to be ordered in from the outside," Robert said. "I am not suggesting that you do this sir; I am only mentioning that such is the listing in the rule book. You had requested the information, sir," Robert added, blinking his signature blink.

"In addition, sir … " Robert offered. Captain Newman indicated for Robert to continue. "I believe the rules specify that, unless the payee is the commandant, the meal must be ordered by a cadre officer of equivalent or higher position. Thus, either you or Commandant

Leary must order the meal, as the law must assume that the payee of the meal might not order a completely *nutritious* one."

"Let's go see Cadre Major Sooner, shall we?" Captain Newman offered, smiling. As the two were leaving Captain Newman's office, Major Sooner was approaching.

"You need to serve two Majors, cadet," Sooner said in a dooming manner.

"Yes, sir. What reason shall I put for the Majors, sir?" Robert asked dutifully as he scribbled in his gig book.

"You just served twenty minors, cadet. That equals two *Majors*, doesn't it?" Sooner answered.

"No, sir. Twenty minors should equal two majors, but I served two majors for the gigs already, sir. Should I put down the reason for the Majors as 'Served twenty Minors,' sir?"

"That's fine! Just do it, cadet!" Major Sooner snarled. Robert continued to scribble in his gig book.

"That's quite enough, Aldus!" Captain Newman exclaimed. "You've been working this cadet to the bone, starving him—*illegally*—and now you want to make him serve double majors? You are *out of line*, Major! *I* am the master of discipline in this academy, and you are *out of line*. You will leave this cadet alone. That is final."

"We can just take this up with the commandant, Cadre Captain," Major Sooner answered petulantly.

"Fine! Right now, *Major*!" Captain Newman answered.

The two cadre officers left Cadet Crandon standing at the doorway of the master of discipline's office. He heard the two go into the commandant's office and heard yelling. It was clear that the commandant did not care which senator Major Sooner had worked for. He did not care if the Director of Academies was called. He sided completely with Captain Newman. He also agreed that the major would have to pay for a meal to be delivered to a certain cadet who had been unfairly denied sustenance.

Apparently, one of the three did, in fact, place a call to the Director of Academies. After some time, Captain Newman came out of the commandant's office and saw Cadet Crandon standing there, as the cadet's last orders would indicate. "Have you been standing here the whole time?" Captain Newman asked. He thought, perhaps, that the cadet was waiting to eat.

"Yes, sir. My last orders were to write the reason for two majors, and I need Major Sooner to sign for the reason. I don't believe that Cadre Captain Toole would believe my reasons given without a signature, so I am required to remain here until the reasoning is initialed, sir," Robert responded.

Captain Newman looked at the cadet with a profound respect. He knew that the cadet must have heard the heated conversation that occurred in the commandant's office, yet Robert had remained standing at the office door, awaiting a signature for two *unearned* Major punishments. His total would have come to four, getting him banned past the Christmas Common Week—yet he waited dutifully. "Come with me, cadet. We need to talk to the commandant." Robert followed the cadre officer, obediently.

Just as they were approaching the commandant's office door, they overheard the following conversation.

"You've crossed over the line this time, Sooner. The director was very clear. You will leave that cadet *alone!* You have been nothing but a pain since you arrived. You nearly sabotaged the entire academic year for Waterline Academy. Now, a cadet who succeeded *in spite* of your efforts, *not* because of them, has been worked non-stop for three days because of your mean-spirited activities. You take one more step out of line, and you are through. I don't care who you know. *I* run this academy, not you!"

"We'll see what Congress has to say about that!"

"Yes, I suspect we will." The tone was quiet and deliberate. It was the kind of tone of voice that Robert hoped never to hear addressed to him. "I also suspect that, given the near disaster of last year, the

Joint Committee on Academies will side with me and our director, not some garbage from a senator's campaign!"

The door opened. "Ah! Crandon! The *major* here was just about to order up a meal for you. Why don't you stick around and eat it in here. That way you won't get your barracks messed up," Commandant Leary said cheerfully.

"Yes … sir," Cadet Crandon answered. He was still stunned that the other cadre officers would dishonor a fellow cadre officer in the presence of a cadet.

Charlie-3 had followed its platoon sergeant's demands to the letter. They no longer routinely received minor penalties. All of the plebes had already gotten three major penalties—but none had four—so they were banned from Thanksgiving Common Week. Cadet Lieutenant Crandon wanted his platoon to succeed. He helped them with each and every task they were required to perform. He continued to drill them on required knowledge. Thanksgiving was the earliest that it could be in 1973, November 22. On the 17th, Cadet Lieutenant Crandon had called his platoon into the common room for a pep talk.

"Okay. Thanksgiving is coming up. For you plebes, don't be too upset about missing it. No plebe has ever gotten their first Thanksgiving off. I plan to return early to help you with your final preparations for First Inspection. It's coming on the 4th of December this year, so you don't have as much time to prepare as in past years.

"It may be possible for you to get Christmas Common Week off. That would be a first. No plebe has *ever* done *that* either. I want all twenty of you to get back to your families for Christmas. If you don't make it, well … that's Waterline Academy. Don't get your spirits down; you're here to redeem yourselves. If you make it here, you'll make it on the outside. You won't be spending your whole life in prison. *That*, cadets, is something to shoot for!

"During common week, those who've been banned are given twelve hours of work. They changed that rule last November. That means that you'll get something like a Battalion Penal Squad day, each day, for twelve hours. They used to be able to work us twenty hours, but that got changed. So, my guess, although I don't know for sure, is that they will work you from 0700 to 1900 hours. You *will* be given time for meals.

"Once you get off at 1900 hours, shower up and then drill each other on required knowledge while getting those boots, shoes and brass shiny. Like I said, I'll try to make it back early. All my sibs have to go to school ... well, except for my baby brother ... the week of the 26th to 30th, so I won't be missing them much anyways."

THANKSGIVING
COMMON WEEK, 1973

On November 21st all the Waterline cadets who were going to see their families for Common Week were in formation. The cadets who had been banned were already taken off to a detail somewhere else in Ft. Waterline. The master of discipline reminded them of the regulations regarding Waterline Cadets who were not on the disciplinary academy grounds.

"Section 1, Rule A," Captain Newman said, "regards cadets who have an altercation with law enforcement personnel. Subsection 1, paragraph a: Any cadet who has an altercation with law enforcement personnel will return immediately to Waterline Academy by whatever means necessary—no exceptions, no excuses. Paragraph b: An altercation includes, but is not limited to, being placed under arrest, being told to halt 'in the name of the law,' being taken in for questioning about an offense alleged to be the cadet's fault and other similar circumstances.

"Subsection 2, paragraph a: A cadet who is returning due to 1.A.1.a. will obtain transportation as soon as feasible to a major transportation system. Paragraph b: Transportation will be obtained from the closest airport that has multiple flights heading to Atlanta, when in Atlanta, shuttle transport or other ground transportation will be obtained to Waterline Academy. Paragraph c: The cadet must remain as close to the terminal boarding gate in any transportation facility as he can. The only exceptions are for water and latrine functions.

"Subsection 3, paragraph a: A cadet who is returning due to 1.A.1.a. will seek transportation from the law enforcement agency engaged in the altercation unless a legal guardian is willing to transport the cadet to the transit system. Paragraph b: A legal guardian consists of a parent, grandparent, aunt, uncle … "

Captain Newman finished up the orders as quickly as he could, but regulations required that he cover them each and every time cadets visited their families during common weeks. When he had finished, he marched the cadets over to shuttle buses, which were waiting to take the cadets to Atlanta. Each cadet carried a duffel bag filled with uniforms. Even outside the academy, Waterline cadets had to wear their uniforms. Usually, they wore PT uniforms or Class A and B uniforms, but some of them used their parade uniforms while working around their parents' houses.

From Atlanta, Robert Crandon flew to Providence, Rhode Island. The airport in Boston, Massachusetts was bigger, but Coventry was about equal distance from both locations and Providence was easier to get into. When his plane arrived and he debarked, he saw his parents and his baby brother waiting for him. Little Patrick was sucking on a pacifier contentedly. His parents gave big smiles when they saw their second to youngest child.

"Did you have a good flight?" Paul Crandon asked his son.

"I guess it was okay. I didn't really notice, sir," Robert answered.

"How did you like it?" Roberta Crandon asked.

"Oh. Well, there was no meal on the flight. They were nice, though and gave me some pineapple juice with ice."

"How are you doing, little Patrick?" Robert asked his baby brother. Patrick just continued to suck on the pacifier. "May I push him?" Robert asked, referring to the stroller his mother was pushing.

"Of course, dear." Roberta answered. Robert got behind the stroller and pushed it to the elevators. The four Crandons made their way to the luggage section and retrieved Robert's duffel bag. They then made their way to the parking area and got into the family car.

"I'm certainly glad they don't have metal detectors when you get *off*," Robert mentioned.

"Why is that, dear?" Roberta asked.

"Well, with all this jewelry on," Robert pointed to the rank and insignia on his dress blues jacket and shirt, "I have to practically undress each time I go through."

"I guess that's Waterline Academy," his father said. Robert just nodded.

The next morning, Robert woke at 0500 and got into his winter physical training uniform. He headed downstairs and outside to conduct PT. John, his brother, came wandering down, wondering what his brother was up to. "What's up, Robbie?" he asked.

"Oh, just doing PT. I don't want to get out of shape while I'm gone." Robert answered.

"Can I join?"

"Surely." He led John through stretches, jumping jacks, push-ups, sit-ups, and isometric exercises. When it came time for him to go running, Robert asked his brother, "Did you want to go on the run as well?"

"Okay," John said hesitantly.

"You really don't have to," Robert offered. John seemed determined so Robert told him about a route he had planned from a map he had found online at Waterline Academy. The route was for four miles, but there was a cutoff that would shorten the trek to two miles.

The two boys got to the cutoff and Robert told his brother to take the short-cut. "I'll be home soon enough. Just go through that apartment complex, up the road, past the school and you know your way from there." John was getting tired and did not argue with his younger brother. Robert continued on his planned route.

When he headed on the last leg of the route, Robert was in the center of Coventry. There were stores all around and a stoplight that had only recently gone from blinking to working. He pushed up his pace until he heard a voice call to him, "Where are you going so fast, son?"

Robert looked around and saw a local police officer. He jogged over to the officer and continued to jog in place. "Were you addressing me, sir? I was uncertain."

"Yeah. Where are you running at this time of the morning?"

"I'm just exercising, sir," Robert answered.

"Exercising on Thanksgiving? What's your name son?" the officer asked.

Robert stopped running in place, stood at the position of attention—just as he had been drilled in Waterline Academy—and answered crisply, "Cadet Lieutenant Crandon, Robert J., Waterline Academy, SIR!"

"Waterline Academy?" The officer asked suspiciously. "Where are you running from, cadet?"

"Sir, I am running as part of an exercise regimen."

"Put your hands onto the hood of the car." The police officer pointed to his cruiser. Robert complied. "I asked you where you're running from, *cadet*. What have you stolen? Whose place did you rob?" The policeman began to frisk the boy and seemed upset that he found nothing in the cadet's clothing. "Where did you stash the stuff, *cadet?*"

"Sir, I have taken nothing and have not entered anyone's residence or business unlawfully. I am just exercising."

"Don't give me none of your lip, maggot!" the officer snarled and hit Robert in the face, causing his lip to bleed. "You *Waterline* cadets are all alike. You're vandals, thieves, and trouble-makers. You tell me what you've been up to or I'm gonna run you in."

"Sir, I have been exercising. You can call my parents' house and ask my brother, John," Robert offered.

"Maybe I'll just do that!" the officer snarled. He took out his handcuffs and bound Robert's hands behind his back. He then pushed the cadet into the back seat headfirst and slammed the door behind him. Robert figured that he could likely pick the locks given a wire and enough time, but he also figured there was no point in doing that just yet.

The police officer called on his car radio and announced that he was bringing in a suspect. Robert tried to sit up in the seat, but his head had fallen between the front driver's seat and the cushion of the back seat, so he could not gain any leverage to straighten out. When they arrived at the Coventry police station, another officer opened the back door of the police car.

"What do ya got here, Sam?" the new police officer asked.

"Don't know *yet*," the first officer answered. "He was runnin' through town and said he was 'exercising.' He's from Waterline Academy. It even says so on his joggin' suit!"

"Did you find anything on him?" the second policeman asked.

"Naw, he either stashed it somewhere or maybe he was spray painting somebody's shop!"

Robert was lifted out of the car by his arms and hustled into the police station. He again gave his name and academy. He insisted that he was just exercising. The police officers did not accept his explanation. They told other officers to search the region where Robert had been picked up. There was no sign of vandalism, no sign of break-ins, and no sign of *any* criminal activity.

After the police had interrogated Robert for nearly an hour, Paul Crandon called to report that his ten-year-old son was missing. The police informed Mr. Crandon that Robert had been caught fleeing the scene of a crime and was currently being questioned. Paul Crandon immediately rushed to the police station and demanded to see his son.

When Paul saw his son in handcuffs, sporting a bleeding lip and several bruises on his face, he went ballistic. "How *dare* you treat my son this way? I'm going to call the chief of police. I'm going to call the governor."

"Sir, we caught him fleeing the scene of a *crime*," Officer Sam stated.

"What crime?" Mr. Crandon asked.

"We're still trying to determine that, sir," the second officer said.

"You beat up my ten-year-old son on the *suspicion* that he *may* have committed a crime?" Paul roared. "This is the United States of America, gentlemen! If you don't have any crime, any evidence or any confession, you are in *huge* trouble! You release my son, *right now!*" he yelled.

The police were in a bind. They were certain that any Waterline Academy cadet must have done something wrong if he was running. Even still, they had no crime, so they released Robert into his father's custody.

Paul was muttering to himself the entire time that he was driving Robert home. "I'm sorry to have caused you any problems, Father," Robert said with tears in his eyes.

"Oh," his father said tenderly. "It's not you, Robbie. It's those idiots back there! I'm not mad at you at all," he insisted. Robert just nodded, tears still coming to his eyes. "What did they *do* to you, son?" Paul asked Robert.

"They hit me to try to get me to tell them what I did. They didn't believe that anyone would exercise on Thanksgiving, I guess," Robert answered. At that time, Paul pulled the family car into the driveway. "I'll get showered and dressed and then you can take me to Boston, sir," Robert added.

"Why would I take you to Boston?" Paul was bewildered.

"I have to go back to Waterline Academy, sir," Robert answered.

"In Heaven's name, *why?*" Paul demanded to know.

"Because I had an altercation with a law enforcement agency, sir. One-a-one-a states that any cadet who has an altercation with a law enforcement agency must return to the academy immediately, no exceptions, no excuses. I have to go back sir."

"What if I say that you stay?" Paul asked.

"I would have to go back to the police and request that they provide transportation to Boston, sir. I really would rather not do that, Father. I would *much* prefer you to take me. If you can't, though, then I'll go back to the police. I just need to get washed up and into dress blues, sir."

Paul was devastated. His son had returned for only the fifth time in four years and now he was being taken away due to the incompetence and bigotry of the Coventry Police. He told Robert that he would drive him to Logan Airport in Boston.

Roberta was hysterical. She just *could not* accept that her namesake son was being taken away from her after less than twenty-four hours. Her sister was not available to watch the other children, so Roberta had to remain in Coventry. She could not even bring her son to the airport. Paul and Robert left her while she was still in tears.

After arriving at the airport, Robert went up to the ticket agency and informed the man working there that he was a Waterline cadet and needed immediate transport back to the academy. The ticket agent checked all flights going to Atlanta and the earliest flight he could book for the cadet would leave in six hours, and the flight provided no meal. Robert checked his duffel bag, took the ticket, and proceeded to the gate.

"If you've got six hours to wait. I can stay with you for a while," Paul offered to his son.

"You don't have a ticket, Father. I have to remain as close to the embarking entrance as possible, sir. The regulations are very specific about that," Robert answered. Paul just nodded his head in resignation. With tears in his eyes, Mr. Crandon hugged his son and wished him well.

"We'll write to you. I promise!" Paul told his son. Robert nodded sadly, turned toward the metal detectors, and removed his jacket and dress blues shirt. He went through the metal detector, retrieved his clothes, put them on, checked them meticulously, and then went to sit in the terminal.

About two hours before his flight was to depart, Robert saw an airline employee arrive. "Have you been here long?" she asked.

"About four hours, ma'am," Robert answered.

"Well, this flight won't be leaving for another two hours, young man. You don't have to worry about missing it," the woman offered.

"Thank you, ma'am. I won't worry about missing it," Robert answered, as cheerfully as he could muster.

When he arrived in Atlanta's Hartsfield/Jackson airport, Robert made his way to the baggage area, retrieved his duffel bag, and made his way to the shuttle that ran to Ft. Waterline. Usually, the shuttle left every hour, but this was Thanksgiving Day. The shuttle ran only three times. Cadet Crandon's flight had arrived six minutes after the shuttle had left. The next shuttle would not leave for another five hours.

Robert sat nearest to the door where the bus would be parked when it arrived. After four hours, a bus came to the shuttle door and disembarked a few passengers. Robert took his duffel bag to the bus. The driver informed him that the bus would not be leaving for another fifty-five minutes, but agreed to allow Robert to put his duffel bag into the storage compartment on the side of the bus. About an hour later, Robert was on the shuttle for the two-hour ride to Ft. Waterline.

When the shuttle pulled up to the Waterline Academy gates, it was already dark outside. Robert had traveled with the bus driver and one soldier. The soldier had been dropped off first, and then the driver drove the bus to the academy gates. Robert got out, retrieved his duffel bag, and went to the intercom system. He pushed on the button that would alert the cadre officer in charge.

"Waterline Academy," Robert heard the voice of Captain Newman through the intercom.

"Cadet Lieutenant Crandon returning as per Article 1.A.1.a., sir," Robert said into the microphone/speaker. There was a long delay.

"You're kidding," Captain Newman's voice said tentatively.

"No, sir, 1.A.1.a., sir," Cadet Crandon answered. Another delay.

"Okay, Rob. Come on in. Come straight to the cadre office. Bring your duffel bag with you."

"Yes, sir," Robert answered. He heard a buzz and pushed the gate open. He proceeded to the cadre office, hearing the gate close automatically behind him. Since the academy had a border with the town of Riverton, South Carolina, they had built a gate and fencing on that border. Usually, the cadets did not go to that side of the academy grounds unless taking the shuttle to the airport for common week. When the cadets returned from common week, the buses were waiting for them and, since the vehicles were filled with cadets, the bus drivers simply drove right onto the academy via Ft. Waterline.

Robert made his way to the middle building that housed Charlie Company, the cadet field grade officers' quarters and the Cadre Office. The Cadre Office was actually a series of offices along with a large central area for the secretaries. Each cadre officer had his own office and computer; some of those offices were located in other buildings. The secretaries had desks and computers but no walls. None of the computers was wired to the outside. That was an Academy rule.

When Robert arrived at the door to the cadre office, he took a very deep breath, let it out slowly, and went into the building. "What the hell is going on, Crandon?" He heard Captain Newman shout. "You only left yesterday. How the *hell* did you manage to get eleven drunked in less than thirty hours?"

"I was running for PT, sir," Robert gave as an explanation.

Captain Newman sat in a chair at one of the secretaries' desks stunned. He thought about the answer for an entire minute, in silence. He knew that this cadet was telling the truth—the *whole* truth. "Which police agency picked you up, Rob?" he asked, mechanically.

"Coventry, Massachusetts, sir," Robert answered. "Do you need me to give you the number, sir?" Robert offered.

"Go ahead. I have to call and confirm it," Captain Newman said. He wrote down the number and told Cadet Crandon to take a seat. Captain Newman then called the Coventry Police Station and tried to get the reasoning for his cadet's altercation.

"What do you mean, 'I don't have any record of it,' officer? My cadet has made his way all the way from Massachusetts to Georgia to South Carolina! You had better have a record of it!" Captain Newman then listened to the telephone receiver.

"Crandon, which officer picked you up?" Captain Newman asked.

"I didn't get a good look at his badge, sir," Robert answered. "However, another officer called him Sam, sir," Robert added helpfully.

"An Officer Sam picked him up," Newman told the telephone receiver. There was a delay. "She's going to check Officer Sam's report files," Captain Newman told the young cadet sitting near him. After a short time, Captain Newman heard some more from the police receptionist.

"I will be informing Commandant Leary of this, officer. Tonight." Another delay. "Good-bye, officer, and thank you for your time, ma'am." Captain Newman hung up the receiver. "It looks like your story checks out, Crandon. Go on to your barracks and get some sleep. You are still on Pass, even if you have been stuffed back into the academy. You don't have to show up for work details or anything like that."

"Thank you, sir," Robert answered. "I was planning to come back and help my platoon get ready for First Inspection anyways, sir. I just came back a little earlier than I had planned." He grabbed his duffel bag, walked out of the cadre office to his stairway door, and climbed the stairs to the second floor of the building. He walked into his room, threw his bag at the wardrobe, took off his dress blues violently, and jumped onto his bed. As an afterthought, he got up, closed his door, and then jumped back onto his bed. Then he cried himself to sleep.

The next morning, Robert went to PT with the cadets who had been banned from Common Week. Since he was the ranking cadet, it fell to Robert to conduct the PT session. He was in a bad mood and took out some of his frustrations by exercising far more than required. In short, he dogged the cadets to the point of muscle failure in most areas. He did two hundred push-ups, three hundred sit-ups, five hundred jumping jacks, and then began isometric exercises. Finally, he ran the group for five miles along the hilliest route he had ever run. He had only been on the route twice, since the cadre did not like running up and down hills any more than the cadets.

By the time he had finished with the run, most of the cadets had fallen out of the run, been picked up by the running formation on the way back, and then fallen out again. He dismissed the group to their showers and morning meals, reminding them that they still had to do the horizontal ladder and pull-ups. There was a universal groan from the banneds. Cadre Captain Newman pulled up in his car with ten cadets piled inside. He let them out and sent them off to their showers as well.

"Come here, Crandon," Captain Newman ordered.

Robert rushed over to his master of discipline and stated, "Cadet Crandon reporting as ordered, sir."

"Robert, why did you try to kill the rest of the cadets?" Captain Newman asked.

"I wasn't aware that I was doing that, sir. I will apologize to them and ensure that I watch how well they are keeping up in the future, sir," Robert answered.

"I didn't quite mean it that way, Robert. Come with me, please," Captain Newman said. He led Robert to the cadre shower area and offered Robert a towel. "Go ahead and get showered, Rob. I'll go get you a uniform. What's your combo?"

Robert gave the cadre officer his lock combination and got showered. When he came out, he saw his dress blues uniform waiting for him. He got dressed and walked into the general office region. "Dress blues, sir?" Robert asked Captain Newman.

"Have a seat, Rob," Captain Newman offered. "Cadets! Go eat morning meal. Now!" Newman shouted to the two cadets who were detailed to clean the office and help answer phones. The two had already eaten their morning meal, but they left quickly and without comment.

"Rob, you have been under enormous stress. You have performed in such an exemplary fashion that every cadre officer except our resident idiot is in awe of your accomplishments. You have a right to be upset about being picked up and beaten by the police for no reason. If you don't start acknowledging your feelings, you are going to crack up. This morning was a good indication of just that. Don't you think?" Captain Newman said.

Robert thought for a while. "Yes, sir. I suppose that I was using PT as a means of getting out some of my frustrations. I'm sorry that the other guys had to be with me when it happened. If I had thought about it, I would have conducted a short PT session, sent them on their way and then gone to the gymnasium to work out my anger and frustration."

Captain Newman was proud of this young cadet. "You've grown up a lot while you've been here. Cadre Captain Sinclair has kept detailed records of your progress," he complimented Robert. "Most of your professors have told me that you will have completed all the academics this academy has to offer by the end of May. Did you know that?"

"No, sir," Robert answered simply. "If they don't have any other academics to teach me, sir, then … "

"The director of academies is working on that," Captain Newman answered the unspoken question.

At that time, Commandant Leary came into the office. "Have you got your bag, son?" he asked Robert.

Robert stood up at attention. "Sir?" he responded. "I don't understand the question, sir," Robert explained.

"You need your uniforms if you're going to Coventry with me, son. Have you got them packed?"

"Yes … sir. I never actually *unpacked* them last night sir." Robert took out his gig book. "How many gigs is that, sir? I mean, is it one for each piece of clothing?"

Captain Newman and Commandant Leary both laughed. "None!" Commandant Leary stated emphatically. "You're on pass, cadet. You can throw your uniforms all over your room and you are not to be gigged. Go get your bag and meet me at the end of the building. I have a car waiting. We are going to go talk to your policemen." Commandant Leary then looked closer at Cadet Crandon. "Did they do *this*?" he asked, pointing to the fat lip and bruises on Robert's face.

"They were trying to obtain information from me, sir. They believed that they needed to coerce me into compliance, sir. I had told them what answers I could, but they … well … found the answers to be either incomplete or unacceptable." After that, he ran to his room, made up his bed, grabbed his duffel bag and ran to where the commandant was waiting. Commandant Leary had Robert put the duffel bag into the trunk and the two got into the car for the trip to Atlanta.

At the airport, Commandant Leary obtained two first-class tickets to Boston. He then checked his and his cadet's bags and headed to the terminal. As the two of them passed a restaurant, Robert Crandon's stomach growled. "Didn't you eat yet, son?" Commandant Leary asked.

"No, sir," Robert stated plainly. "Not since Thursday morning, sir," he added.

"Thursday morning?" Commandant Leary exclaimed.

"Well, sir. I had to wait six hours for a flight out of Boston and five hours for a shuttle to Ft. Waterline. I never got a chance to get anything to eat, sir. This morning, I got showered in the cadre area while Captain Newman got my dress blues. I never got to morning meal either."

Commandant Leary ran through what Robert had just told him. After a few seconds he commented, "They don't give you any provision for obtaining a meal, do they?"

"No, sir. The regulation stipulates that only latrine visits or water are exceptions to 1.A.2.c., sir."

"Then let's go get some breakfast."

After he made sure that his cadet had eaten enough, Commandant Leary led him to the terminal for their flight. The flight was elegant. Commandant Leary was offered champagne and Robert was offered a variety of drinks. The cadet chose to have pineapple juice with ice. Upon arrival in Boston, Commandant Leary headed to a section titled *Avis*. Robert had no idea why they had gone there, but gathered that the agency rented cars. The two made their way to baggage and retrieved their luggage.

"How do I get to Coventry, cadet?" Commandant Leary asked.

"I suppose you could drive there, sir," Robert answered plainly.

Commandant Leary laughed. "Ask a cadet a stupid question…" he muttered. "Do you happen to know the way to Coventry, Robert?"

"Oh! I'm sorry, sir. I didn't understand you at first. I believe that Coventry is off of an interstate road numbered 495. I think that you can take Interstate 93 to Interstate 95 to get onto Interstate 495, sir. After that, well … I don't really know the *town* roads, sir," Robert explained.

"Don't worry, cadet. I think that the car I rented has a GPS system in it. We'll get there," Commandant Leary assured.

"Sir, what's a GPS system?" Robert asked as they boarded the Avis shuttle to the parked rentals.

"Global positioning satellite," Commandant Leary answered. "The military has been using them for a few years, and I ordered one to be placed in our rental car when I was back in Ft. Waterline. It's a device that shows you where you are located on a map. It also helps you find certain landmarks. The technology is new, so you need to be in the general area of your destination. It tends to mess up for large distances. Since you gave me the general directions to Coventry, we should be able to get exact instructions from the GPS to find the police station. At least, we can once we get near there."

Robert took in the information quietly and was eager to see the device mentioned. The two drove out of the Callahan tunnel and got onto Interstate 93. They followed the directions that Robert had given to Commandant Leary and eventually came to an exit for Coventry. Commandant Leary turned on the GPS system and punched in his destination (the police station). "You might want to specify 'Coventry Town Police,' sir. There is also a state police barracks there," Robert commented. Commandant Leary changed the destination and the screen on the device showed a street map of the region with red dots showing the suggested route.

When they arrived at the Coventry Police Station, Commandant Leary told Robert to come in with him. The commandant walked up to the desk and demanded to see the chief. "He's not here, sir," The police receptionist stated. "He's on vacation."

"You contact the chief and tell him to be here in one half hour, officer. You tell him that if he's not here in thirty minutes, I will call the governor of Massachusetts to order his arrest. I am the commandant of Waterline Academy. That is a federal facility, and I outrank nearly every federal law enforcement officer save my director, the head of the FBI and the attorney general of the United States. You tell the chief that I will wait thirty minutes and at thirty-one minutes from now, I will have the state police or the FBI pick him up, in restraints if necessary!" Commandant Leary was not a man to be trifled with.

In twenty-four minutes, Coventry's chief of police came into the police station. He was in his mid forties; he had thin, balding, white hair, was overweight but not obese, and carried an expression that suggested that the world had never been fair to him. Commandant Leary was not impressed. "May I help you, sir?" the chief said in a nasal tone.

"Yes. I believe you can at that, chief. May we go into your office?" Commandant Leary asked.

"Of course, of course," the ingratiating chief offered. "Please, come right in." Commandant Leary motioned for Robert to follow, so he did. As the chief closed the door to the office, he asked, once again in his nasal tone, "What may I do for you this fine day, sir?"

"Take a good look at this cadet." Robert was standing at attention, since he had been given no other orders. "Here is his picture in this uniform, another in his Class B's, and a third in his PT uniform. Take a long, hard look at them, chief." The chief did as ordered.

"You may keep those copies. I have others. You, in fact, *will* keep those copies. You will ensure that each and every officer who works for you has this face in his or her mind. This cadet goes to Waterline Academy. One of your officers picked him up yesterday for the offense of *attending* Waterline Academy."

"I'm sure that none—" the chief began.

"Are you questioning *my* integrity?" Commandant Leary snarled.

"Oh, no, sir! It's just that … "

"That's very good, because discriminating against a ward of the federal government is an offense that carries a one-year jail sentence. Furthermore, your officers attacked my cadet because he answered their questions *honestly*. He was running for exercise, as any good cadet does. Your officer *arrested* him, beat him, threw him into a cruiser, and then interrogated him for an hour without so much as allowing him a phone call or calling his parents!

"I can easily charge your officers with false arrest, discrimination against a ward of the federal government, police brutality, assault of a minor, and assault of a minor who is a ward of the federal government. As their chief of police, I can charge you with conspiracy for each of the above. Furthermore, I can charge you and them with falsifying police records and obstructing justice. As far as my attorney friend can tell, the total sentencing could put you and your officers behind bars for … what was it?" Commandant Leary appeared to be trying to remember. "Oh, yes. You could be sentenced to twenty years and nine months plus fines of up to 755,000 dollars! Would you care to challenge my figures, sir?"

The chief of police of Coventry was humbled. He sat in his chair, silent and unmoving.

"Robert, would you please take a seat out there?" Commandant Leary indicated the general office area. Robert immediately left the office, closing the door behind him. He took a seat as far away from the chief's office as he could find.

The commandant spent another fifteen minutes talking and, sometimes, yelling at the chief. The police receptionist, a brunette woman in her mid twenties went over to Cadet Lieutenant Robert Crandon and introduced herself. "I'm Officer Jane Sutton." She offered her hand to Robert, and he shook it.

"I would greet you standing, ma'am, but my commandant ordered me to sit," Robert answered. "My name is Cadet Lieutenant Robert J. Crandon of Waterline Academy, ma'am."

"Well, cadet. Welcome to Coventry."

"Thank you, ma'am. I used to live here before I was sent to the academy. My family still lives here."

"Oh. Then you're still a resident here, aren't you?"

"I … don't exactly know, ma'am."

Just then, the two heard the commandant's voice get louder for a short while and then softer. "Why's your commandant reading the riot act to the chief?" Officer Sutton asked.

"I think it's because of my arrest yesterday, ma'am," Robert said. "The arresting officer and another officer seemed to think that I needed coercion in order to tell them the truth. They also seemed to think that it was impossible that a cadet could be running on Thanksgiving morning without having committed some sort of crime."

"That's just *terrible!*" the woman exclaimed softly. "They beat you up just because you were running?" Robert nodded. "It's no wonder your commandant is so mad. I hope he throws the book at those jerks. Do you know who they were?" she asked.

"Well, one of them was called Sam. I heard the other officer use that name. They usually kept a light in my eyes, so I could not read their badge numbers or anything. My father may know the names. He came here to pick me up yesterday before I had to go back to the academy."

"Why did you have to go back, Robert? That is your name, right?"

"Yes, ma'am, Robert Crandon. Article one-a-one-a states that any cadet who has an altercation with a law enforcement agency must return immediately to the academy, no exceptions, no excuses. I couldn't even stop to eat. Only to drink water or go to the latrine, ma'am."

"You mean you didn't get to eat on Thanksgiving until you got back to your academy?" the officer exclaimed.

"No, ma'am. I did not mean that," Robert answered.

"Oh, that's good," Officer Sutton said, cheering up a little.

"I didn't get to eat at the academy either, since I arrived too late, ma'am," Robert explained. Officer Sutton's happier expression fell to the shocked expression again.

Soon Commandant Leary emerged from the chief's office and had Robert follow him to the rental car. "Next, we need to stop at the state police barracks," Commandant Leary explained. "We need to make sure that they know who you are as well."

Robert punched in the letters, *S-T-A-T-E-P-O-L-I-C-E* and the red dots showed the path to the nearest Massachusetts state police barracks. Commandant Leary followed the directions and they arrived in about ten minutes. When they entered the building, there were three officers sitting at desks. One of them had a computer, which was apparently tracking the various squad cars that were on patrol.

"May I help you two?" an officer asked. Robert noticed that the State Police had their last names attached to their uniforms. This man was apparently Officer Higgins.

Commandant Leary answered. "I would like to see someone in charge. I have a cadet here from Waterline Academy, and I don't want him to be picked up by *accident* when he is on pass."

"You got eleven drunked?" Officer Higgins asked knowingly.

"Just yesterday," Robert answered.

"That's rough," Officer Higgins replied. "I take it, sir"—Higgins was now addressing Commandant Leary—"that the boy was *not* involved in illegal activity, not that I would expect that from a Waterline cadet anyways."

"You've had some experience with them?" Commandant Leary asked.

"Actually, a close acquaintance," Officer Higgins answered. "He's my partner and sergeant, as a matter of fact. He's in the back right now. He'll be out shortly."

After a few minutes, another Massachusetts State trooper came into the room from a rear entrance. He had the telltale three stripes of a sergeant on his sleeves.

"Charlie! The commandant of Waterline Academy would like to see you. Looks like they're taking you back there again." Higgins laughed at his partner and friend.

"Hmm … might be able to resist. I've got a revolver *this time*." Charles Kupfer fingered his weapon and then gave a big smile toward Commandant Leary. "On the other hand, I suppose it won't hurt to talk first and shoot later … if necessary." He smiled some more.

Sergeant Kupfer walked over to where the commandant and cadet were standing. "How's it going, cadet?" he asked Robert Crandon. "A lieutenant already? They must love you at the academy … unless things have changed a *whole lot*. I made it as far as a captain. I graduated in 1968 from there and went to the Massachusetts State Police Academy in Framingham. Waterline was the best beginning for that place that I could ever have attended. I breezed through that training." He then addressed the commandant. "Sorry, sir, I didn't mean to ignore you. I am guessing that this Cadet Lieutenant"—he looked at Robert's uniform—"Crandon must have gotten eleven drunked?"

Robert nodded.

"Which weenie town picked him up, sir? I'll go have a talk with the police chief and straighten him out concerning *senior officer cadets!*" Sergeant Kupfer had fire in his eyes as he spoke those last words.

"Actually," said Leary, "I have already taken the liberty of putting the fear of God into them. It was Coventry. I don't think Robert will have any more trouble with them. I also suspect that you will see one or two town policemen replaced in the very near future. I just wanted to leave Robert's photographs with you so that the state troopers would know what he looks like. He got picked up because he was on a six-and-a-half kilometer run, exercising."

The look of anger that passed over Sergeant Kupfer's face was quick, but both Commandant Leary and Cadet Crandon noticed it. "When did this happen, sir? Just yesterday?" Robert nodded. "On *Thanksgiving?*" Sergeant Kupfer's intonation was more a threat than a question. "Those … individuals"—here, the sergeant was visibly

controlling his words—"will stop at nothing to …humiliate someone, won't they?" The Waterline graduate took a deep breath to calm
down. "It's probably a good thing that you already told them, sir. I
might just have been forced to put someone in the hospital in order
to get *my* point across. Of course we'll disseminate Cadet Crandon's
photo, sir. You can count on that!"

Robert Crandon had seen the hot tempers of some cadets,
senior officers included. Now he knew why the academy needed
to exist. It helped the cadets learn to control their often volatile
tempers. He appreciated the restraint that the sergeant had shown
in his choice of words regarding the Coventry police officers; he
knew that profanity would likely have been used had Robert not
been there. Clearly Sergeant Kupfer wanted to keep a certain cadet
honoring authority, no matter what.

Commandant Leary gave copies of the same three photos to
Sergeant Kupfer that he had given to the Coventry Police Chief.
Sergeant Kupfer promised to copy them and let any officers he
encountered know that they should leave Robert Crandon alone unless
they were absolutely certain that he had done something wrong. He
wished the cadet a pleasant *remaining* common week. Commandant
Leary and Cadet Crandon then left the state police building.

"Next stop, your parents' house. Punch in the address, Robert,"
Commandant Leary offered. Robert punched in the number and letters and the dots showed a new route. After about three minutes, they
arrived at the intersection where the Crandon house was located.

"The driveway is on the side street, sir," Robert offered helpfully. "So
is the back door. We always use the back door through the porch, sir."

Commandant Leary drove around to the driveway and parked
behind the car that was already there. He got out and told Cadet
Crandon to get his bag. Robert picked up the duffel bag; a smile
was spread across his face that made his cheeks bulge out the side.
The two then walked to the house, entered the porch and then

Commandant Leary knocked on the door. Paul Crandon came to the door and opened it widely.

"Robbie?" he asked, dumbfounded.

"I brought him back to you personally, Mr. Crandon. I also took the liberty of informing the police that should they find need to pick him up again, he had better return to the academy unharmed and with felony charges pending against him. Your chief of police seemed to be accommodating." Commandant Leary was smiling a toothy, mischievous smile.

The homecoming was ecstatically joyous. Mrs. Crandon came rushing out of her first-floor bedroom and swept her son into her arms. Robert's siblings all gathered around and hugged him. Even Patrick came over and tugged on Robert's pant leg, to which Robert responded by picking up his baby brother. Patrick then sucked on Robert's nose for a while.

"He'll be staying until next Sunday. I have his return flight right here." Commandant Leary announced. He handed the ticket to the cadet. "You usually fly out of Providence, right, son?" he asked.

"Yes, sir. Begging your pardon, sir, but … my platoon? I was going to return early to help them prepare for First Inspection," Robert announced.

"Already taken care of," Commandant Leary assured his cadet. "Cadre Captain Newman told me about your plans and said that he would help your plebes prepare while you were home. We want you to get some time away from the academy, son. You've earned it—much more than you can imagine." Since his commandant had ordered it, Robert would not have questioned the order anyways. He just wanted to give input. He had not expected that his own concerns would have been alleviated. He was very, very grateful.

"Thank you so much, sir," Robert choked out. He was hugging his baby brother with a force and tenderness reminiscent of a mother trying to protect her child from an abductor. "I promise to stay as you ordered, sir. I … I … well, it's not as if I don't like the academy, sir … "

"No need to continue, Robert. I know how you feel. I admire your devotion to your duties, and I'm sure that everything will be all right. I'll be heading back to South Carolina tomorrow. I'll see you next Sunday or Monday. Make sure you have fun." With that, Commandant Leary took his leave and drove away.

The Crandons celebrated Thanksgiving for three days. It didn't matter to them that the *traditional* Thanksgiving was on the fourth Thursday in November; they were going to celebrate the return of the second to youngest member of the family. On that Sunday, Mrs. Crandon planned to invite her sister and sister's family, the Werstons, over for a large family gathering. Mrs. Crandon's parents and brother, the McPhees, were also coming. Mrs. Crandon decided to cook another turkey for the occasion.

Robert was watching his mother prepare for the meal and asked, "Why don't you put the turkey in a plastic bag to cook it?"

"Why would I do a fool thing like that, young man?" his mother asked, teasingly.

"Well, my chemistry professor told me that this certain kind of plastic foil will heat up to 220 degrees without burning or melting. That would mean that you could cook the turkey in the bag, with maybe some slits to prevent the air from getting trapped, but it would keep all the liquid in," Robert answered.

"Well, dear, a turkey is cooked at 350 degrees … " his mother said.

Robert interrupted. "I mean 220 degrees centigrade, Mother, not Fahrenheit. That's much more than 350 degrees Fahrenheit."

Mrs. Crandon thought about what her son had suggested. "Have you ever seen anyone actually *try* this before?" she asked.

"Oh, surely, lots of times. That's the way they cook turkeys in Waterline Academy now. Since they have to cook a bunch of them at one time, they put them all in bags and that way the birds cook faster—and taste better—or so I'm told … " Robert finished rather tentatively, shrugging. "Um … it's just a suggestion?"

"Well, my little chemist, how about if you and I go to the supermarket and try to find some plastic bags that might work?" Roberta offered to her son.

It was more difficult to find the correct kind of plastic than Robert had expected, but eventually he discovered a plastic wrapping that was made of the right material. He gave it to his mother to purchase. When they got home, he sewed the wrapping into the shape of a bag large enough for the turkey his mother was to cook. He took a cigarette lighter and carefully melted the plastic to weld it together. He then put about a handful of flour into the bag and shook it.

"It's ready for use, Mother," Robert announced.

"Well, I'm not quite ready to use it yet. I still have to make the stuffing," Roberta answered. Robert helped his mother make the stuffing, stuff the turkey, get the turkey into the bag, and put the entire thing onto a wire rack inside the turkey pan.

"You need to cut some openings so that the bag won't expand due to the hot air," Robert suggested. "Those *might not* be needed since I sewed the bag up, but … "

Mrs. Crandon gave her son a paring knife. Robert made the cuts in the top of the makeshift bag. "How long should I cook it?" she asked her son.

"I think about two thirds of the usual time," Robert offered. "I think that the cooks in Waterline use thermometers, but not the kind you take somebody's temperature with. They have long, metal ends to them."

"I have a meat thermometer, dear," Roberta assured her son. "I just wanted to have some idea as to when to start checking."

Robert helped his mother clean up the kitchen. He then proceeded to wash, dry, and put away the dishes. After that, he found a mop and washed the floor. Mrs. Crandon was surprised at this activity. Her other children only did chores when they were told to and sometimes not even then.

The Sunday dinner was a big success. The turkey came out very moist, as Robert had predicted. Roberta Crandon gave all the credit to her son, even though it embarrassed him to have such praise given to him. His grandparents wanted to give Robert some money for "missed birthdays" but he would not take it. "I can't, Grandfather," Robert tried to explain. "I'm not allowed to own *anything*. I can't even wear any other clothes than what the academy provides to me." Justin McPhee gave up after he received his grandson's explanation.

"You can call me Grandpa, you know," Justin offered to his grandson.

"Oh! I couldn't do that, Grandfather. I'd get gigged from here to the moon! We always have to be *very* formal. Well … that is … we do at the academy … and I wouldn't want to get into bad practices." Robert was nearly in tears, explaining his speech patterns to the only grandfather he had ever met.

"It's okay, Robbie. I don't mind. You go ahead and call me Grandfather, or Mr. McPhee, or Justin, or anything else you have in mind. I'm just glad to be able to give you hugs and see you," Justin said as he was hugging his grandson.

That Monday, Robert had a mission. He spent the morning cleaning the house, whenever his mother didn't chase him away from doing chores. At 1455 hours, he asked his mother if he might be permitted to walk to South Side Elementary School. She agreed, telling him to be careful.

Robert walked down the familiar street in his dress blues uniform. He waited for the school day to end. When the school bell rang, he went into the upper section of the school, where the principal's office and secretary's desk were located.

"I would like to speak to Mrs. Rowell, if I may, please," he asked the secretary. He did not recognize the woman; she must have been hired in the last four years.

"I think that she's in her classroom," the woman offered. "You just need to go down those stairs and turn right. Her room is at the end of the corridor." The woman pointed to the open staircase to her right. Robert followed the familiar pathway; he had never forgotten that once dreaded route.

When he arrived at room A1, he looked inside and saw a familiar figure straightening out desks. He entered and helped her set all the desks into neat rows. He also routinely picked up papers and other small objects, storing them in his left hand to put into the wastebasket. Soon enough, Mrs. Rowell noticed his uniform and the help he was giving. "Thank you very much, dear. May I help you?"

"I had just come here to talk," Robert answered.

Mrs. Mary-Ann Rowell had not seen the boy in over four years, yet she still saw something familiar in his face. She looked at him for a short while and noticed the name tag over his right breast pocket. "Robert?" she asked. "Is it really you?"

"Guilty," Robert answered. "I would have visited earlier, but I didn't get a pass until last year, and I was too injured then," he explained. "I wanted to come see you. I wanted to let you know that I'm doing okay in Waterline Academy."

Mrs. Rowell's face fell a little. Robert continued. "I knew it wasn't your fault after about a year and a half. I'm sorry that I was angry with you before that. I was hurt, confused. I felt betrayed. It took me some time to figure out what *really* happened. You see, I wasn't able to contact anyone from the outside for three years, so my parents were not able to tell me that Roger Granson had switched letters."

"How did you know then?" the woman asked.

"Well, two of the claims in the letter my parents received said, 'throwing papers around the class, tearing up his school books.' Obviously, I had never done such things. Finally it occurred to me that I had known someone who *had* done those things. Since he sat right next to me in your class, it wasn't too difficult to put two and two together and come up with three point nine, nine, nine repeating," Robert answered, blinking in his conspiratorial way and smiling.

"*Anyways*, I wanted to let you know that my parents showed me your real letter about me. I was very touched by what you said. It healed a lot of hurts. I loved you, and it was so hard for me to understand what I thought was betrayal. I still love you, Mrs. Rowell, and whether you realize it or not, you have done me a great service. I can't say that I like being in Waterline Academy—I don't consider that *any of your fault*, by the way—but I have been able to learn there much faster than I would have here. So, even though I didn't get to go to Bethesda Academy, I did sort of get the quick learning that I would have gotten there."

"Look at you!" Mrs. Rowell said. "You are so grown up since I last saw you. You look very handsome in that uniform, Robbie. How *have* you done at Waterline, incidentally? Is it as bad as I have heard? And what are all these things on your uniform? Do you have time to sit and talk?"

"Yes, ma'am. I'm on common week. That means that I get to leave the academy for a little while. As for how I have done ... " here the boy thought hard about what he should and *should not* tell his former first grade teacher. "How much do you *really* want to know, ma'am? Some things are not all that pleasant, but others are not too bad."

Mrs. Rowell took a deep breath and thought for a while. "Go ahead and tell me *everything*. You don't have to go into details where you don't want to, but I think I can handle it."

"Well, to sum it all up quickly, I was taken away in the van just as you and my mother were crying in each other's arms—my mother told me about that. I was going to write you—to try to comfort you—but I didn't know what address. *Anyways*, I got the best platoon leader I could have possibly gotten, so God must have been looking out for me there. I got promoted faster than any cadet in history—well at least Waterline history, that is. I was made a fire team leader after only six months and was a squad leader after only a year. When I started my fourth year, I was already a *senior officer!*

"Things were pretty rough at the academy, but I did okay. I made sure to play the Game, and that helped a lot! Umm … you won't know what *the Game* means. Well, to sum *that* up, it's how cadets are able to handle being at Waterline. They purposely try to make sure they don't complain or grump about anything. If they can do all the stuff without grumping, then they win. If they cry or complain, then they lose. There are other parts, but they're not that important. Basically, we try to play pranks on the cadre whenever we can get away with it.

"In my fourth year, I got attacked by one of my cadre officers. That's why I couldn't come visit you last November. I was too injured. It was my first pass, too!" Robert made a face indicative of a child who had just been given bad news or eaten something he did not like. "*Anyways*, that cadre officer put me into the hospital. He got arrested and I have to testify, probably some time in January."

"How badly were you hurt?" Mrs. Rowell asked.

"Pretty badly, ma'am. I won't lie to you. The doctors thought I was going to die," Robert answered. "I didn't though!" he added, happily. "I beat Mr. Gerralds in *that*, too! I liked beating Cadre Captain Gerralds in his own punishments. It kind of made Waterline … bearable? Is that the right word, Mrs. Rowell?"

"It's probably as good as any, Robbie. Please go on."

"Well, *anyways*, Cadre Captain Gerralds was fired and arrested, so now that makes him *Mister* Gerralds. It took me a while, but I got all healed up and my platoon took the top honors at the June assembly!" Robert finished with a big smile.

"So what are all these things on your uniform?" Mrs. Rowell asked. She pointed to the lieutenant bars and his medals.

"Well, these gold bars show that I'm a cadet lieutenant—that means I'm a senior officer. The lieutenants kind of keep all the rest of the rowdies in line. These are medals," Robert answered.

"How did you earn each of the medals?"

At this point, Robert had a difficult time continuing. He was still a very shy, humble, little boy when it came to praise. "Well … this one"—here he indicated his achievement medal—"actually stands for five achievement medals. You get an oak leaf cluster added to the ribbon for each additional one after the first. You can only get five, though. After that they give you commendation medals." Robert pointed to the ribbon next to the achievement medal. "After your fifth commendation medal, they start giving you silver bars to go with the oak leaf clusters. *Anyways* … you usually get those for doing well in class, passing inspections really well, that sort of stuff. These ones mean that I was in the top platoon for a given year. I've been in the top platoon for three of my four years there." Robert smiled.

Mrs. Rowell looked closely at the medals and saw two silver bars and two oak leaf clusters on the commendation medal. She did a mental calculation, came to the number thirteen, and tried to grasp the quantity of times her former pupil had been honored at Waterline Academy. "How did you earn this last one?" she asked Robert.

Robert had hoped she would forget about that one. He took another deep breath and said, "Well, you remember Mr. Gerralds, ma'am?" The teacher nodded her head. "Well, when he attacked me … and the injuries put me into the hospital … well, I was kind of protecting another cadet from him. He—Cadre Captain Gerralds, that is—had decided to punish the two of us by hitting us with a metal swagger stick. The other boy, Johnny—that is, Cadet John Freeman—well, I kept holding off Cadre Captain Gerralds until Johnny escaped.

"*Anyways* … as it turns out, Captain Gerralds wasn't *supposed* to be hitting us with sticks. I didn't know that, exactly. I had a feeling that something wasn't right, but since all the complaints always went through Cadre Captain Gerralds, all the cadets had stopped bothering to try sending complaints. *Anyways*, I was given this"—here Robert pointed to his Medal of Freedom—"for bravery in saving Johnny from harm. It's called the Medal of Freedom. It's the highest medal that the Academy System can award. There are only three other recipients, ma'am." Robert finished his explanation.

Robert changed the subject. "I was hoping to see you during the other times that I get to come to Massachusetts. The only problem is that you usually have vacation at those times. I was wondering if there was some way that we might get together during the other weeks. If not, that's okay, really." Robert added the last part quickly.

"I would *love* to get together with you, Robbie," Mrs. Rowell answered.

"I figured out a way that you could know when I was coming here," Robert offered. "I can write to you and let you know when I'll be at my parents' house. Then you could come visit any time that's okay with you." Robert was very enthusiastic. "I'm sure that my parents wouldn't mind. They spoke really highly of you."

"Well, then, Robbie, let's go see where you live. You used to walk to school, didn't you?"

"Yes, ma'am. I can show you the way. It's just down the street, Wildwood Avenue, that is. We live at the corner," Robert offered.

Mrs. Rowell had finished with her room preparations for the next school day, so she went with her former pupil and walked down Wildwood Ave. When they arrived at the Crandon residence, Robert offered to have her visit his family. Mrs. Rowell graciously accepted and the two went in. The reunion between Robert's mother and his former teacher was both gracious and happy. Robert's siblings were all busy doing homework, except for Patrick, of course. He was sleeping in his crib contentedly.

After the visit, Robert walked Mrs. Rowell back to the school and her car. She had told him that such an action was unnecessary, but he accompanied her anyways. He had been drilled in proper etiquette, and it was second nature to him to follow all the lessons he had learned. Mrs. Rowell offered to give him a ride home, which he turned down since the distance was so short.

Robert considered his mission to be accomplished, and he was very, very happy at how it had turned out.

Soon, the week ended and Robert was brought back to the Williams Airport in Providence. He left his parents at the metal detector, taking off his jacket and outer shirt, as usual. He had no problems with the rest of his trip back to Waterline Academy and arrived about 1400. He went up to his room, unpacked, and sought out his platoon members. He was going to make sure that this inspection went *really* well.

THE RESULTS OF FIRST INSPECTION

The visiting cadre officer was from Washington, DC; that meant that he was working in the Directorship of Academies. Cadet Lieutenant Crandon was not all that worried. His platoon from the previous year had taken top honors, in spite of the fact that two of the four inspections had been conducted by directorship cadre officers. They usually did not ask as many questions of required knowledge because they did not know the answers themselves. That meant that only the required knowledge of the *entire* academy system would likely be asked (not Waterline specific stuff), albeit in very detailed form.

Cadet Lieutenant Crandon drilled his cadets as the day went on; it seemed that his platoon would be sixth in line for inspection. "This guy is probably going to ask detailed questions about chain of command, locations of US military installations, various battles and outcomes, that sort of thing. Remember the songs that I taught you and remember to answer *slowly*. If you answer slowly and deliberately, he won't gig you. He'll just keep waiting for you to finish.

"Everyone repeat after me," Robert Crandon ordered. "Sir ... the ... last ... word ... in ... the ... Pledge ... of ... Allegiance ... is ... 'all'" The cadets repeated with delays in each word. "Sergeant Cadet Lorte, do you have all five copies of our work order requests?"

"Yes, sir!" Donald Lorte answered.

"Does everyone know the chain of command? Say it together!" The platoon leader ordered.

"Cadet Lieutenant Crandon, Cadet Captain Smith, Cadet Lieutenant Colonel Marks, Cadre Captain Toole, Commandant Leary, Director Cord, General Davis, the honorable Phillip Harrison, President Robert Kennedy," the cadets said in unison.

"What is the primary infantry weapon of the US Army and Marines?"

"Sir ... the ... primary ... weapon ... of ... the ... infantry ... is ... the M16A1 ... assault ... rifle."

"Where was the final battle of the US Revolutionary War fought?"

"Sir ... the ... last ... battle ... of ... the ... Revolutionary War ... was ... fought ... in ... Yorktown, Virginia."

The drill kept up from the time they had finished morning meal (about seven a.m., or 0700 hours, until 1000 hours, when they all heard, "Charlie-3 platoon leader, post!"

Cadet Crandon immediately answered, "On my way, sir!" and hustled down the stairs to greet the cadre officer. Upon arriving at the bottom of the steps, he saluted and said, "Sir, Cadet Lieutenant Crandon reports as ordered. Third platoon, Charlie Company of Waterline Academy is ready for inspection, sir!"

"We shall see, Lieutenant. We shall see." Robert noticed the golden oak leaves on the cadre officer's shoulders, signifying a Cadre Major. He also noticed the nametag, which read, "Zade." The major led the way up the stairs, bending down occasionally to wipe his white gloves on the stairs or guiding board. Robert Crandon was reassured when no smudges showed up on the gloves.

"I would like to inspect your room first, Cadet Lieutenant," Major Zade declared.

"Yes, sir!" Robert answered. He pointed the way into his quarters and watched as the major checked out everything from how far from the pocket Robert's nametag was to whether or not there was dust coming from the vent. Robert Crandon was very glad that he had thought to clean out the ventilation system before Thanksgiving Common Week. Major Zade asked various questions to the cadet lieutenant, as was required, but he did not really expect a senior officer to fail in any required knowledge.

After he inspected the platoon leader's quarters he started on the left side of the barracks and made his way down to the platoon sergeant's quarters. The first room he came to after the platoon sergeant's had a broken window. "Broken window, cadet?" he asked.

"Platoon Sergeant!" Robert prompted. SFC. Cadet Lorte produced the five carbon copies of the five work orders submitted.

"Five times?" Major Zade asked.

"Six, actually, sir," Robert corrected. "We didn't think to carbon-copy the first submission, sir."

Major Zade nodded and continued down the corridor, inspecting each cadet and each room. He noticed three damaged wardrobes, each with four carbon-copy work-order requests that had gone unheeded. After Major Zade had finished with the individual cadets, he checked the common room. Again, a broken window was noted and five carbon copies for work orders were shown to him. Finally, Major Zade made his way into the latrine.

"What have we got here, cadet?" Major Zade asked Robert.

"It's a Gerry-rigged hose to prevent floor damage, sir," Robert explained.

"Floor damage?" Major Zade asked. " ... And just how did you make it, cadet?"

"Sir, back in August, when we moved into this barracks, the sink was dripping, and there was no pipe leading to the drainage system. The previous platoon routinely used a bucket to collect the water. However, they also routinely had accidents, causing the tiling to come loose and weakening the flooring underneath. I therefore determined that until the work order was completed that we would need a better system for draining the water.

"I collected used toilet paper rolls and duct-taped them together. I expected that the cardboard would not likely last, but the duct tape would withstand the constant water. Whenever a leak occurred, we patched it up with extra duct tape. The reason for the toilet paper rolls was so that the original duct tape would have a surface on which to stick. Without the cardboard rolls, the tape would have collapsed on itself and the glue would have rendered the hose unusable."

After the cadet had finished his explanation, Major Zade said, "Very ingenious, young man. You may very well have saved the academy system thousands of dollars in repairs." Major Zade inspected the commodes. One of them was labeled, "Out of Order, DO NOT USE." SFC Cadet Lorte produced the requisite copies of the work orders. Finally, the major inspected the shower. He ran his gloves along the floor and next to the fixtures.

After he finished his inspection, he headed toward the doorway to the stairs. "Come with me, alone, cadet," he ordered Cadet Lieutenant Crandon. The two made their way down the stairs. "These are the first gloves I don't have to change before my next inspection, Crandon. Well done."

"Thank you, sir," Robert responded.

"Which is the door to Bravo Company, first platoon?" The major asked.

"The same as this one, sir, on the opposite side of the building over there," Robert answered pointing to B Company's barracks.

"You're Charlie-3 here, and they're Bravo-1 there?" Major Zade asked incredulously.

"Yes, sir. Our cadre officers like to try to confuse us as much as possible, sir. They change the location of each company and platoon each year. In addition, there is never a corresponding floor to platoon match from company to company. This is general Waterline Academy procedure, sir," Robert answered.

"Thank you, cadet. You may return to your platoon. I should finish up with Bravo in about one hour. You will be able to get the overall results shortly after that. I will give your Cadet Adjutant the *platoon* results immediately after I finish. The individual results will have to be entered by the secretarial staff before they are released," Major Zade said.

"Yes, sir. Thank you, sir," Robert answered, saluting. Major Zade returned the salute and proceeded to Bravo Company.

Robert Crandon went back up to his platoon and told them to relax for an hour. The cadets gave a collective sigh of relief, especially the plebes. After about sixty-five minutes, a cadet summoned Cadet Lieutenant Crandon to the cadet adjutant's quarters. Robert nearly flew down the stairs, around the building and into the field grade officers' section.

Cadet Major John Stevens was waiting for him. "You passed!" John said. "As a matter of fact, your platoon had a 99 percent, the highest in the academy!" John handed the Charlie-3 results to Robert. The paper showed a total of seven gigs amongst six cadets. In addition, there was a mark that he did not recognize.

"Hey, sir, what's this mean?" he asked the adjutant.

John looked at the report paper and saw the marking. He did not recognize it either. "Maybe you can ask Captain Newman. He ought to know since he's discipline," John suggested.

Robert took the report into the cadre office. The secretaries were busily typing in the results of First Inspection. Robert made his way down the corridor of cadre offices to the master of discipline. He knocked and heard Cadre Captain Newman answer, "Come!"

Robert opened the office door and said, "Sir, Cadet Crandon wishes to address the master of discipline."

"Come on in, cadet. Close the door if you wish," Captain Newman offered.

"I don't think that will be necessary, sir," Robert answered. "I'll close it if you want me too, of course, sir," he added.

"Not at all, not at all," Captain Newman answered. "I trust your judgment, cadet."

"Sir, I received my platoon's score for First Inspection. I was wondering what one of the marks meant, sir. My battalion adjutant said that he could not identify it, sir," Robert said.

"Let me take a look," Captain Newman offered. He looked at the inspection results, noting that the platoon had scored a ninety-nine percent. "That, cadet," he stated, "is a sign for *merits*."

"Sir, what does a merit on an inspection mean?" Robert asked.

"It means, Lieutenant, that you have gone above and beyond the norm. You must have done something to impress Major Zade. Merits count against gigs and, in some cases, minor punishments. He gave your platoon three merits. That means that each platoon member gets thirty gigs wiped out, if need be," Captain Newman answered.

Cadet Lieutenant Robert Joseph Crandon's eyes widened in amazement. He did not even know that such a thing was possible in Waterline Academy. Gigs were gigs, and nothing had ever erased the consequences before—at least not by *joint* effort.

"One of the happy consequences of the merits for your platoon is that each member will receive a commendation medal for outstanding achievement. Since no one had more than two gigs, the merits make the individual scores perfect. Congratulations, cadet! You managed to do what every cadre officer in Waterline, including one *misguided one*, believed impossible," Captain Newman added. "Your entire platoon, regardless of *banned* or *passed* status, has permission to go to the PX until 1600 hours. They may also obtain stamps and write letters to their families. Those on banned status must submit the letters to the cadre platoon officer. That's to make sure that they are only writing to their families—no friends.

"Once again, Robert, congratulations! You faced the most difficult job I've ever heard of in the history of the academy system, and you found a way to make it work."

"Well, sir, I would be remiss if I did not thank you for your help in the past week," Robert offered.

"My help was minimal, cadet. Your platoon had all the tools to succeed. I just helped to guide them a very little bit. You are the one who deserves the credit, Robert. By the way, have you told your cadre officer of the results yet?"

"No, sir. I haven't had the opportunity yet, sir. I came straight to your office to ask about the *merit* symbol, sir," Robert answered.

"Let's go tell him," Captain Newman offered.

The two made their way to the other end of the hall, and Captain Newman knocked on the door. "Come!" they heard Captain Toole order. Captain Newman opened the door. Seeing his cadet platoon leader with the master of discipline, Captain Toole stood up immediately and asked, in a rather concerned manner, "He didn't take all the gigs again, did he, Roy?"

"Wouldn't matter if he did," Captain Newman answered. "The platoon passed with a ninety-nine percent and was given three merits to boot. Charlie-3 was the top platoon in the academy, Pete."

Captain Toole relaxed and sat back down on his chair. "Are those the results, Robbie?" he asked.

"Yes, sir," Robert answered, handing the paper to his cadre officer.

"The most was *two*?" exclaimed Captain Toole. "With twenty plebes, the most gigs anyone got was two?" he repeated.

"Yes, sir," Robert answered. "I hope to do better in the Second Inspection, sir," Robert added, confidently. Both of the cadre officers smiled.

"I owe you guys a party, Lieutenant," Captain Toole offered. "Go ask your platoon what they'd like. Pizza, ice cream, tacos, whatever they want is okay. We'll have it in the common room in a few days. Just let me know what you guys decide. Oh, and go tell them to get their butts off to the PX. Make sure they're in their Class *A*s."

"Yes, sir!" Robert answered excitedly. He ran down the hallway, out of the cadre office and up the stairs to his platoon.

"Sergeant Lorte, assemble the platoon in the common room," Robert yelled down the hallway. He entered his room and shut the door. As a matter of protocol, the platoon leader waited for the junior officers to assemble all the cadets before entering such a gathering.

In a few short minutes, SFC Cadet Lorte knocked on the platoon leader's door three times and called, "Charlie-3 assembled sir!" Robert Crandon opened his door and entered the common room. The platoon was in Class-A uniform since that was the inspection uniform and no one had ordered otherwise.

Cadet Lieutenant Crandon produced his copy of the inspection results. "I have here a copy of Major Zade's inspection," he said in a falsely ominous tone. "Charlie-3 had a grand total of seven gigs amongst six cadets. That means that the platoon passed inspection with a ninety-nine and the lowest individual score was a ninety-eight. In addition, we received three merits, which easily wipes out any of those gigs!" Robert finished in a very excited and happy tone of voice.

Charlie-3 burst out in cheers. After about thirty seconds, Robert quieted them down and continued. "Due to the outstanding inspection results, Charlie-3 cadets all have permission to go to the PX until 1600 hours. You must be in Class-A uniform if you are off campus. In addition, all plebes may obtain stamps and write letters to their family members *only*. Cadre Captain Newman didn't say it, but I think that means you'll also be able to *read* mail from your family as well, so the first letter you send should tell your folks to list all family members with different last names." Once again, the platoon cheered.

After the noise died down again, Cadet Lieutenant Crandon spoke to his platoon in a more serious tone. "Okay. You all did great. Now, as for the rules of the road: in order to go to the PX, you have to pass the cadre adjutant and salute. You don't have to say anything; you just salute and move on. Every cadet has a certain amount of credits stored up for buying Icees, pretzels, smoothies, and some other things. All the Icees are made from juice, but you can get combinations put together. If you don't know what to order, just ask one of us veterans and we'll try to help.

"The cadre officers will not be at the PX. There will be some armed guards there to ensure that nobody gets too rowdy. Don't piss off the armed guards; this is NOT a game. If you hear a whistle, then the guards have called for all cadets to return to the academy grounds. Just get up calmly, make your way to the academy barracks at an even walk and don't stop to look at anything. If you are called over by any *adult*, you will report to that person as if he or she is the president of the United States. Don't get too worried about this talk. All platoon leaders have to give it to first-timers to the PX. There hasn't been an incident there in years.

"*Anyways*, after 1600 hours, you will change into extended PT *winter* uniform. That means sweats and your Field Uniform hat. Until then, go have some fun and be on your *absolute best* behavior. Cadre Captain Toole wants you guys to think of what you want to eat for a party, so talk it up amongst you, and let me know tonight. Remember, you all represent Charlie-3! Now get your butts down to the PX. Platoon, attention!" The entire platoon immediately stood up. "Dismissed until 1600 hours!"

The cadets bolted out of the common room and down the stairs. They made their way to where Cadre Major Sooner was seated at a table. Each cadet turned, saluted the major, and left in the general direction that the others were headed. Robert Crandon pulled the sleeve of Donald Lorte, signaling him to remain.

After the Charlie-3 barracks was empty save for the platoon leader and platoon sergeant, Robert said, "If you don't mind, I'd like you to wait a bit."

"Sure, sir. What's up?" Sergeant Lorte asked.

"Oh, I just don't want to gum up the works. I don't want all the guys to worry about saluting me on their way, so I figured we could wait a bit. I need to figure out some stuff with you, so if you don't mind, we can walk there together."

"No problem," Sergeant Lorte answered.

After about five minutes the two cadets began to make their way to the PX, in a somewhat more dignified manner than their underlings. "What I'm getting worried about is that we have a broken window in one of the *cadet* rooms," Robert began. As the two passed Major Sooner, they saluted the cadre adjutant automatically and simply continued to talk. "It's now December, and the blue blotter paper isn't going to keep the *cold* out. Yes it worked for dust and bugs, but those guys are going to freeze if we don't do something—and soon."

Donald Lorte thought about the dilemma. "I don't suppose there are any open rooms anywhere?" he suggested.

"Nope, the whole academy is filled. We'd have to use one of the extra rooms in the field grade officers' section or the company commanders' section, and those are usually saved in case somebody can't get up the stairs. You can bet that the cads aren't going to change a room for a broken window."

"Maybe one of our work orders will get through?" Donald asked.

"Not a chance," Robert answered gloomily. "I checked the secretary files and not a single work order of ours has even been filed! They probably threw them out—by mistake, I'm sure—as usual! That means that we have to come up with something else." By this time, the two had reached the PX and went up to the counter to order.

"I'd like a triple mix, please, sir," Robert asked.

"Me too, sir," Donald added.

"Do you want any pretzels or crackers?" Robert asked his platoon sergeant. "My treat," he added.

"Pretzels are good," Donald suggested, "but I can sign for them," he offered.

"I get more credits than you, and mine don't get reduced for polish and brass cleaning stuff. Also, I had three years to build up!" Robert explained. "I'll sign for them." After the two cadets got their pretzels and drinks they sat at a table that had a commanding view of the PX. Robert had been sitting at that particular table whenever he was at the

PX. Since he had made Cadet Lieutenant, it was expected that he, as a senior officer, would maintain discipline at the facility.

"We have also got to find a way to get some metal piping. Our makeshift hose isn't going to last forever." Robert continued his previous conversation. "I just wish that we could somehow *force* the issue."

"Why don't they get new secretaries if they can't seem to file simple fix-it jobs?" Donald asked.

"They're political appointees," Robert answered. "They got their jobs because they are the wives or relatives of congressmen, top military officers or something like that. Some of them may have worked on campaigns for congressmen as well, like Cadre Major Sooner," Robert added. "Oops … that's secret, Don. No repeating that. Not even to me, okay?" He whispered.

Donald winked at his platoon leader. "You can always count on me, sir."

"So, have you got any other ideas … hey, isn't that Morse over there?" Robert changed the subject abruptly.

Donald looked over to a table about five meters away. "Yeah. Hey, what's Morse doing with those idiots?" he asked.

"Recruitment, probably," Robert answered. "Why don't you go invite young Cadet Norman over here? I'll go get him an Icee."

Donald Lorte went over to his cadet plebe who was talking with Cadets Hersh, Alexander, Gendron, and Hayes. These cadets were notorious, and all the cadet officers, junior and senior, hated what they did. The only one of the lot who seemed even remotely useful was Cadet Arthur Alexander, and he appeared to be falling under Gendron's spell. "Excuse me, gents. My platoon leader would like to talk with his plebe. Hope I didn't interrupt anything too important," Donald said snidely.

He led Norman Morse over to the table he was sharing with Robert Crandon. When the two arrived, Crandon offered the drink to his cadet. "Here, it's on me. Would you like some pretzels or crackers?"

"Umm … yes, sir," Morse answered.

Robert nodded his head over toward the counter for his platoon sergeant to get the snack. "Bring me the slip to sign." he added to Sergeant Lorte. He then addressed Cadet Morse. "The reason I asked you over here, Morse, is that you are playing with fire. I don't want you to get your fingers burned." Cadet Morse looked at him uncomprehendingly.

"Let me see if I can put it another way," Robert offered. "You see those four cadets over there?"

"Yes, sir."

"Well, Gendron has this nasty habit of collecting plebes and leading them into trouble. He then goes and tells the cadre officers and laughs at the fact that he got plebes into trouble. The other three have sort of joined his little clique. They all do the same thing, except for Cadet Alexander. He's just dumb and likes to hang around with them.

"To give you an idea of how much of a problem they are, I'll bet that at least three of the four aren't even supposed to *be* here."

Norman Morse's eyes popped open. Donald Lorte had returned with the pretzels and the two junior cadets shared them. "Why don't you go report them, sir?" Norman asked.

"Because cadets *help* cadets; cadets don't turn in cadets," Robert said. "I'll go tell their platoon leaders that they're here when I get a chance, but then it's up to them. I don't *technically* even know that they shouldn't be here. Alexander probably got a pass, but I remember the other three in PT two Fridays ago. It's a pretty good bet that they didn't earn PX privileges during inspection. Even still, they aren't in my platoon, so I leave the dirty work to their platoon sergeants and platoon leaders. That's just how we do things here at Waterline.

"As I was saying, I don't want you to get your fingers burned. I can't *order* you to stay away from them. Well ... maybe I could, but I won't. I'm just *suggesting* it to you, for your own good."

"Thank you *very much*, sir," Norman answered. "I'm really glad you told me about *those* guys. I may have earned my way into Waterline, but I sure as hell don't want to earn my way into *reform school!* Somebody ought to punch those guys lights out!" Morse almost made a move to accomplish that feat.

"Easy there, cadet," Donald cautioned. "Those *guys* are much older and bigger than you. They would eat you for breakfast. Just try to stay away from them. If they give you any problems, come tell me or any other platoon sergeant. We have ways of keeping these guys from causing too much trouble"—here, SFC Cadet Donald Lorte clenched his fists—"and we do it together. That way it's not four on one."

"You can count on me, sir," Norman assured his platoon leader. "I'll let the other guys know, too. We're not about to let *those* cadets spoil Charlie-3, sir."

Pleased with his efforts in keeping Cadet Morse on track, Robert went back to the window and pipe dilemma. "So, we can't seem to get work orders through the secretaries and we can't ask the cadre for the repairs because they'll just tell us to submit work orders. There has to be some way around this."

Robert thought for a while and then exclaimed, "I know! I'll ask for an acetylene torch!"

"A *what?*" Sergeant Lorte thought that his platoon leader had gone mad. The cadets were not allowed to have so much as a single match or lighter, never mind an industrial torch.

"I'll submit for an acetylene torch," Robert repeated. "I'll have to ask for a mask, a canister of acetylene, some glass shards and some piping too." He took out his gig book, something he usually only used for notes, and began writing. "I can melt the glass … oh yeah, I had better ask for a metal pan to put the glass in and a metal stick to move it. Then I can melt the glass and blow it to fix the windows. I can then weld the pipe onto the sink and solve the problem of the drips threatening the floor." Robert finished his notes and began to get up.

"No offense, sir, but what makes you think they'll let you have an acetylene torch? I mean … this is Waterline Academy…"

"Ye of little faith," Robert answered cryptically. "Remember, any such request has to go directly to Commandant Leary."

"I can't see Commandant Leary offering to let you burn down the barracks either, sir," Donald said.

"You'll see, Don. You'll see. I've got to get back and create the paperwork. You guys go ahead and stay here. I'll be back after I go see a commandant about a torch. Don, you're in charge unless and until a senior officer shows up." With that, Cadet Lieutenant Crandon turned and walked toward the exit. "You guys can all remain," he assured the other cadets in the PX. He then walked out the door.

After a few minutes, Sergeant First Class Cadet Donald Lorte heard whistles being blown. He had not heard them for five years, but he knew exactly what they meant. "Time to go home, Norm," he said to the cadet sitting at the same table. "Remember what Lieutenant Crandon said. Just walk out calmly, like in a fire drill and head to the barracks. If you are called over by an adult, report as ordered, do what they ask and then head to the barracks." The two cadets got up and followed a throng of cadets out of the PX.

Four army military police soldiers, armed with M16A1 assault rifles, were looking all around. Another MP was rapidly copying down the names of those cadets who were exiting the PX. "Keep it moving, cadets," one of the armed men was saying, trying to keep the situation from getting out of hand. "You don't need to slow down. Just head calmly to your academy."

Sergeant Lorte heard the telltale whine of an ambulance approaching. He then heard several more similar whines. As he walked toward the barracks with his young underling, he noticed that three of the MPs were shielding a pile that had the blue tint of Cadet Class As. He began to help the vocal MP. "You heard him, cadets. Keep moving to your respective barracks. The cadre will want to question us later. Just keep moving and go straight to your platoon's floor. Make sure to avoid any automotive traffic, but otherwise, keep going." Donald did not know if his encouragement was necessary, but he felt that he should try to help in *some* way. "Keep a slow, steady pace. The MPs are just writing down your names so they know who to ask questions to later."

When he arrived at Charlie-3's barracks floor, Donald noticed that his platoon leader was missing. He waited until all the cadets had come back from the PX and then counted his platoon. He counted forty-one, with only his platoon leader missing. That was not welcome news.

Ten minutes later, Cadre Captain Toole arrived. "Platoon leader, post!" Captain Toole commanded. Donald Lorte came out of his own quarters and ran to the end of the hall.

"Sergeant Cadet Lorte reports in the place of his platoon leader, sir!" Donald announced.

"Where is Cadet Lieutenant Crandon, sergeant?" Captain Toole asked.

"Unknown, sir. There are forty-one members of Charlie-3 present, sir. Only Cadet Crandon is unaccounted for, sir," Donald answered.

"You are currently in charge of the platoon until further notification, then, sergeant. Tell the rest of the cadets to rest easy until we find out what happened. Get into extended PT uniform. For your own knowledge, cadet," he continued in a soft voice, "there was a fight with weapons at the PX. Five cadets are injured and currently in the hospital. There is no word on their conditions. You guys will get PX privileges tomorrow, if possible." With that, Captain Toole descended the staircase.

"I want to know when I can speak with my cadets, doctor," Commandant Leary pleaded. "I have to find out what happened. The director of academies is waiting for a preliminary prognosis on each of the boys, and he wants to know *what happened!* Do you have any idea when I might be able to come over there and speak with them?" Commandant Leary listened at his phone receiver. "That's great, Doctor. Thank you very much." More listening. "No, I must insist that a guard remain at the door where any of the boys are located. The regulations are very strict on that accord." More listening. "Yes. I will be there in thirty minutes doctor. Thanks again. Good-bye."

Joseph Leary did not even have any idea of which cadets were in the hospital. Evidently, the MPs had not taken down the names even though the nameplates had to be pinned to each cadet's chest. The hospital personnel had not seen any name plates, so he had to wait for a roll call of each platoon until he would have that answer. He considered whether or not to call the director and let him know about the thirty-minute delay. He decided that he would rather not talk to Director Cord just then and walked outside his office door.

"Aldus, don't you have the names yet?" Commandant Leary demanded in an angry voice.

"These things take *time*," Major Sooner answered petulantly. "I've told the battalion adjutant to get me the roll call."

Commandant Leary decided he was not going to wait. He stormed out of the cadre office and around to the field grade officers' quarters. As he entered he heard a cadet call the others to attention. "As you were," Commandant Leary said. "Where's the battalion adjutant?" he asked.

"In here, sir." Leary heard a voice call.

Commandant Leary proceeded into Cadet Major John Stevens's quarters. "I'm just finishing up *triple*-checking, sir," Major Stevens announced. "I took so long, sir, because it just doesn't make any sense."

"How is that, cadet?" Commandant Leary asked.

"Well, sir. I understand that an … incident … took place at the PX. The problem is that three of the missing cadets aren't even supposed to be off *campus*, sir. They were banned from common week and failed the inspection. The other two were permitted to go to the PX, but I find it hard to believe that a senior officer would be involved in a fight with weapons, sir." John Stevens was visibly distressed. "Actually … I find it hard to believe that any Waterline cadet could even *find* a weapon."

Commandant Leary took a few moments to grasp the implications of what he had just heard. "Names please," he asked.

"Yes, sir: Cadets Robert James Hersh, Arthur Thomas Alexander, David Matthews Gendron, Albert Phillip Hayes, and Cadet *Lieutenant* Robert Joseph Crandon, sir," John Stevens answered.

"Cadet Crandon?"

"Yes, sir, Charlie-3 platoon leader. Sergeant First-Class Cadet Donald Lorte is currently in charge of the platoon, sir."

"Which three were not supposed to be off campus?"

"Hersh, Gendron, and Hayes, sir," Stevens answered. "I sent a runner to check their platoons, sir. They are definitely not on campus."

"Those are the only five missing?"

"Yes, sir."

"Good work, cadet," Commandant Leary said. He then left the field grade officers' section and returned to the cadre office.

He placed an urgent, person-to-person call to Matthew Cord, Director of Academies. The telephone call was more productive than Commandant Leary had expected. He hung up the phone and went to Captain Newman's office. The door was open and Newman was scouring through histories of every disciplinary academy in the system. "Newman, you can do that later. I need to know if you're up to doing double duty. I can't promote you, but I *can* assure you that a promotion will come by next August. I can also give you overtime pay."

"Sure, Joe. What's up? Why do you need me to do double duty?"

"Come with me and find out," Commandant Leary offered, smiling.

Captain Newman followed his commandant to the door of the cadre adjutant. Commandant Leary did not bother to knock at the closed door; he simply went in, showing a notable lack of protocol. Cadre Major Sooner was seated at his desk, looking at a computer screen.

"You won't need to look at that anymore, Aldus. I checked with the battalion adjutant. At least I have one adjutant who knows his job. You are fired. Furthermore, you are prohibited from leaving the greater Ft. Waterline area pending investigation. If you want to call the senator, do it on your own facilities. Get out!" Commandant Leary held a steady voice throughout the entire speech.

"Just who do you think you are?" Aldus Sooner demanded. "You don't have the authority to fire me!"

"No, but the director does. The order is being faxed over right now. Actually, I believe I hear the fax machine just finishing up." Commandant Leary moved over to the machine and took up the printout. He immediately photocopied the document several times and then went into the cadre adjutant's office once again. "Here it is all nice and official looking. You are facing dereliction of duty charges, Aldus. The military will likely be court-martialing you. Now get out of my academy!"

Major Sooner looked at the order. He got up and stormed out of the cadre office. He was definitely going to call Senator Bronson on *this* one. How dare they accuse him of dereliction of duty just because some stupid Waterline cadets got off campus illegally? That couldn't possibly hold up. Could it?

As he got to the end of the PX building, Robert Crandon felt a pull on his arm. He then felt a crash on his head and bent over, reflexively. He immediately kicked back and upward, scoring a hit on something. He looked forward dazedly and saw a figure armed with a stick. The figure swung the stick into the right portion of Robert's chest, and Robert felt his ribs break. He also heard the words, "This one's for Gerralds." He charged forward, heedless of pain, and began pounding forward at the assailant's chest. When that person fell, he saw another holding a stick in two hands.

Robert grabbed the stick the next figure was holding and wrestled with the unknown holder. He kicked the figure's left leg, popping the knee. The figure let go of the weapon with a groan and Robert swung the stick into the figure's left arm.

Robert turned around and saw a cadet coming at him with yet another stick. He parried the blow, kicked hard with a backwards thrust toward the boy's chest and saw that assailant fall. He then saw one more cadet—he assumed this was the one who had clubbed him in the head since the end of the stick was red—charging toward him. He again used the stick he was holding to parry a blow from his assailant's weapon. Robert then grabbed the attacker's right arm and twisted him around, dislocating the shoulder. Robert then whipped his stick around onto the boy's right leg, causing the boy to fall to the ground.

Robert fell over the last attacker, straddling him on his hands and knees. When he heard a whistle blowing, Robert looked up quickly to identify himself as a cadet senior officer. It was a mistake. The blow to his head caused his brain to scramble when he moved it too quickly, and he immediately passed out.

When Cadet Lieutenant Robert Crandon first woke up again, he noticed a familiar figure and face. "Ma'am," he asked hopefully, "I don't suppose, by any chance, that you have changed jobs in the hospital in the last year?"

"No, I've been working here in ICU for three years, cadet," she answered.

"Aw, boogers! Not again!" Robert said and then passed out again.

Robert Crandon woke up with a blinding headache. He had been getting migraine headaches for over a year, but this one was by far the worst he had yet experienced. He groaned involuntarily and tried to hold his head. He figured that there must be a balloon in his head, trying to pop.

A nurse came over and asked him, "Where does it hurt, son?"

Without taking his hands from his eyes, Robert responded, "My head. It feels like it's going to explode!"

"I'll call the doctor and see if I can give you something for it," The nurse promised.

Another voice said, "Hey, sir? Do you think that you'll be awake for a while this time?"

"Probably," Robert answered. "Vianelli, is that you?" he asked, recognizing the Italian accent.

"Yes, sir. I've been waiting for you to wake up. We all have. That is, all eight of us, sir."

Robert opened his fingers a little to look out into the room. "All eight of you?" he asked the corporal cadet, seeing only one boy in the room.

"Yes, sir. All of your squad leaders and fire team leaders. We've been taking three-hour shifts for the last two days, sir. We volunteered once the commandant told us he needed someone to watch you."

"Umm … why did you—" here, Robert groaned again. Throughout the continuing time he continued to have problems controlling his response to the pain. "Why did you want to know if I would be awake?"

"The commandant wants us to call him once you are awake, sir. He says that it's very important," Art said. "Is it okay to go call him, sir? He said to only call him if you'll be able to talk to him. He said not to bother you if you aren't up to it."

"Go ahead and make the call, Art. I won't be sleeping with this headache!" Robert answered.

Commandant Leary was actually tired of hearing testimony concerning the "incident." He believed that he knew *exactly* what had happened. You don't get three *identical* testimonies with the same words. It just doesn't happen. Meanwhile, he had heard over fifty cadets tell a similar story with nary a one using the same exact words.

His telephone rang. He lifted the receiver and heard a voice that he had been hoping for. "You're sure he'll be awake?" He listened. "Okay, cadet. Good work. I'll be right over." He left the pile of police reports on his desk and immediately headed out of his office, out of the cadre office and to his car. The hospital was only two kilometers away, but he wanted to get there as fast as possible.

He entered the hospital and asked the receptionist if Cadet Crandon was still located in the ICU. "Oh, no, sir. They moved him to a semi-private room in neurology. It's, let me see ... room 412. May I let them know that you're coming?"

"That will be fine, miss. I'll find my own way there, thank you." Commandant Leary headed to the elevators and punched in the fourth floor. When he exited, he simply looked around for an armed guard. He was fairly certain that Crandon would be the only patient in the neurology section who was under guard. He went down the corridor and the guard stood up from his chair.

"Oh! It's you, sir. I understand that the cadet lieutenant is awake. The nurse has given him some Demerol to calm his headache. She said he might be woozy but will probably be awake for a while still."

"Thanks, soldier. I'll be sending the other cadet back to the academy. Please see that he has an escort. It *is* nighttime, after all."

"I can take him myself, sir; if you're going to stay with Cadet Crandon until I return," the sergeant offered.

"That's a deal, Sergeant." Commandant Leary graciously accepted.

Commandant Leary entered the hospital room. "Attention!" Corporal Cadet Arturo Vianelli called out instinctively.

"Sorry Art, but I can't do that," Robert replied weakly. "Who just arrived?" he asked.

"Commandant Leary, sir."

Robert waved his hand in the general direction of the door. He had a cold pack on a wet towel over his face. "Hello, sir. Nice of you to come visit," Robert offered.

"It's nice to see you conscious, cadet," Commandant Leary said warmly. "Art, there is an MP outside who will walk you back to the barracks. Tell the others that they no longer need to keep up the vigil." With that, Commandant Leary dismissed the cadet.

When the fire team leader had vacated the room, Commandant Leary began performing a duty that he felt was likely unnecessary, but required. "Okay, Rob, I am recording this. You have the right to remain silent. Anything you say may be used against you in a court of law or military court martial. You have the right to have counsel present when questioned. You have the right to refuse to answer any question that you believe may be incriminating against you. Do you understand your rights? Just say yes since I can't imagine *anybody* who is *still* in authority actually trying to prosecute you."

"Yes, sir. I understand my rights," Robert Crandon answered. "I'd tell you if you asked anyways, sir. If I've done anything wrong, I'm willing to take my lumps."

"I kind of figured you would regard things that way," Commandant Leary agreed. "Okay, you know that there was an … altercation, shall we say … a few days ago at the PX?"

"Yes, sir. I didn't exactly know that it was a few days ago until Corporal Cadet Vianelli mentioned that he and my other junior officers had been keeping a vigil for two days. However, I did know that an incident occurred—without anyone messing up my testimony," Robert agreed.

"Okay, good. So Vianelli didn't discuss anything with you?"

"No, sir."

"You consider that anything you tell me will be your own viewpoint?"

"Yes, sir."

"All right, Robert, go ahead and tell me what you remember. Use your judgment on where to begin," Commandant Leary more asked than ordered.

"I remember getting up from my table at the PX, sir. I had been talking with Sergeant Cadet Lorte and Cadet Morse. I had been mentioning to Norm—that is, Cadet Morse—that he was … associating … with people who would likely try to get him into trouble. Anyways, I went out of the PX and headed back to the barracks.

"I remember getting my arm grabbed and then being hit on the head. Now that I have had time to think about the incident, I can probably place names if you want, sir," Robert offered.

"Yes, go ahead and do that, but explain why you believe the names fit," Commandant Leary asked.

"Okay, well, something I had noticed was that the 'Gang of Three Plus One,' as we have come to label them, had left their table at the PX. The Gang of Three are Cadets Hersh, Hayes, and Gendron. We have been tracking them since I was made a Cadet Lieutenant. Lately, Cadet Alexander has been hanging around with them. Since he hasn't taken up any of their ... bad habits ... we used the term 'Plus One,' kind of as a way of saying, 'He may not be one of them.' These were the cadets I was warning Norm to stay away from.

"When I was leaving the PX, I had noticed that the table the Gang of Three Plus One had been sitting in was empty. I wasn't too worried about it. In retrospect, that may have been very dangerous."

"Go on, Robert," Commandant Leary encouraged.

"Yes, sir. Well, as I said, I left the PX, and when I got to the end of the building, I got grabbed by the arm and knocked on the head with a stick from behind. I back-kicked and made contact, probably with Hayes's groin. I saw Cadet Gendron in front of me. He smashed his stick into my right side, breaking ribs and probably collapsing my lung. It's kind of bad luck having the same ribs broken and the same lung collapsed, don't you think, sir?"

"Probably," Commandant Leary said.

"Well, anyways, now that I think on it, I thought I heard Gendron say, 'This one's for Gerralds.' That seems odd, since Cadre Captain Gerralds was not any more lenient on Cadet Gendron than anyone else. *Anyways*, I charged David Gendron and punched him in the chest a bunch of times as hard as I could. I'm not sure, but I think I may have given him more broken ribs than he gave me, sir.

"After I took down David Gendron I charged the next guy in line. I think it was Artie Alexander. I want to make it clear sir that *I charged him.* He had a stick in his hand, but he never swung it at me. Now that I think on it, I believe that he didn't want to have any part in this whole mess. I grabbed Artie's stick, kicked him, wrenched the stick out of his hands, and swung it at his left arm. I think I heard a crunch, so I may have broken his arm.

"I turned around and saw Bobby Hersh coming at me. I blocked his stick and did a back kick into his chest. Apparently, Hayes had recovered enough to give me another try. I dislocated his right shoulder and smacked his leg out from under him. After that, I was kind of spent. I fell down on my hands and knees. I heard a whistle blow, so I looked up to tell the guards that I was a cadet senior officer. As far as I know, I never got the chance. I don't remember anything else until I woke up for a short while in the ICU.

"I knew I was in the ICU because I recognized the nurse from last year. She confirmed that I was in the hospital in the ICU, as well. That's about it, sir. If you have questions"—here Robert gave a yawn—"I think I'll be up to answering them for a while, sir."

Commandant Leary looked at his notes. He had recorded the conversation, but he had also taken notes to remind him of questions he might want to ask. "You said that you were headed back to the barracks. Why were you heading back to the barracks so early? It was, according to the MPs, about 1115 or 1120 hours. Noon meal wasn't going to start for another forty-five minutes. A meal you were not even required to attend, at that."

Robert reached his hand to his left breast. "I don't have my gig book, sir!" Robert gave as an answer, his eyes bulging.

"I'm not interested in gigging you, cadet," Commandant Leary laughed.

"No, sir, I mean that I have stuff written in the book. I don't get that many gigs, so I kind of use it as a diary and reminder. Cadre Captain Toole said that I could do that," Robert answered.

"Oh, okay, let me look around here." Commandant Leary looked around the hospital room and found Robert's bloody dress-blues jacket in the closet. Inside the left breast pocket was Robert's gig book. "Found it." Commandant Leary assured his young charge.

"Well, sir, I was heading to the barracks to ask for an acetylene torch and all the stuff on the most recent page in the book. If I remember right, it included a metal pipe, glass, acetylene, and a mask," Robert explained. "Oh yeah, it also should include a metal stick to move melted glass and a fireproof mitten," he added.

"You forgot that you added welding metal and a tray to hold melted glass. Other than that, you seem to have remembered well. Now what I'd like to know is why the hell you'd think I would *approve* any of this! I'll admit that I happen to like your spunk and creativity, but I don't think I'd give you the tools to burn down my academy." Commandant Leary chuckled a little, mostly to let his cadet know that he was not angry at the request, just a little surprised.

"Oh! I never expected you to *approve* it, sir. I just expected you to *see* it. Then you would ask me why I wanted the stuff. I have two broken windows and a broken sink in my platoon barracks, sir. I've submitted six requests for work orders and nothing has happened. It's starting to get cold, and one of those windows is in the bedroom of two of my cadets, sir!" Robert explained.

"Why did you expect that the work orders would not get done?" Commandant Leary asked.

"Sir, the tape recorder," Robert said. Commandant Leary caught on and turned off the recording device. "I checked the files, sir. None of my work order requests have even been *filed*, sir!"

"Are you sure? Never mind, don't answer that question. Of course you're sure. Do you have any proof that you filed the requests?" Commandant Leary asked.

"Yes, sir. I got some carbon paper from Captain Thomas and copied the last five requests. The secretaries wouldn't let me use the photocopier, sir. I also have carbon copies of all of my other requests: broken furniture, tiles missing, that sort of stuff," Robert assured his commandant.

"Time to record again, Rob," The commandant stated and turned the device back on. "So you made carbon copies of the requests in order to prove that the work orders had been submitted?"

"Yes, sir," Robert agreed.

"Where are the carbon copies?"

"Sergeant Cadet Lorte has access to them, sir. We showed them to Major Zade, sir."

"Cadets Hersh, Hayes, and Gendron all testified that you ordered them out of the PX. Is that correct?" Commandant Leary asked.

"No, sir. I did not see them when I got up from my table. I could see everyone in the PX at that point, and they were definitely not there," Robert answered.

"Do you have any idea where the weapons came from?"

"No, sir. Now that you mention it, that is really, *really* strange. That they had weapons, that is, sir. I mean, there aren't any trees around for just that reason. Nobody in Waterline Academy should have been able to get sticks larger than toothpicks. I wonder where they managed to get them … " Robert answered.

"Okay, Rob. I think that's all I need for now." Commandant Leary turned off the recorder. "How are you feeling? I realize that you had a headache just a little while ago, but how are you doing otherwise?"

"Honestly, sir, I think that the knock on my head may be more serious than when Mr. Gerralds attacked me. My chest doesn't hurt as much. The nurse told me that my kidney was bruised. Strange that I don't remember any blow in the back. *Anyways*," Robert continued, "I think that my head is the real problem. Whenever I move it, my whole head acts like it's twirling around. I don't know exactly what's happening, but I think it might be serious. As a matter of fact, sir, I was kind of hoping that you'd find out for me."

"All right, cadet. I'll see if I can get some answers." Commandant Leary laughed.

Cadet Lieutenant Robert J. Crandon was in a very bad mood. He had just gigged his platoon sergeant, ungigged him, and then verbally chased him from the hospital room. He knew that it was the pain in his head that was the real problem. He had already pressed the button for the floor nurse, but she had other patients and might take a long while. "Sergeant Lorte, please come back in here!" Robert pleaded.

SFC Cadet Donald Lorte peeked into the room from the doorway. "I promise I won't get mad at you! Actually, I'm not mad at *you* anyways. I'm just in *lots of pain!*" Robert yelled. Robert bit himself on his right hand. He needed to find a way to stop yelling, and besides, the pain that he caused in his right hand just might overwhelm that in his head and give him a welcome distraction.

Lorte took a few tentative steps back into the room. "Are you *sure* you want me to come back, sir?" he asked.

Robert started to nod his head, thought better of it, and mumbled "Uh-huh" in a confirmatory manner while holding his head. Lorte took a few more steps into the room. "Donald, you and I have to have an understanding," Robert began. "When we're the only two in this hospital room, there are no protocol rules, okay. That means you don't have to call me sir, you don't have to salute, you don't need to ask for permission—since I'm your platoon leader, you never really needed to ask me for permission anyways—and most of all, you have to remember that I'm going to be in pain and that I don't *really* mean to be such a twit. Got that?"

"Okay, sir."

Robert extended his left hand and motioned Donald over to the bed. Donald obeyed, and Robert motioned him even closer. "Yes, sir?" Donald asked when he got about five centimeters from his platoon leader's face.

"Do me a favor," Robert asked.

"What's that, sir?"

"Stop calling me sir and start calling me *anything else*. I'll accept Rob, Robert, Robbie, You Twit, You Slime head, you obnoxious moron, just about anything except sir. Okay?"

"All right, sir," Donald agreed.

Robert rolled his eyes, which caused the pain in his head to instantly intensify. "Where's my nurse?" Robert yelled rhetorically.

Lt. Tangora, a nurse in the neurology section of Ft. Waterline Hospital, was busy that day. She knew what the red light flashing under the number 412 meant. She rushed to the room and saw a child in extreme pain. She took the syringe and needle in her hand and immediately went to his intravenous unit. She injected the fluid into the medicine section and increased the drip to get the powerful narcotic into the boy's bloodstream.

It wasn't until she had finished drugging her patient that she noticed another boy, probably in his early teens, standing next to the bed. "He'll be all right in a few seconds," she assured the older boy. "He keeps getting headaches from the blow he took to his head," she explained.

"Lt. Karen?" Robert asked. "If that's the case, then why do I get my headaches on the *left* side of my head, and in a place where there aren't any pain receptors?" Robert really, really wanted an answer to *that* question.

"I don't know, Robbie. I just don't know," she said apologetically while shaking her head. "I'll call Colonel Moore and tell him that you got another headache. He may want to come check you again," she added. She waited until her patient's breathing had normalized and the tightness in his face relaxed. She had seen the pain meter readings from Dr. Moore's tests. Her patient was not just feeling pain; his pain was often off the scale! That was definitely not good, to say the least.

After the nurse left, Donald asked, "Are you feeling any better, sir—I mean, Rob?"

Robert took a deep breath and relaxed some more. "Yeah. The stuff they give me is really strong. They're worried I'll get hooked, but Dr. Moore figures that it would be better for me to be hooked on my painkiller than in the quantity of pain he measured. He said it would even be more merciful to get me hooked on heroin than to have me go through the pain, although I think he was kidding about *that* part." Robert gave a weak smile toward his platoon sergeant. "Don't worry Don; I'm not going to get hooked on this or any other medicine. I promise," he added.

"Isn't that what all the addicts say?" Donald asked.

"Yeah, but they're not as strong as me!" Robert said and pretended to make his bicep bulge.

"I have got to get an assistant platoon leader." Robert changed the subject. "Are you sure you don't want a promotion? I'm sure I could get Captain Toole to approve it." Robert looked pleadingly into the other boy's eyes.

"Since the beginning of December, I've had a chance to compare platoon leader to platoon sergeant," Donald answered. "I prefer platoon sergeant … by a wide margin!" he added.

"Okay. Then the next thing we have to do is figure out who would make a good platoon leader out of those available," Robert said.

"How about Sergeant Flynn?" asked Donald.

"He's fifteen!" Robert exclaimed. In a calmer voice, he added, "He's probably the same as you. He won't want it."

"That means Frank Hunt will also not do it, I suppose," Donald said.

"We need to think of the *squad* leaders, Don. They're the ones who might take the job. The platoon sergeants are sitting fat and happy. They don't want the responsibility," Robert said.

"How about Ronnie Logan?" Donald suggested.

"I'm not sure that Tom Peters would even give him up. Of course, I could try to *force* the issue. Okay, write him down," Robert suggested.

"Roy Powers might do it, too. He's kind of young, but … " Donald suggested.

"Young?" Robert giggled. "He's two years older than me! Anyways … do you think he could pull it off? I mean, if I helped him?" Robert saw a possibility emerging.

"He was my fire team leader two years ago, when I was first a squad leader. He's got his head screwed on right, at least. He's not a bully, either," Donald said.

"That's the kind of guy we need," Robert agreed. "Bullies make bad leaders. You might get away with one as a platoon sergeant or squad leader, but they make really bad senior officers. They let the *supposed* power go to their heads. Being a cadet senior officer is more about serving than ordering guys around.

"If you think he's okay, then go to Major Stevens and tell him that *I* recommended him. It'll go over better that way. It's not that he wouldn't listen to you. He and Darryl would talk about it all night and come to the same conclusion we did. We're just saving them the conversation—maybe. They respect a senior officer's suggestion more. That's just the way they think, okay?"

"No problem," Donald said. "Anything else, s ... uh, Rob?"

"Yeah. If you don't get either Powers or Logan in three days, come back here and let me know. If you get somebody *else*, get back here immediately—well, as soon as you can. I don't want some idiot screwing up *my* platoon. Keep drilling the guys on the required knowledge stuff and the marching. Have them sing the songs I made up whenever you get the chance. By the way, did you say we finally got our windows replaced?" Robert asked.

"Yeah, and all the furniture, and they're working on the plumbing now too! They cause an awful mess, but we clean it up every night," Donald answered. He added in a whisper, "Sometimes we even work in the dark after 'lights out.'"

"Don't worry about that," Robert assured his platoon sergeant. "Cadets have been doing that since before we were born, before Darryl was born, even."

Robert closed his eyes to rest. "Hey, Donald," he prompted.

"Yeah, Rob?"

"Thanks for putting up with a grumpy little snit."

"Hey! That's what platoon sergeants are for. We do that all the time." Donald smiled.

"Yeah, I suppose. When you go ask for Powers, ask Colonel Marks to come visit me?"

"Okay, Rob. I'm sure he'll want to."

"Good night, Don."

"It's 0900 hours, sir."

"That's okay. Good night Don." With that, the ten-year-old boy succumbed to the powerful pain medication and fell asleep.

A CADET HOMECOMING

"May I go back? Please?" the little boy pleaded.

Cadet Lieutenant Robert Crandon is nothing if not persistent, thought Dr. Moore. "Just *why* would you *want* to go back there?" Dr. Moore asked his patient. He had heard enough about Waterline Academy to know that the cadets were not usually fond of returning.

"Because my platoon *needs* me!" Robert pleaded.

"I'll make a deal with you, cadet," Dr. Moore continued, holding up two fingers, "I'll let you travel back there for two hours—just two hours—each day for the next week. If you make it through without any big problems, then I'll consider allowing you more time." As a military doctor, he understood the desire to help those in one's command. He just could not believe that a ten-year-old boy would feel the same way.

"It's a deal, sir!" Robert agreed. "You let me know what you want me to do. I won't even *try* to get around anything. I promise!"

"Okay, then listen carefully. Your cadre said that you have an eidetic memory, so I won't even bother writing down all the restrictions. I'm just going to write, "Restricted" on your profile. You will tell your cadre what restrictions you have *and need*. Is that a deal?"

"Yes, sir!"

"You will not do anything that causes your head to move rapidly. You will not do anything to cause the blood to pump too rapidly. You will return if you fall to the ground. You will not climb nor have others carry you upstairs. Those are your restrictions. I'm *trusting* you, cadet. Don't let me down."

"I won't let you down, sir. If I have any problems, I'll come right back to the hospital. I promise," Robert assured the doctor.

"I'll call your cadre and have someone bring some uniforms for you. I will also let your cadre officer know that he has to transport you back and forth," Dr. Moore said.

Cadre Captain Peter Toole carried a suit carrier into Ft. Waterline Hospital. He went directly to the elevator and pushed the "four" button. When the elevator opened again, he made his way to Room 412. He was looking forward to this return more than he wanted to show. He stopped before he reached the end of the hallway and tried to get his composure. *No matter how stupid his assignment to Waterline was, I still have to treat him as a Waterline Cadet,* he thought to himself. He put on a neutral, although not stern, face and went into the room.

"Cadet Crandon, I'm here to take you to the academy. You have two hours to check out your platoon and then I'm bringing you back. Any questions?"

"Yes, sir."

"What is it?"

"Are those my convalescent PJs?" Robert asked.

Captain Toole could not contain himself. He chuckled a little and answered, "Yes, cadet. That's what is in here." Captain Toole unzipped the suit carrier and took out the uniform that Jim Thomas, the Waterline Academy Quartermaster, had given to him. He helped his young charge get dressed. "All set?" he asked.

"I *think* so, sir," Robert answered honestly. "I have to take it really slowly, though. The doctor doesn't want me to get too woozy."

Captain Toole had been briefed on Crandon's condition. Three days after he had been attacked, Robert had gone back into emergency surgery to repair a broken blood vessel in his brain. Robert was suffering from migraine or cluster headaches, exacerbated by the trauma to his head. He still had broken ribs that were trying to heal as well. Colonel Moore had actually bet Robert that he could not walk. After Robert proved that suggestion wrong, Colonel

Moore had made a deal with the boy: no more than two hours at the academy each day for a week.

"I've seen devotion to duty," Colonel Moore had told the commandant, "but this is ridiculous." Commandant Leary had passed on that part of the conversation to Captain Toole.

"He's your responsibility, Pete. Let him come back and help his platoon, but keep a *very* close watch on him. Do *not* let him try anything outside his profile limitations."

Do not let him try anything outside his profile? thought Captain Toole. *His profile just says, "Restricted—ask cadet." How am I supposed to even know if he tries anything outside his profile?*

The cadre officer and the cadet walked slowly to the elevator. "I've been on the elevator, sir," Robert assured his cadre officer. "It goes slowly enough for me. I don't get nauseous or anything." Instead of that statement being reassuring, it actually alarmed Captain Toole. Captain Toole had not even considered that the movement of an elevator might have the potential to cause this boy harm.

"Are you *sure* you're up to this?" Captain Toole asked.

"I won't know until I try it, sir," Robert answered. He considered the answer obvious, but had learned that many things *he* considered obvious, others had never even thought about. "If I have *any* problems, I *will* tell you. I promised Dr. Moore, sir."

The two made their way to the government car that the academy had procured from Ft. Waterline. Captain Toole drove so as to minimize any abrupt changes in speed. He parked in the Charlie Company lot and got out. Robert Crandon opened his door and got up very carefully. Captain Toole went to the cadre office; Robert Crandon went to Charlie-3's stairway door.

"Charlie-3, time to assemble outside!" Robert called. He moved away from the doorway, just in case some of his platoon cadets were too enthusiastic in their rush down the stairs. Third Platoon, Charlie Company was, in fact, very excited to get their platoon leader back.

They rushed down the stairs like a herd of wild elephants. They quickly formed up into platoon formation and awaited further instructions.

"Charlie-3 ready for your inspection, sir," Cadet Roy Powers said. His status had not yet been determined, so at the moment, he was unofficially given the rank of 3rd Lieutenant.

"At ease!" Lieutenant Crandon ordered. The platoon went into the more relaxed stance. "I've been hearing some good things about your progress," Crandon continued. "I've also been hearing about some problems with your academics. We are going to form study groups so that you can all help each other out. I want you to begin concentrating on your academic grades. You passed First Inspection. I believe that you will also pass Second Inspection. So long as you all keep your noses clean, we may be the first platoon in the history of this academy to see everybody get passes for Christmas Common Week." There was a cheer from the platoon.

"I want you to give Lieutenant Powers just as much cooperation as you gave to me. I have been giving him some ideas of things to check, and I know that he's been doing his best. You guys have got to help him, though. If you think something *may* need to be done, tell him. Don't get lazy just before Second Inspection! If we pass that well, we are well on our way to finishing the year as the top platoon!" Robert took a long pause to let his speech sink in.

"I still can't go up the stairs, so you will all have to look for anything that can be gigged. You know what we did for First Inspection. Repeat it! Third inspection doesn't come until March, so this is it for three months. The inspection is in one week. I expect all of you to do your *own* stuff. Last time, we had groups doing the polishing of boots or brass, the waxing of floors—that kind of stuff. You can't make it in this academy if you don't learn to do the things yourself. You are to prepare your own stuff for inspection.

"You can ask for directions or techniques, but you are *not* to ask for help in getting the stuff done. Each room is to be waxed by the guys living in it. The only things that are to be done by group are the common stuff ... the corridor, latrine, and common room. Before you get too skittish, is there anybody who thinks he can't pass inspection on any particular item?" Lieutenant Crandon asked.

Several boys raised their hands. Lieutenant Crandon began taking notes about who needed help with boots, brass, placement of uniform items and other needs. After he compiled the list he said, "Platoon attention!" The platoon responded immediately. "Cadets will fall out and go back into the barracks, cadet officers will remain here for further instruction. Charlie-3, fall out!"

After the other cadets had remounted the stairs, Lieutenant Crandon addressed the junior officers. "I meant it when I said that each cadet must do his own stuff. I'll have Lieutenant Powers give you the list of guys who need to learn techniques better. You are to help them learn, not do it for them. Is that clear?"

"Yes, sir!" the Charlie-3 officer corps responded.

"I also expect *you guys* to do your own stuff. That should go without saying, but I'll say it again anyways. You lead by example. You do your own stuff. Now, changing the subject, do we have any discipline problems?"

The cadet officers thought about that for a short while. Sergeant Lorte responded for the group. "We seem to have anger management problems taken care of, sir. They stopped clobbering each other a few weeks ago and Juan takes the more ... umm ... hostile?" Sergeant Lorte was looking for the right word, "guys to the gym every day just before noon meal and evening meal. That seems to get out their need to punch things. We haven't had anybody 'slip on bars of soap' since you went into the hospital—earlier than that even."

"Okay, squad leaders and fire team leaders head up to the barracks; I need to speak with the platoon sergeant and assistant platoon leader." The squad officers immediately made their way up to the Charlie-3 barracks. "Okay, you two. What do we need to do in order to get a one hundred on Second Inspection?" Robert asked.

"Well, sir," Lieutenant Powers began, "Second Inspection is pretty much the same as First Inspection. If the platoon passed that one, shouldn't we pass Second Inspection as well?"

"If that were the case," Robert explained, "then all the cadets who ever passed with a one hundred would always get a one hundred. Yet, we know that each year, they all seem to start from scratch. Granted, the cads change the rules each year, but even still, you'd expect a better showing. It just doesn't happen. That's why platoon leaders go nuts in September and October. They just can't believe that guys they had the previous year can be so dumb as to forget everything they learned.

"I want this inspection! I want every guy to pass with a one hundred percent score! It's never been done before, so I want us to win! That's the only way to show up *former* Cadre Major Sooner. I get to keep coming back each day, probably about 1900 hours like today. I'll try to get my brains to unscramble enough to get up the stairs in a few days. I need you two to take really, *really* good notes. I can only tell you what to look for. I can't do all the looking. That's why you guys get paid the big bucks, right?"

"We'll get the platoon to one hundred percent, sir," Donald Lorte assured his platoon leader.

"Roy, do you need anything? I mean like cleaning stuff, polish—that sort of thing?"

"No. Your suggestion that I go see the quartermaster officer paid off. He gave me all sorts of extra stuff! Does he do that for all the senior officers?"

"No, only the ones smart enough to ask," Robert answered as he winked. "Okay, I guess I'll go see Captain Toole and tell him that I'm ready to go back." Robert appeared less than enthusiastic about that prospect. "At least I may get to come back in a week if I can keep my head unscrambled. Don, how about spotting me to the cadre office?"

Robert finally got Dr. Moore to allow him up the stairs. When Robert looked at the barracks he knew he had to get his platoon in shape! They were not cleaning the place well enough, the floors were not polished to the glass shine that Robert wanted. He began to get them organized and working to his specifications.

He also began to check out their marching. During Second Inspection each platoon would have to perform marching drills. Charlie-3 was clearly not ready yet. Robert met with Roy Powers daily before the former's visits to the Academy. They went over the paperwork required to be kept by each platoon leader. Since paper work for plebes was more extensive, the work was beyond Roy's ability to cope with it.

The strain of trying to get everything perfect was starting to show up in the cadets' attitudes. In addition, Robert's headaches kept coming back as he strained to get his platoon members to the perfection he believed they needed. Robert reminded them that a cadre officer could ban them from common week for any reason—they had to keep up positive attitudes. He warned them that if they wanted a pass they would have to shine out. Just passing would not be enough.

One evening, as Robert was about to head to Captain Toole to be taken back to the hospital, a voice from the base of the stairs called, "Formation!"

Robert began to head down the stairs. That was a mistake. His platoon had been well-drilled on the requirement to get into formation as quickly as possible. Robert was heading down the stairs carefully when a stampeding herd of cadets charged down the same stairs.

Robert's world began to twist and turn. He felt a few bumps to his head and body, but nothing too serious. Meanwhile he regained the knowledge that he was likely in a stairwell. He tried to reach out and grab the hand railing. Eventually he was able to grab onto something solid and not moving—at least as far as he could tell.

"I've got you, Rob," a caring voice said. Robert opened his eyes and saw the world spinning uncontrollably. He also recognized Roy Power's face. "Are you going to be okay?"

"Maybe eventually?" Robert suggested.

Cadre Captain Toole arrived. "What happened?" he asked.

"The platoon headed down the stairs for formation while Rob was there," Roy explained.

Captain Toole understood immediately. "Come on, cadet. We're heading back."

Robert was no longer allowed to head to his academy. The stairwell incident had caused too much damage. Dr. Moore was adamant. The cadet would not be heading back to the Academy until after Second Inspection. No matter how much Robert grumbled about it, Dr. Moore would not budge.

"Why are you so upset?" Lt. Tangora asked the cadet.

"My platoon needs me!" Robert insisted.

"Well, you had a lot of time with them. Didn't they learn?"

That got the cadet to thinking. Why was he so insistent on being there? Roy Powers visited him each day. Donald Lorte came quite often as well. Surely they could get the platoon to pass the inspection.

But I need them to get to their families! Robert told himself.

Then he began wondering again. No cadets had ever gotten a pass their first year. In fact, Cadre Captain Gerralds had specifically banned Robert during his first Christmas Common Week. Why was it so important to him that they get passes?

We have to show up Cadre Major Sooner! Robert told himself. Then he wondered about why he would be so concerned about a defunct former cadre officer. Major Sooner could not possibly ban any of his cadets—not anymore! Why was he so afraid that something terrible would happen to them?

That is when he came to an epiphany. He was afraid. He had always assumed that he had been banned for not doing well enough. He had tried and tried to be perfect, but something always seemed to hold him back.

No, that's silly, he told himself. Commandant Leary specifically told me that I would have gone on pass my first Easter. Why should I worry that they would get banned?

He finally realized the he was afraid that *he* would not get a pass. He was afraid that any poor performance by his platoon would reflect *his own* failure. Now he knew his mistake. These guys were, for the most part, psychopaths. They *needed* to be at the Academy. Harry Tromp had once tried to explain it to Robert. Now Robert remembered those words and finally understood them.

"Robbie these guys are not like you and me. We care about others. We can understand the pain that others are feeling. We think about what our actions will do to others. They don't get it. They *can't* get it. Even Darryl and John (Stevens) can't get it.

"That's why they're here. The Cads make them try to guess what they want. They make all the guys worry about anything that any Cad might find wrong. It gets them used to thinking about what someone else is thinking. It's the best that they can do with these guys.

"You know why I'm here?" Harry asked.

"Because you lit your school on fire, right?" Robert asked.

"Yeah. This is the only place where they figured I couldn't get my hands on matches and stuff. There are some other guys who are fire-bugs too. You know who they are as well, I assume. All cadet officers have to know.

"Anyways, like I was saying, most of these guys—all except us fire-bugs—are here because they don't feel other guys' pain. First we get them to realize that they need other guys' help. Then we get them to realize that they won't get the help they need if they don't help others."

Robert had his second epiphany of the day. Robert finally understood the simple yet sublime design of the Academy. The cadre officers were specifically trained to make the cadets have to think about what they (the cadre) were thinking. In order to replace their incapacity to feel for others, the system forced them to constantly think about what others needed. Clearly it worked. Graduates of Waterline Academy were model citizens. Robert finally understood why the things he had put up with for over four years had been done.

He wondered how Harry could have known that he was not like the others. Harry was very smart but usually slow on the uptake. Perhaps Harry could just sense that Robert did not have the psychopathic tendencies of their Academy mates.

Then Robert thought about his own role in the Academy. Why was he there? Why had the cadets made sure that he got promoted so quickly? Those answers would have to wait for another day to be solved.

Robert Crandon's mood was changing by the day and the hour. He was reading novel after novel and was vocally expressing his emotions. Lieutenant Karen Tangora watched as the boy tore through his entire reading list. He shouted at the obnoxious behavior of Tom Sawyer; then he laughed and cried during Huckleberry Finn and Jim's trip down the Mississippi River—once again shouting at Tom's antics. He yelled at King Lear, "You idiot! Why change your mind about your third daughter just because she doesn't give you a bunch of words!" He finished the play, but considered the following four acts to be utterly predictable. He cried when Ophelia and Hamlet died. He cheered on Mark Anthony during *Julius Caesar* and yelled at him in *Anthony and Cleopatra*.

He changed authors and read James Fennimore Cooper. He was laughing throughout the novel and Lieutenant Tangora asked why. "How can an Indian miss a twenty-foot barge going slowly down the river when he's on an overhanging branch?" Lieutenant Tangora decided not to answer. Finishing that novel, he switched again, this time to Charles Dickens. Lieutenant Tangora had to threaten him twice about his yelling. "But … why? Why did he have Oliver give half his inheritance to Monks? Monks squandered more than what was left trying to get Oliver *executed!*" During his reading of *Great Expectations* Lieutenant Tangora *did* give him a sedative. He proceeded to *A Tale of Two Cities*, and told Lieutenant Karen, as he called her, that it was a good thing she did give him a sedative.

"It's almost Christmas, Robbie. Why don't you try *A Christmas Carol?*" Lieutenant Tangora suggested, hoping it would improve the boy's mood. That worked. He loved the redemption tale, which, Lieutenant Tangora thought in retrospect, only made sense. Unfortunately, that only worked for one night. The next day, he began reading *Moby Dick* by Herman Melville. He began grumping about halfway through the book.

"What's wrong *this time?*" the nurse asked.

"Lt. Karen, this guy seems to think God is the cause of all *his* problems. He needs to get his head out of his butt and realize that God isn't limited by time. All this predestination stuff is dumb. If Ahab wanted to avoid the whale, why didn't he just move to Michigan? It's a pretty good bet that the White Whale wasn't going to go after him there!" Later on, he actually cheered when Moby Dick wiped out Ahab and *The Pequod*.

Lt. Tangora was worried when the boy took up his next Melville novel, *Bartleby the Scribner*. To her great surprise, Robert seemed to agree with Bartleby. When she asked the boy why there was a difference in his readings of the two novels, he replied, "Well, I wouldn't say that I agree with Bartleby's tactics, but I can understand his motives. He finally decided that he didn't want people to push him around anymore. He was willing to take the consequences and didn't whine or complain like Ahab did. I wouldn't just give up, but at least Bartleby was willing to face the consequences with honor."

As the days passed, Robert's headaches became less frequent, if not less severe. He was finally placed on medication that could be taken by mouth, in an attempt to break him free from his dependency on being near the hospital. The medication appeared to work without too many bad side effects. Robert was hoping that he would soon be allowed to leave the hospital. He had already finished his reading list and did not expect to receive any more books from Professor O'Connor, his literature professor.

December 19, 1973 was the date for Second Inspection at Waterline Academy. Cadet Lieutenant Robert Crandon was in a very sour mood. He could not be present for the inspection on that Wednesday; he was stuck in his hospital room. He looked at his trigonometry problems once again. He wrote down all twenty answers without showing any work. *If he wants to see the work, I'll show him the hole in my head and say, "It's in there, professor,"* Robert thought. He turned the pages of the book and began doing the problems on the following pages as well. He continued this for a few hours, trying to ignore his increasing pain.

Lt. Tangora entered his room just as he was completing one of the pages of problems. "I thought you might like to know that your inspection is finished," she said.

"Did they give you the results, Lieutenant Karen?" Robert asked eagerly. He noticed that the clock showed the time to be 1400 hours.

"I'm sorry. They said that the results wouldn't be ready until tomorrow, Robbie. I'm sure your platoon did well," she added cheerfully.

"I think so too." Robert grumped. "But I don't want well, I want perfect!"

Lt. Tangora shook her head. *Just what kind of cadets are they breeding these days?* she wondered to herself. To Robert, she asked, "How much pain are you feeling in your head and chest?"

Robert thought about the question for a moment; then he did a mental examination of himself. "Probably a level-seven headache and level-three chest pain," he answered. He had been taught the one-to-ten scale that Dr. Moore wanted him to use. Level five was enough pain that it could not be ignored.

"If you have that bad of a headache, then why didn't you call for me? I can give you some more medication." The nurse immediately took a syringe and needle from her carrying case and moved over to the boy. "Give me your left arm," she commanded. Robert obediently followed the order and received the shot.

"Why not the pills?" Robert asked.

Lt. Tangora smiled. "Because you didn't tell me when you got the headache. Maybe this will teach you to mention that you're in pain," she teased the boy. She squeezed his nose ever so slightly.

"I wanted to get my homework done before the drugs made me too sleepy," he offered as an explanation. "After I got started, I kind of lost track of time. At least I've almost finished the book," he added with a smile.

Lt. Tangora looked at the book title. "You almost finished *Advanced Mathematics, 11?*" she asked incredulously. She looked at the problems in the book and reasoned that the *11* meant grade, not age.

"Well, I know that I should have gotten through this sooner, but my head hurt," Robert offered as an explanation. "Besides, I'm not eleven … yet. I'll try harder if you think I'm not doing enough, ma'am." Robert appeared worried that the nurse was going to report him for laziness.

"That's okay, cadet. You go at your own pace. I'm sure that your teacher will … cut you some slack," Lieutenant Tangora offered. She left the room shaking her head.

Robert Crandon continued to work on his trigonometry problems, just in case. Even though he could feel the effects of the drugs slowing down his thought processes, he spent the next hour finishing up the last twenty pages. When he finished, he put the book aside and lay back in his bed to rest. He thought about the inspection that he had just missed. *Did they do it?* he wondered silently. He ran over every instruction he had given to Donald Lorte and Roy Powers. *If they did, I hope that Captain Toole puts them in for a commendation medal.*

Having finished his trigonometry book and his reading list, Robert was bored. He lay back and let the drugs take effect, falling asleep. He did not wake up until 0500 the next morning. When he awoke, he got up and performed his daily ritual of exercise. He was still *strictly* prohibited from conducting any kind of intense physical activity: that meant no push-ups, sit-ups, or running. He had decided, days ago, to substitute his physical training regimen with isometric exercises instead.

After completing about thirty minutes of the self-resistance movements he had been taught in his various self-defense courses, he took his shower and went to the closet in his hospital room to find which uniform had been left for him.

He was surprised to see a uniform that resembled dress blues; up to this time this academic year, he had only had convalescent parade uniforms. The trousers and shirt were made of soft cotton that resembled the pajamas that he was so used to for convalescent uniforms. He took the shirt; the only pieces of insignia that were not made of cloth were his lieutenant bars. The dress blues Jacket reminded him of a bathrobe. It had all of his medals and insignia sewn into the cloth, once again other than the gold lieutenant bars. The convalescence dress blues were nearly the same as last year. He looked at the right breast pocket and saw the name "CRANDON" in capital letters, so he knew it must be meant for him. He looked around for socks and dress shoes but could only find some black, fuzzy slippers. He tried those on, and they fit perfectly. He then greeted his guard and went for a walk around the hospital ward.

As he walked around the hospital ward, he looked into the other rooms to see if any other patients were awake. He found one soldier sitting up and asked if he might join the man. "You're from Waterline Academy, huh?" the soldier asked.

"Yes, sir. This is my fifth year there, sir," Robert answered.

"Well I'm pleased to meet you, cadet. My name is Specialist Carney. What brings you into the hospital, son?"

"I got hit in the head with a stick."

"Better than what happened to me," the specialist answered. "I got hit in the head with a bullet. Dr. Moore says that I'll be all right though. How about you?"

"He told my cadre officer that I got a broken blood vessel in my brain. He had to operate a second time because of that. I get headaches, but I don't think that they're from the stick. I mean, that may have made me get more of them, but I've been getting headaches for a long time before I got hit with the stick."

"Somebody conk you?" the specialist asked.

"Yes, sir. Another cadet. Actually, three other cadets, but only one hit my head," Robert explained. "I think that they're in really big trouble."

"What happens to them?" Specialist Carney asked.

"Well, it depends on the cadre, sir. If they go by past occurrences, then they only have maybe three incidents in all the academy system. We had a cadre officer who used to like making us copy down the past offenses and punishments of cadets, so I know most of the incidents.

"*Anyways*," Robert continued, "there was this one time when three cadet lieutenants took out their company commander. He was a cadet captain, sir. I don't think my case will follow that one. The cadre gave each cadet lieutenant a minor punishment and expelled the captain for being such a pain. That was in Boise Academy.

"The next one was when two cadets from Baton Rouge attacked their platoon sergeant with sticks out in the field. He easily took them out, but the cadre gave them fifty major penalties, expelled them and confined them to Reform School until they were eighteen.

"The only other incident was from my academy. A single cadet attacked a cadet lieutenant, hitting him on the head with a history book. That guy was given fifty majors, expelled, and confined just like the Baton Rouge guys. So ... if my cadre follows precedents ... then those guys are probably headed to reform school." Robert had tears in his eyes after telling this news to the specialist.

"Why so sad?" asked Carney. "They're getting what they deserve, aren't they?"

"Probably, sir. But Waterline Academy is there to *redeem* us, not to condemn us. The rate of incarceration out of Reform School is one hundred percent! I don't like to see any cadets fail, sir," Robert said, wiping the tears from his eyes. "Even if they did attack me and increase my headaches and collapse my lung," he added.

Specialist Carney nodded his understanding. "So how did you get shot, sir?" Robert asked him.

"I was rescuing some other guys who had been caught in an ambush," Carney answered. "We were stationed near Hue, in Vietnam that is, and were on patrol. When they got hit they called for a medic. That was me."

"Wow!" Robert exclaimed. "Then you're a hero!"

"I guess..." Spc. Carney said. "I just did what I thought I needed to do."

"Isn't that what heroes are made of, sir—people who do what they need to do when the chips are down?"

"I never really thought about it that way, cadet. I guess you're right. Heroes don't plan to be heroes. They just get caught up in a bad situation and do whatever looks like it might work."

"How are things going over there, sir?" Robert asked. "I know some of the history since I took *Modern World History*, but I don't get much by way of current news."

"Then you know that we sent thousands of troops into Vietnam when they invaded Cambodia and Laos?" Spc. Carney asked. Robert nodded yes. "Well the Vietnamese had dug all sorts of tunnels when they were fighting the Japs and later the Frenchies. It's been hard as hell to get them out of those places. The openings are hid all over the jungle. Whenever we fight in Laos or Cambodia, we win easily. In Vietnam, the tables are turned on us. We're still kicking their behinds—don't get me wrong—but it's not easy at all."

Robert took in all the information stoically. He wondered if the world would find a way to peace before his brothers came of military age. "Is that what you guys were doing, sir?" Robert asked. "Searching for tunnel openings?" he explained.

"Yeah. Stupid Viet Cong!" Spc. Carney exclaimed. "They killed two of my friends over there. They've hurt a lot more. At least the docs and nurses are able to save a lot of the guys who get hurt."

"And the medics!" Robert added cheerfully.

Spc. Carney smiled. "Yeah. Us too." He yawned and then said. "Thanks for talking to me, Crandon. It really cheered me up. Sorry, but I'm getting sleepy. I'm still on Cambodian time."

Robert took his leave and continued to explore the hospital ward. At 0700, he heard his name being called. "Over here!" he answered. "I'm on this side." He began to move toward the caller, remembered not to run, and slowly made his way back to room 412.

"You need to eat your breakfast," Nurse Olivia Frazier ordered. She had the double silver bars of a captain on her lapel. "Your cadre officer will be here to pick you up in about an hour," she explained.

"Where's Lieutenant Karen, ma'am?" Robert exclaimed. "I promised I would say good-bye to her."

"Lt. Karen?" Captain Frazier asked. "Oh! You mean Lieutenant Tangora. She said that she has to go to an assembly today. I'm sure your cadre will allow you to return to say good-bye on another day, cadet." Robert was less than certain, but he said nothing further about it.

About the time that Robert finished eating, Dr. Moore came in. Robert instinctively stood up. "As you were," Dr. Moore said. Robert sat back down and finished the last few morsels of his peach. "Your cadre is coming to retrieve you today, Robbie. I've already told them your further restrictions, so they won't have to ask you. I know that Christmas Common Week is coming up. I have approved you to take the train. You can't fly in an airplane just yet. Commandant Leary is looking into the wherefores and hows to get you back home."

"I thought you said that I was going to the academy *today*, sir," Robert said.

"You are."

"But you just said that Commandant Leary was looking into how to get me there, didn't you sir?"

"I meant how to get you to Massachusetts, Robbie, not Waterline Academy. Do you really think of Waterline Academy as your *home*?" Dr. Moore asked.

"Yes, sir. I mean, it's where I live. I visit my family ... and some friends," he added, remembering Mary-Ann Rowell, "but that's not home, sir. Not anymore, it isn't. I'm stuck in the academy until I turn eighteen. That's my home. It's my whole world, sir."

"That's a pretty small world, Robbie."

"Yes, sir. That's why I've gotten to know every pebble and blade of grass. I want to know everything I can about my world."

"What happens when you have to join the rest of us?"

"Then I'll probably be a chemist, sir. Maybe I'll join the army first. I don't know. I definitely want to be a chemist, though."

"You could be a science officer," Dr. Moore suggested. He moved over to the stack of books piled next to Robert's hospital bed. He began to read the titles. "What are these?" he asked.

"Homework, sir," Robert answered. "but I've already finished all of those. I'm kind of hoping that my professors will have something else for me to read when I go to my parents' house."

Dr. Moore nearly choked. He saw before him more books than he ever had to read in a single year during his years in the university. He noticed the physics textbook and asked, "No biology or human physiology?"

"I took those last February through May, sir. I'm all done with *those* classes. I finished up Chemistry II last month. Well ... really two months ago, sort of. I finished it at the end of October, sir. Captain Newman said that I've just about finished all the academics that Waterline Academy has to offer. I'm also taking French, Spanish, and German, but they didn't send those books to me. I guess they figured that I wouldn't have anyone to teach me the speech patterns," Robert answered.

"Are you sure you're in the right academy?" Dr. Moore asked.

"Well ... my first-grade teacher, Mrs. Rowell, and my parents told me that there was a big mix up. They wanted me to go to Bethesda, but, as they say, once in the van, there's no turning back, sir. Not only that, but due to a computer glitch, I'm stuck *here*. I can't even leave after my six years are up. DOD rules won't allow it. I got eight bans after the first year, so I have to stay here or go to reform school, and I *definitely* don't want to go *there!*" Robert answered.

"How could a computer glitch keep you in Waterline Academy?" Dr. Moore wondered aloud.

"Well sir, it has to do with all those *bans*. It turns out that I should have gotten *passes*, but since the secretaries typed in zeroes instead of *O*s, I got banned. Once the data was put into the computers in the Pentagon, it couldn't be changed. That means that, by law, I have to attend Waterline Academy until either I turn eighteen or Congress changes the rules. I've been told that Congress is not going to change the rules, so..." Robert offered his explanation, shrugging.

"There are times when I really *hate* bureaucracies," Dr. Moore growled.

"It's okay, sir. I believe that I won't spend my life in prison, so Waterline Academy has *helped* me, sir. And ... I have been able to help others because I was sent here. I helped to get rid of *Mister* Gerralds, sir. That would be worth any punishment the academy wanted to give me. He's a real monster, sir."

"*You're* the cadet he attacked?" Dr. Moore asked. Robert nodded yes. "We don't get to know the names of cadets. Well, that is, the papers don't. It's illegal to print their names or show their photographs in the papers, for privacy purposes. I didn't know that you were the cadet he attacked. That does explain the healed damage to your skull, though. I guess he hit you just behind your right eye?"

"Yes, sir. With a metal swagger stick. My headaches started coming more often after that. I didn't mind too much, because I only got a headache maybe once or twice a month. Dr. Salwart said that they were migraines and that I should just take Tylenol."

"I'm hoping that their frequency dies down. We should have a pretty good idea in about a month. I want you to keep up your headache diary. That's very important."

"Yes, sir! It's right here." Robert pulled out the gig book in his left, breast pocket. "I keep the diary in my gig book, sir. I'm supposed to have it at all times ... except during PT, that is ... and you won't let me do PT anyways. So I have my diary at hand all the time, sir."

"Good boy!" Dr. Moore praised him. "You keep that up and whenever you get a headache mark the time and how painful it gets. If it dies down, write that up ... and why it died down. Just make abbreviations for the meds you take. Put a big *T* for Tylenol. Use an *F* for Fioricet. Use *F/C* for Fioricet with codeine, like that. I'll review your diary from time to time and change the medication as needed."

"I will, sir. Of course ... you'll have to give the pills to one of my cadre officers, sir. We're not allowed to have any medications on us, not in Waterline Academy. That's probably for the best, sir," Robert answered.

At 0800 hours Cadre Captain Toole entered the hospital room to pick up his charge. Cadet Crandon and Dr. Moore had finished talking. "Are you ready to go, Robert?" asked Captain Toole.

"No sir," Robert answered. "I don't have any socks, and I didn't find a lieutenant's hat," he explained.

"Oh. Well "—Captain Toole looked at the cadet's feet—"you don't need socks. Did they leave any dress blues hat?"

"Yes, sir. There's a field grade officer's hat, but I'm not supposed to wear that," Robert answered.

"Well, we don't have enough time. Just wear that one, and if anyone asks, tell them that I gave the order. We have to go to an assembly. It starts in fifteen minutes, so we'll just take you as you are," Captain Toole ordered.

Robert retrieved the hat from the closet and looked at his stack of schoolbooks. "We'll send someone to get those later," Captain Toole assured him. The two then followed their usual routine of going slowly to the elevator and then to the Ft. Waterline car. Captain Toole drove directly to the assembly parade grounds. Robert had been there only ten times before. One of those times he received his Medal of Freedom. When the car stopped, the two exited. Captain Toole guided the cadet toward the podium. "You'll be up here, today," he explained. "No marching for you, cadet."

Robert remained standing as he watched his fellow academy cadets march onto the assembly grounds. He watched proudly as Charlie-3 went by in perfect step. Cadet Lieutenant Powers was leading that platoon. Robert hardly noticed the extra security around the podium. He had gotten used to dignitaries coming to address the academy cadets. When the cadets were all positioned, a four-star general went up to the podium. As Robert took a closer look at the speaker, he recognized the face of the chairman of the Joint Chiefs of Staff, General Ray Davis.

The general gave some opening comments including praise for the US military personnel who were fighting abroad and about the need for patriotism. Robert was caught by surprise when he heard the general order, "Cadet Robert Joseph Crandon, post!" Captain

Toole took Robert's arm to help him up, thinking that the boy was having troubles standing.

Robert finally understood that he had been called and made his way to General Davis. "Cadet Crandon reports as ordered, General!" He saluted the general crisply.

General Davis saluted back and both dropped their arms. "General, please read the citation," General Davis ordered another officer sporting stars on his shoulders. The other general was Brigadier General Suarez.

General Suarez read:

"Cadet Robert Joseph Crandon, of Waterline Academy, has consistently shown outstanding leadership, bravery and intelligence in the execution of all assigned tasks. He was the first cadet in the history of Waterline Academy to have earned a pass during a common week in his first year. He was the youngest member of the academy to ever achieve the ranks of Corporal, Sergeant, and Lieutenant.

"While a Cadet Lieutenant, Cadet Crandon demonstrated spectacular leadership skills. His first year as a platoon leader, his platoon received top honors for achievement and scored the highest of all the platoons in the academy.

"In the start of his second year as a platoon leader, Cadet Crandon led his platoon to the highest score of the academy for First Inspection and then led his platoon to a perfect score for Second Inspection. Cadet Crandon also successfully inspired his cadets, including twenty first-year cadets, to all earn passes during the second common week, known as Christmas Common Week. He accomplished these goals in spite of severe injury causing convalescence.

"For the many achievements he has accomplished, including those mentioned above, Cadet Robert Joseph Crandon is hereby awarded the Bronze Star."

The entire academy cheered as the general pinned the award onto Robert's housecoat/jacket. Robert's day, however, was not finished. As General Suarez retreated from the microphone after shaking

Robert's hand, the chairman of the Joint Chiefs of Staff approached and began reading from another paper:

"By order of the president of the United States: Congress, the President and the Joint Chiefs of Staff have imposed special trust and confidence in the person of Robert Joseph Crandon. Cadet Crandon is hereby promoted to the rank of Cadet Colonel and assigned as the Cadet Brigade Commander of Academies. The order is effective as of this 19th day of December, 1973. Signed: President Robert F. Kennedy."

When General Davis finished reading, he said to Robert, "Congratulations, cadet. I understand that this is considered to be long overdue by your cadre." As the general removed the lieutenant bars from Robert's shoulders and replaced them with golden eagles, the academy cadets burst out in a roar of enthusiasm. There had always been a slot in the chain of command for cadets labeled "Brigade Commander," but to date, no one had *ever* filled that post. The brigade commander was technically the head of all the academies in the entire academy system.

Cadet Colonel Robert Joseph Crandon was stunned. His platoon had all received passes for Christmas Common Week; they had scored 100 percent on Second Inspection, and now he, their platoon leader, was being promoted to Cadet Colonel in his fifth year at the academy. He looked around and saw Lieutenant Karen Tangora, US Army nurse in the bleachers cheering his achievement. He looked some more and saw his parents cheering in the bleachers as well.

"I think that they will expect you to make a speech, Robert," General Davis suggested.

Robert Crandon took in some deep breaths while waiting for the crowd to quiet down. "General Davis, General Suarez, Commandant Leary, ladies and gentlemen and cadets of Waterline Academy," he began, "many of you, especially our visitors, may not understand the true intent of Waterline Academy. It has been suggested to me that Waterline Academy exists to punish its cadets or that the purpose of sending us here is to impose negative consequences to our previous actions. Nothing could be further from the truth."

Robert then thought about all the information that Commandant Leary had told him regarding the purpose of the disciplinary academies.

"Many years ago, during a nasty war known as World War II, the military noticed that some of the men they drafted seemed incapable of adjusting to the discipline. Some generals and admirals invited some very smart teachers to a conference and asked them why this occurred. Those teachers helped research the backgrounds of the men in question and they saw that early on, those men had been pegged by their teachers as children who were at risk of not being able to make it in your society." Here, Robert indicated the visitors and dignitaries.

"The teachers suggested to the generals and admirals that if something had been set up for the boys long before they turned eighteen, that they might have been able to make it in society. The military leaders listened and suggested to President Roosevelt that the academy system be created. They reasoned that it was cheaper to get to the children early rather than imprison them for life or execute them."

Robert faltered for a short while, remembered his required knowledge and continued.

"We cadets have, in most cases, come to realize that a 'required knowledge' that we are always required to be able to repeat is actually true. We are at Waterline Academy to learn to function in society. Most of us are very grateful to all of you who have given us this chance. I believe that I speak for all cadets when I say, thank you so much, to all those who have made Waterline Academy possible. Those people include the commandant, the cadre, the staff and professors, the military, and, finally, the government—that means all of you, since this is the United States of America."

Robert faltered again. Inwardly he thought, "So far, so good—now how do I end?"

"I am honored by the medal and promotion I have been given. I'm not sure yet what my duties as the Brigade Commander of Academies are, but I suspect that my cadre will inform me soon and then probably try to gig me by immediately questioning me." There was laughter amongst the guests and cadets, as well as the cadre. "The honors I have been given are not my accomplishment alone. I could *never* have accomplished these things without the help of my fellow cadets. These achievements are achievements of Waterline Academy far more than they are the achievements of a ten-year-old boy. My cadet platoon leaders, cadet officer corps, and, especially, the cadets who I am privileged to have served as a platoon leader, squad leader, or fire team leader all share in these honors.

"I hope to be able to serve well in my new position, not just because I wish to honor my academy, but because I want to repay society for the chance it has given me. I hope to remember always that I owe you all a great debt; one that I want to spend my entire life repaying. I hope to inspire all my fellow cadets to do the exact same thing: repay our debt and prove your trust well founded. Thank you."

There was applause after Robert's speech, but not as vigorous as the cadre had expected. Many of the visitors were dumbfounded. They had not expected such understanding and knowledge from a young boy. They continued to clap, standing one at a time. Eventually, the applause was very vigorous as the crowd of visitors seemed to come out of their shock and contemplation. The cadets also seemed to have started in shock and also came out of their contemplation slowly but surely. The clapping went on for quite a long time, slowly rising to a crescendo. Finally, the listeners began to quiet down.

Robert had moved away from the microphone and was replaced by General Davis. General Davis announced that there would be a reception at the Ft. Waterline Officers' Club following the assembly. Robert Crandon was informed that he would be expected to attend.

Robert considered this obvious, but said nothing about that. The academy cadets marched back to their barracks region and Captain Toole went over to collect Cadet Colonel Crandon. "I'll drive you to the barracks first and then, later, to the reception, Robbie."

"Thank you, sir," Robert acknowledged. "Will I get a chance to speak to the cadets, sir? Privately, I mean?"

"I'm sure that can be arranged," Captain Toole answered. As he drove his cadet back to the barracks, Captain Toole began to give Robert some idea of what his responsibilities might include. "You will generally have the same authority as a member of the cadre. The cadets are expected to treat you as such. You are still a cadet, of course, but you are also in a special position. You can give many of the same orders and permissions that I could give. Since you are still a cadet, you can't give yourself permission to leave the academy grounds, but nearly anything else that I could allow, you can allow.

"We expect you to use your head when using these authorizations. Even still, we *do* expect you to actually *use* them. You can schedule items yourself, subject to the review of the adjutant and commandant. You have full authority to cancel classes or order cadets to perform tasks during school hours—please use *extreme* discretion when doing that. You can order inspections, changes in meal times, changes in uniforms, all sorts of things like that.

"None of us actually know what the director has in mind for you. We do know that you are expected to visit each of the other academies, starting with Baton Rouge right after Christmas Common Week. I think that you will probably create your own job, cadet. I believe that you are the one best able to determine what you should do, and I think that those who promoted you feel the same way."

As the cadre officer parked the car in Charlie Company's lot, he told Robert, "You are now a field grade officer, so you will be permanently in those quarters. We already moved your things to your new quarters, since we expected you to be there due to your injuries. You will need to get new uniforms from Captain Thomas. He was probably already told of your promotion beforehand, so I suspect that he already has them ready. Any questions?"

"Not right now, sir," Robert answered. "Actually, sir, there is one … " he added. "Can I bring Darryl with me to the reception, sir?"

"If you say so then you can." Captain Toole smiled. "You have the same authority that I have," he added.

Robert walked into the cadre office and saw a cadet waiting who was apparently serving a Minor Punishment by being used as a lackey. "Come with me, cadet," Robert ordered.

"Yes, sir," the cadet responded and immediately went to his brigade commander. Robert led him to the Quartermaster building. The two went in. Captain Thomas, the Quartermaster Officer, was busily checking paperwork. He looked up and saw Robert.

"Ah … you've finally come for some uniforms?" the quartermaster officer asked.

"If now is convenient, sir," Robert answered tentatively.

"Now is fine, cadet. I take it that you brought Cadet Lavelle along to carry the stuff?"

"Yes sir."

The quartermaster officer began taking uniforms off of a shelf. "I think that these will fit you correctly."

"All convalescent PJs?" Robert said dismayed.

"PJs?" Captain Thomas asked. He considered for a while and then laughed. "I guess they *do* resemble pajamas. I think I'll change the name of them to that!" The quartermaster officer wrote down a note to himself and then began removing the prior insignia. He punched Colonel Crandon's last name and rank into a computer and a sewing machine immediately began to print the nametags for the uniforms. Captain Thomas then put the uniforms on the sewing machine one at a time and the machine automatically placed the nametags onto the shirts and jackets and sewed them in place.

Next Captain Thomas obtained the golden and black cloth eagles signifying the cadet's rank. He placed those into the machine and fixed the shirts and jackets at different angles. The machine attached the rank to the lapels and shoulders of the respective garments. "When you switch back to regular parade uniforms, I'll have the insignia sewn in again. You won't be using the black-colored brass anymore, Rob. By the way, *congratulations* and well done!"

"Thank you, sir," Robert responded. "I'm still a little bit in shock, I think. Nobody told me this was coming."

Captain Thomas smiled. "You'll get over it, I'm sure. Well, that's it, Robert. Here's a new duffel bag. Your other uniforms were returned a few days back so don't worry about them. Please sign." He handed the cadet paperwork designating the items he had just issued. Robert checked the list with the contents of his duffel bag and signed for the items. "I'll be checking with DOD about any other uniform requirements. I'll also send a memo out to the other academies to stock up on *your* size uniforms. You never know when you might need to replace one."

Robert Crandon led Cadet Lavelle to the field grade officers' quarters and had him place the duffel bag down. "Okay, thanks, cadet. You can go back, now, if you want."

"I can help you put the stuff away, sir," Lavelle offered.

"Okay. If you want to … " Robert answered. "I just don't want you to think that I'm requiring it. I mean, I may be the brigade CO, but I'm still also a cadet."

"Oh, it's not a problem, sir," Lavelle answered. "They didn't have anything else for me to do, and the longer I help you, the less chance that a cad will come up with something."

Robert grinned. "Well then, cadet," he said happily. "Let's start getting these uniforms placed in their proper places."

"Yes, sir!" Lavelle answered enthusiastically.

After some time of putting uniforms into the wardrobe had passed, Robert said, "You go ahead and continue, Lavelle. I have to talk to Colonel Marks, okay?"

"No problem, sir," Lavelle agreed.

Robert walked to the end of the short hallway and knocked on the battalion commander's door. "Come," a voice answered.

Robert opened the door and Darryl Marks and John Stevens immediately stood at attention, with one of the boys calling the order. "As you were," Robert commanded. "Is Harry around?" he asked.

"I'll go check, sir," Cadet Major John Stevens offered. He left the room and Robert entered and sat down next to Cadet Lieutenant Colonel Darryl Marks.

"What's up, sir?" Darryl asked.

"Well, for one," Robert answered, "I need to come to an understanding with my bunkies." When both cadet majors entered the room, Robert motioned to chairs as a suggestion that they sit down. "Okay, guys, I guess the cadre has told you about my status. We're going to be living in close proximity, so I need to get some house rules set.

"First of all, unless it seems *really needed*, don't call attention or stand up for me. You don't do that for Darryl, so don't do it for me," Robert said.

"But we've been told to give you the same respect as a cadre officer," Cadet Major Harry Tromp offered.

"Yeah," Robert agreed. "And that means that I can *order* you to do exactly what I just said. So, that solves that. I want all of you, especially you, Darryl, to remember that Darryl is *still* the battalion commander. I may outrank him, but I am *not* going to replace him. As far as I'm concerned, I happen to be a higher ranking officer in Darryl's battalion."

Darryl nodded his understanding. The other two cadets seemed to have less grasp of the situation. "What it means," Robert explained, "is that you don't come to me with any problems that you used to bring to Colonel Marks. He's still in charge. If you have problems that you would bring to a cadre officer, you can ask me first if you think I can solve them, but not the stuff that Colonel Marks is supposed to handle. Meanwhile, he'll bring stuff to me that he thinks I can help with. Got it now?" Robert asked.

"Oh, okay," John answered, finally comprehending.

"Umm … I'm still lost," Harry answered truthfully.

"Don't worry, Harry. I'll help you as we go along," Robert assured him.

"Darryl, you're going to the reception, so get into dress blues. I'm giving the order, so I'll sign you out in the Cadre Office. Captain Toole said he'll be driving me there, so you can come along with us, okay?"

"Yes, sir!" Darryl answered and began taking his dress blues Uniform out. "Any particular reason?"

"Yeah, I want you there."

Robert then changed the subject. "You guys planned this all along, didn't you?"

"Of course," Darryl agreed. "We didn't know you would get there so soon, but we planned it ever since the second week you arrived, little guy."

"I thought you were planning to make me Battalion Commander at some point," Robert confessed.

John spoke up, "Well, we sort of expected that that would happen *first*, but we wanted you to get where you are now! We need you there. You'll be in personal contact with the Director."

"Gerralds, Snider and their bunch? Is that why?" Robert asked.

All three of the other cadets nodded. Then Darryl said, "Even if they hadn't stayed here, we need someone who can talk to the outside. If we don't have you—or someone else—then the Gerralds and the Sniders will come again. We needed you—more than you can possibly realize."

At the reception in the officers' club, Robert and Darryl tried their best to be inconspicuous. They felt like fish out of water. The two had talked with Mr. and Mrs. Crandon initially, but Paul Crandon eventually suggested that the two cadets needed to "mingle with the crowd." Eventually, Robert was hailed by General Davis.

There were a number of officers of varying ranks surrounding General Davis. Commandant Leary was also present. "I've heard a lot of things about you, young man," the general began cordially.

"I hope not too many of the bad things, sir," Robert offered, jokingly. Those present laughed a little.

"Oh, come now. You cadets can't be as bad as they say," the general offered.

"I'm not privy to what 'they say,' sir," Robert answered. "We can be hellions when we put our minds to it, sir. We also have a deserved reputation for some of our capabilities, sir, although not necessarily the habits."

"Well, I've heard some claim that you are thieves, thugs, druggies, gang members, muggers, and killers," the general said, only half jokingly. "I'm sure that Waterline probably cures you of most of those ills."

"Yes, sir. We don't have too many muggers or thugs anymore, and *no cadet ever steals.*"

"Why do you say that, cadet?"

"Because we're not allowed to *own* anything, sir. There's really no point in taking stuff that, once found, is going to be taken away from you. Later on, I guess leaving other people's stuff alone just becomes a habit."

"It's not that you're afraid of getting caught?"

"With your permission, sir, I'd like to be excused for a few minutes. I'll be able to answer your question once I return, sir," Robert said. The general agreed. Robert found his fellow cadet and told Darryl his plan.

Darryl headed toward the doorway that was guarded by one of the MPs usually assigned to Waterline Academy. "Hey, sir," Darryl prompted. "Please ask anyone who is planning to leave to remain until Cadet Crandon addresses the room," the guard agreed.

Robert headed into the crowd. In about five minutes he accomplished his task. Darryl had also moved amongst the guests and tried his best to follow his brigade commander's lead. When the two returned to General Davis, the man was a little perplexed. He had assumed that Robert needed to use the men's room. Robert announced to the crowd loudly, "Excuse me everyone! The general challenged me about a particular skill. I thought that the best way to answer the general's question was a demonstration." Robert then looked at General Davis, "With your permission, sir?" he asked.

"Go ahead, cadet; it's your show," the general answered. Commandant Leary finally realized what was going on and sported a huge smile. He also unconsciously checked for his wallet and keys.

"General Davis had wanted to know if the *reason* that Waterline cadets don't steal is from a fear of getting caught. Well, I suppose there are some who worry about that, but not most of us." At that point Robert began taking items out of his bathrobe/coat pockets. "Major Castillo? I believe that this wallet belongs to you, sir. Captain Haddad, this one is yours. Colonel Gemmie, your keys and wallet, sir." Robert then addressed a woman who was not in uniform. She wore a floor-length dress. "Ma'am, this is your bracelet. I didn't find out your name."

Darryl then began his list. "Col. Hershey, these are your wallet and watch, I believe. Captain LaCaire, these are your ID and wallet, sir. Major Lee, your wallet and keys, sir."

The crowd applauded the demonstration. "I guess you've shown me there, cadet," General Davis conceded.

"Your wallet and ID, sir." Robert handed the items to the general.

"How? When did you get these?" The general was dumbfounded. "Just now, while you were watching Cadet Marks, sir," Robert answered.

"Don't worry, sir," Cadet Darryl Marks commented. "As he said, we never, ever *steal* anything. We are pretty good at taking things if we want to, but we never keep anything. We don't *want* to, sir."

Paul, Roberta, and Robert Crandon were on the Amtrak train headed for Boston. Paul was keeping a close eye on his son, checking to see if the boy was suffering any signs of dizziness. He knew that Robert would try his best to conceal any difficulties. He also knew what Dr. Moore's instructions meant. "Don't let him jostle around too much. His concussion is much worse than he lets on. You also need to check if he is trying to hide pain. His migraine headaches are somehow linked to his injuries. You may need to insist that he take the Fioricet—he seems reluctant to take any pain medications, but he shouldn't worry about it. He's not likely to get hooked on them."

Paul looked at his son again, very closely. The boy was all smiles, no doubt due to being with his parents. "So, young man, what happens after your Christmas vacation?" Paul asked.

Robert looked up quickly at his father. He closed his eyes, showing signs of catching his balance. "Well, my orders say that I'm supposed to meet Commandant Leary at the airport in Atlanta on January 2. I'm supposed to go with him to visit another academy—the one in Baton Rouge. I guess that I'll be visiting all the academies now!" Robert looked animated and eager. "It'll be great! I'll get to meet lots of other guys this way!"

Roberta asked, "Will you be able to fly at that point, Robbie?"

The boy looked nervous. Paul cut in, "We'll send you back by train and have you take a taxi to Hartsfield/Jackson. That way, your commandant can decide if you're able to fly. Don't worry, Robbie,

I'm sure that *this* commandant has your best interests at heart. He seems really fond of you, you know."

"Yeah, that's true." Robert agreed. "We ate a lot of meals together last year. He taught me all sorts of stuff about interrogations that he worked on when he was in the Air Force, too. I like Commandant Leary a lot, lot, lot."

Roberta smiled. "I'm sure he likes you too, Robbie."

Paul asked, "How did your friends take to your new promotion?"

"Oh, they think it's great! Actually, Darryl told me that they wanted me to be made the Brigade Commander all along. I hadn't actually known that. I figured they were just setting me up for the Battalion Commander of Waterline, you know? But Darryl told me, 'No way, little guy! We wanted somebody who could talk to the director. Anything else would have left us all at the mercy of the cads.'

"I guess they figured that I'd be able to stop all the yucky stuff from happening. I hope they're right. Of course, we don't have any yucky cadre officers left at Waterline Academy."

"Thanks to you, son." Paul insisted. "All thanks to you."